Smith's MONTHLY

Every Month Original Novels, Stories, and Articles

USA Today Bestselling Writer
Dean Wesley Smith

TABLE OF CONTENTS

Smith's Monthly Issue #3

Thanks for the Support

Dean Wesley Smith

Introduction

Happy Holidays and Moving On

ISSUE #1 OF *SMITH'S MONTHLY* has been out now for a month and Issue #2 is in proof and will be selling and shipping to subscribers next week as I write this. Thanksgiving is still three weeks away and Christmas four weeks beyond that. Yet this issue will be getting to subscribers and bookstores a week or so before Christmas.

So, in a way, this is a holiday issue. But actually, it's not at all.

Nope. There is not one holiday story in this issue. Not even a mention of holidays in any story or article except this introduction.

That's right, I put out a magazine right in the middle of the holidays without one holiday story in it.

You are welcome.

The reason, of course, that I can do such an unheard-of thing like put out a magazine in December without holiday stuff all through it is because this is my magazine. WMG Publishing, the publisher of this crazy experiment, has given me free rein to do what I want (within public decency standards, of course).

However, over the years, I have written and published a ton of holiday stories because other magazines love that sort of thing. And for a long time, most of my jukebox stories were set on Christmas Eve.

So if you want a holiday story from me, I would suggest a story called "Jukebox Gifts." It's a story about friendship and giving the gift to friends of a second chance in their life. It was first published in *The Magazine of Fantasy and Science Fiction* back in the 1990s and people have tended to like it.

Unlike all the original stories and novel I have in this issue, that story was written a while back. But if you need a holiday fix from me, give that one a try. I think you'll find it worthwhile.

And until next year, meaning next month in this ongoing craziness, I hope everyone has a fun season, whatever that means to each of you.

For me, that means I'll be here writing. It doesn't get better than that for me.

Dean Wesley Smith
November 10, 2013
Lincoln City, Oregon

USA *Today* Bestselling Writer

DEAN WESLEY SMITH

A STORM FROM THE RELIC

A Poker Boy Story

USA Today *bestselling writer Dean Wesley Smith writes about many regular characters, the most popular being Poker Boy.*

In this adventure, Poker Boy starts off spending a quiet evening in his favorite casino, playing poker and wining a little money as he waits for his girlfriend, Patty Ledgerwood, to get off work.

Then a man walks in and sits at the table with a lucky charm that would turn out to not be so lucky for all of humanity. Can Poker Boy and his team act quickly enough to stop an ancient war from erupting once again?

A STORM FROM THE RELIC
A Poker Boy Story

GOOD POKER PLAYERS never really believe in luck. Good players know that luck levels out over time and that skill always wins in the long run.

But as Poker Boy, I knew luck very much existed, and I had met her many times over the years. I even saved her life once. Lady Luck, known as Laverne, was a very real and a very powerful god.

But most players, especially newer players, had never had the chance to meet Lady Luck, so they often used something lucky to try to get her attention in some way or another.

That was silly, of course. Laverne had far, far more pressing matters to deal with than rewarding some idiot for bad play because he had a polished rock on his bad cards.

But players of all types used talismans of one sort or another to put on their cards when in a hand.

There was a practical reason for it, of course. It was called "protecting your cards" in case a careless dealer tried to take them before the hand was over, or some careless person tossed their cards and hit yours. If your cards were protected with a chip or something on top of them, they were fine.

Over the years of sitting at poker tables, I had seen players use polished rocks, polished bones, chess pieces, Risk pieces, lucky tokens, and so much more.

It was almost two in the morning on a late Saturday night. Outside it was a beautiful fall evening in the Oregon Mountains. The sounds of bells ringing and excited people at the craps table drifted in from the main part of the casino along with the faint smell of smoke. It was legal to smoke on the casino floor, but not in the poker room, a rule which I was very thankful was in place.

I had only thirty minutes to keep playing in my favorite small poker room at Spirit Winds Casino before I had to teleport to Las Vegas to meet my girlfriend, Patty, aka Front Desk Girl. I had managed to get a couple thousand up for the evening. Considering how small the room was, and how few tourists were in the casino at this time of the year, I felt as if the night had been a success.

Then a man wearing a large winter coat and black stocking cap came toward the table carrying a rack of red chips worth five hundred dollars, the maximum buy-in to the table.

Normally seeing someone like that coming would get me excited and force me to stay a few more hands to see if I could nab some of those chips.

But suddenly every danger alarm I had went off at once, almost rocking me back in my chair. I had never gone from completely calm and with no alerts to completely on alert in such short notice before.

The guy put the rack of chips on the table and took off his coat. He wore regular jeans and a plaid shirt under the big winter coat. He seemed trim and in shape.

He nodded to one of the other men at the table, took off his stocking cap and

stuffed it in his coat, then hung his coat on a nearby coat tree against one wall.

I couldn't figure out what about the guy was causing the danger signals. He just seemed like a regular guy, clearly from outside the area. I had never seen him in this casino before. And considering he was about to sit down in a no-limit game with five hundred dollars, the guy clearly wasn't that worried about money.

There was nothing at all about him that seemed dangerous in the slightest.

The guy turned from his coat, then seemed to remember something and dug something small out of one of the coat pockets.

And when that item came into the light, I almost had to put my hands over my ears to try to cut down the screaming alarms of all my warning superpowers going off at once.

Everything inside me just shouted "Run!"

That was not a feeling I was used to having.

I pushed back from the table. "Got to go pick up my girlfriend," I said to the dealer.

The dealer, a nice guy named Carl, motioned for James, the room's brush, to come over and rack up my chips.

I stood and stepped a few feet away from the table to try to catch my breath and think.

The guy set a golden-looking piece of metal on the table and sat down and started to stack his chips.

Whatever that thing was on the table, it was frighteningly dangerous.

The guy wasn't dangerous.

The talisman was.

How the heck was that even possible?

I froze time around myself, but it did nothing to calm my alarms. Basically what I did was just step between two moments in time, but it felt like I had frozen time since all the noise from the casino stopped and everyone looked frozen in mid-step. Besides teleportation, stepping between instants of time was my favorite superpower.

I wanted to get a better look at that talisman, but as I stepped toward it, every warning alarm I had as a superhero went off even louder than before.

> *I stepped toward it, every warning alarm I had as a superhero went off even louder than before.*

And that was a lot of alarms.

I felt as if a thousand little voices were all shouting at me at once. All inside my head.

All of them shouting for me to turn and just run.

Nothing like that had ever happened before.

I staggered back like a drunk coming out of a bar at closing time. I almost bumped into James frozen on his way toward the table with empty racks to get my chips.

"Stan!" I shouted toward the ceiling, even though I didn't need to shout upward to get his boss, the God of Poker to come running.

Stan appeared beside me and before I could get a word out he staggered slightly and spun around, staring at the table.

"What is that thing?" I asked.

Stan shook his head and pulled me a dozen more steps back away from the table.

With each step away from the talisman, the warnings faded slightly. It was no wonder the guy could get so close to the table with that thing in his pocket before I felt it. Whatever it was, it had a limited range.

"So you don't honestly know what that thing is?" I asked Stan.

Stan just shook his head. "Never felt anything like that before. But it feels very, very old."

I realized Stan was right, it did feel old. And powerful. And evil, all rolled into one tiny little shiny piece of metal.

"Can you get Ben?" I asked. "He might know what it is."

Stan nodded and vanished.

I stepped even farther away from the frozen table. Ben was an old god who loved to read. He looked like an old man you would see shuffling down the street in baggy pants and an old ill-fitting jacket. His hair was gray and very thin. He had been the god of lamplighters for centuries until that profession faded and he faded with it. I had managed to get him in with the gods of books, since he loved to read and remembered everything he had ever read since the beginning of printing and even before.

He was a gentle man and very nice and very shy. He was the newest member of my team, but so far we hadn't had a mission that we needed him on yet.

And at some point I was going to get him to show me the Library of Alexandria.

Stan and Ben appeared beside me. Ben smiled at me and I could tell he was recovering quickly from his ghost state. He looked almost solid now and much healthier, although still very thin.

He started to say something to me and then froze.

He turned in the direction of the table, staring.

"Do you know what would cause that?" I asked. "It's coming from that gold talisman on the table."

"The Relic," Ben said, his voice so soft that if I didn't have time frozen and all the noise from the casino gone, I never would have heard him.

"Oh, shit," Stan said and vanished again, leaving me standing there with Ben.

"What is the Relic?" I asked.

Ben indicated we should move even farther away from the table and I was glad to do so. We moved back so that we were almost out of the poker room and onto the casino main floor.

My danger alarms were still going off strong, but more distance from that thing eased them even more. Clearly Ben and Stan had the same kind of thing.

"The Relic was a spaceship," Ben said. "The legends have it that the ship crashed here in the early days of humans on this planet. It was filled with the vilest of evil aliens. The Titans, the Giants, and the early days of the Gods all banded together to fight the creatures of extreme power who came off that ship."

I looked at him and all I could say was, "Oh."

Ben said nothing more and I went back to staring at the table, wondering just where Stan had gone to.

Finally, my mind cleared enough so that I had another couple of questions for Ben. "How did that guy get a piece of the ship? And why is it still dangerous?"

"In the final great battle, the evil aliens were pushed back into their ship," Ben said. "With that kind of pressure, the ship exploded, scattering the ship and the aliens into millions of pieces. Every piece of the ship contained an essence of an alien. The evil creatures still inhabit the remaining pieces."

"And that's why it feels dangerous?" I asked.

"No, it doesn't just feel dangerous, it is dangerous," Ben said, his voice firm and clear. "The man who has it clearly has no magical powers, but he is being controlled by the entity in the metal. If a magical person touches that piece, the evil will escape from it and inhabit that person."

"That's happened in the past?"

Ben nodded. "Hitler."

"I thought he was a troll," I said, completely shocked.

"He was," Ben said. "Inhabited by the evil from that ancient battle."

Now I finally understood something. "That's why Hitler was always searching for more magic and religious items?"

Ben nodded. "He was looking for more of his kind to bring them back. He found a few of them before he was stopped and they were all killed."

I just stood there staring at the frozen poker table. It was common for a player to show other players their "lucky" talisman, especially if it had a cool look to it. So a poker table was a perfect place for the alien in that piece of metal to find someone even slightly magical.

> ### *"That's why Hitler was always searching for more magic and religious items?"*

"I wonder how he found it," I said out loud.

"That's the most important thing we need to learn," Ben said. "We must get that man away from that piece of the Relic to find out."

Stan and Lady Luck appeared.

She was wearing her standard business suit and had her hair pulled back tight. She turned to the table. "Oh, my," was all she said.

I had never seen Lady Luck look worried before, but right now she was clearly upset and very worried.

I looked at the table and at James frozen in place as he headed toward where I had been with empty racks for my chips.

"I assume none of you dare go in there," I said to the three gods standing beside me.

Laverne and Stan and Ben all nodded.

I had a hunch that was going to be the case. The more power, the more that evil would push them away. I was barely able to just be near the table.

I turned to Stan. "I need Patty and Screamer."

Stan nodded and vanished.

"So we need to get that man away from that piece of the Relic, right?" I asked Ben. "To find out where he found it and if there are more pieces."

Ben nodded. "Critical."

"Will the evil be able to go through him to get to anyone here?" I asked.

This time both Laverne and Ben said no.

"And if we get him away from the Relic piece," I asked, "what can we do with it then?"

"Without the man close to it," Laverne said, "we can send it into the sun as we have done with all the other pieces. But we first must disconnect anyone attached to the piece, otherwise the evil flows back instead of being destroyed."

"And you can do that?" I asked.

Laverne nodded. "Given enough distance between the two, I can break the bond the piece has over the man."

"And it won't transfer to anyone else?"

"Not unless another person touches it," Ben said, and Laverne nodded.

A moment later Stan appeared with Patty and Screamer.

Patty had on her uniform from the front desk of the MGM Grand Hotel and her long brown hair pulled up and back. She looked as beautiful as ever.

Beside her Screamer looked as Screamer always did in his jeans, long-sleeved shirt and short brown hair. Both of them were looking worried. I was sure Stan had told them nothing.

"Oh, oh," Patty said as she appeared, turning toward the table.

She could clearly feel it as well.

"What the hell is that?" Screamer asked, also turning toward the table across the poker room.

"Part of the Relic," I said.

Screamer looked puzzled, but Patty softly just shook her head. "I had hoped to go my entire life and never have to deal with another piece of that evil."

"All right," I said to my team. "It's going to take all three of us if we're going to go drag that guy away from that table and out here. Without breaking the time bubble."

Patty nodded and Screamer looked like he had about a thousand questions, but kept them to himself.

"Stan, Laverne, can you hold the bubble?"

"Got it," Stan said, nodding.

"The evil in that piece will not want you doing what you are going to attempt to do," Laverne said. "It will fight you."

"How?" I asked.

Laverne shook her head. "I do not know."

"You will need a magic-based shield," Ben said.

Now all of us turned to look at him. Both Stan and Laverne were looking as puzzled as I felt.

Ben nodded. "A magic-based shield is an old and almost lost art, but Poker Boy, I think you could do it, with help from Patty."

Ben turned to the table. "Feel the evil coming from that piece like waves of energy?"

I nodded. Once I had my warning powers cut down, I actually could sense the energy waves coming from the piece.

"Hold Patty's hand now," Ben said, "and focus about a foot in front of you both all the good energy you can muster. Hold it there like a wall. Imagine it a wall. Patty, focus as much good and calming energy as you can into Poker Boy."

I could feel Patty's energy coming into me and I did as Ben had told me to do, building an imaginary wall with good energy in front of me, between all of us and that table.

Suddenly I could barely sense the evil. And I could almost see the shield shimmering in front of me.

"Stan," Laverne said, "you and I funnel him more energy."

Suddenly I could no longer feel the evil at all as energy poured through me from Stan and Laverne and Patty.

"Screamer, behind me," I said. "Let's go get that guy out of there."

I kept hold of Patty's hand and kept the image of the shimmering screen between me and that piece of metal sitting on the table.

The closer we got, the more I focused on the shield.

I could feel the evil in that piece pushing back, fighting to keep us away.

It felt like I was pushing a wide board against a river current, working it upstream.

We came in behind the guy frozen at the table. I did not let go of Patty's hand, but with my free hand I took one side of the guy's chair and tipped it back while Screamer took the other side.

The energy coming from Laverne and Stan and Ben now increased as the energy from the evil fought us.

I felt like I was caught between two intense currents and that imaginary shield in front of me was all that was keeping us in place.

The evil in that piece of energy was very, very powerful.

We pulled, moving the guy back from the table, dragging the chair along the carpeted floor.

I wasn't sure how much longer I could hold up that imaginary shield, but I somehow did as we got the guy back away from the table and Ben and Stan came ducking in to help as we beat a full retreat, the frozen guy not even having a clue that he was being pulled away from the table in an instant of time.

We pulled the guy clear out onto the casino main floor.

I could almost not feel the energy from the evil, so I dropped the screen, panting.

"Ben," I said, looking at our newest team member, "will it be safe for us to go into the guy's mind and find where he found the piece?"

"At this distance it should be if we don't release the time bubble. But it wouldn't hurt to have the screen back up as well."

"Got the time bubble solid," Stan said, indicating the time bubble that kept us out of the normal flow of time.

I took a deep breath and could feel the energy coming back into me from Patty's grasp as I again imagined the screen between us and that piece of metal on the table.

Then Screamer touched me and I could feel all of us linked inside Screamer's head. It was such a familiar thing now, it didn't even bother me.

Keep that screen up, Screamer thought at me.

Then he touched the poor guy we had hauled away from the table.

I was right. He wasn't from around here. He was from a mountain town in Northern California, just south of the Oregon border. And he wasn't a poker player either. And he didn't have the five hundred to lose. He had been forced to sit at that table to find someone with magic. Clearly the evil entity in the piece had felt me sitting there and thought I would be an easy mark.

Screamer dug down into the guy's mind as I held the screen between all of us and the evil Relic piece.

First published in More Stories from the Twilight Zone *edited by Carol Serling.*

Elliot knew the world would not end in 2012. But his wife thought it would, so on the morning of December 21st, 2012, Elliot went out for a drive to avoid her.

And found himself in the Twilight Zone.

Now available in paperback and electronic editions from your favorite bookseller.

I could see where the evil had taken over, the darkness in the guy, the unexplained actions, everything. Normally, he was a good man, but he had been controlled to go in search of magic.

Then the image became clear and I damn near let go of everything I was so shocked.

Patty thought clearly, *Oh, oh. Hold on.*

The guy had found the piece in an old mine in Northern California, just south of the Oregon border. He had dug down and ran into a cavern. And there in that underground cavern were many, many more pieces of the Relic. A vast number as far as I could see from the guy's mind.

Thousands at least.

If just one piece had caused Hitler, I could only imagine what all those pieces could do if let lose with magic in the world.

Screamer got the exact location of the cavern, then backed us out of the guy's head, then let go of me so the contact between the three of us was broken.

"Bad?" Laverne asked, looking worried.

"Really bad," I said, holding up the screen. "An entire cavern of pieces of the Relic."

"But he's the only one who knows about it," Patty said.

"I have the exact location," Screamer said.

"Stan, Ben, stay here," Laverne said. "Poker Boy, hold that screen up for as long as you can."

I nodded and Patty gripped my hand even tighter as Laverne, Screamer, and the poor miner from Northern California vanished, chair and all.

We all stood there like that for at least a minute. I was doing my best to hold that wall of good energy up between all of us and that piece of metal on the table.

Then suddenly there was a white light, very bright, that formed on the surface of the poker table and then vanished.

I could feel now that the screen I was holding up was no longer getting attacked from the other side.

A moment later Laverne appeared again with the guy in the chair.

"We broke the connection and that piece has been tossed into the sun," she said.

I sighed and dropped the shield I had just learned how to do, feeling the relief of the lack of energy drain.

And I realized I was suddenly very, very hungry.

"I got him," Stan said.

He touched the back of the chair and teleported the guy to his position at the table.

"What is happening with the cavern?" Patty asked a moment before I could.

"We're going to teleport them all into the sun," Laverne said. "After I broke the connection with the Relic, Screamer and I got the information from the man's head as well. They will all be gone within the next few minutes."

"That place was flat scary."

"We came very close to another major war with the Relic," Lady Luck said, nodding. "Great job once again, to all of you."

And then she turned to Ben. "It sure seems Poker Boy was correct. You are greatly needed on his team."

Ben smiled and I could see him gain energy. "It feels good to be needed."

He turned to me and said simply, "Thank you."

Then he vanished.

Lady Luck smiled at me once again. "Yes, thank you."

And she vanished.

I turned to Patty. "See you in about twenty minutes when you get off work?"

"Dinner is on me," Stan said. "Steaks. We'll meet in the lobby at the MGM in thirty minutes."

Then my boss looked at me.

"You got it?"

"I got it," I said and took back over the time bubble as he and Patty and Screamer vanished.

I moved back over to the table and tried to remember where I was standing when I took myself out of the time stream.

Then I let the time bubble go.

The sounds of the casino crashed in on me again. Amazing how loud a casino can be and how I only really notice it when the sounds are gone.

The guy who had the Relic suddenly looked around, clearly very puzzled.

I turned to James as he approached. "Rack that guy's chips back up first. He doesn't belong at this table."

James looked puzzled, but went around and did as I suggested as the guy stood, clearly very, very puzzled and with only a fuzzy memory of how he had got-ten seated in a poker game four hundred miles from his home.

"Better call your wife," I said to him, smiling and sending him a calming influence. "She's going to be worried."

James handed him his chips.

"Help him cash those out," I said to James. "I'll rack my own."

Then I handed James a twenty-five dollar chip and he nodded, leading the guy from the table.

"What just happened?" Carl the dealer asked, glancing back at the guy walking away as I started racking up my winnings for the night.

"Besides stopping an alien invasion and saving the world from being taken over by great evil, not much."

Carl laughed, shaking his head as I took my chips. I tossed Carl a twenty-five dollar chip as a tip and went to the coat tree and got the guy's coat and took it across the room to him.

Sometimes telling the truth seemed funny.

Even when it wasn't.

~

Written in the fast-paced style of James Patterson, Dead Money *takes readers into all aspects of poker, from high-stakes private games to one of the largest tournaments of the year at the Bellagio Casino in Las Vegas.*

Considered a sport by the courts and television, the prize money given away in major poker tournaments far exceeds the total of golf and tennis combined.

But when one of the greatest poker players of all time dies, the stakes rise even higher.

USA *Today* Bestselling Writer

DEAN WESLEY

SMITH

I Take Out
The Garbage
of Humanity...

I KILLED
ADAM CHASER

USA Today *bestselling writer Dean Wesley Smith writes not only science fiction, but many thrillers and mystery stories.*

In "I Killed Adam Chaser" he introduces us for the first time to a very special secret agent. An agent who kills. An agent who prides himself in taking out the garbage of humanity.

The agent likes his job until the day comes along that he meets one of the wives of the garbage he needs to send to the curb. And everything changes, but only in a way Dean Wesley Smith can imagine.

I Killed Adam Chaser

THERE ARE A LOT of people like me, and not enough people like me.

I kill people. It's what I do. It's my job, although I do not need the money and seldom accept it.

Unless I make a mistake, which I never do, no one knows that I have killed a person. Or that anyone has been killed, for that matter.

I am a hired contractor for Clean Sweep, a simple company with a simple slogan: We Take Out the Garbage.

Human garbage.

So let me tell you the story about one sack of human garbage named Adam Chaser. It's a heartwarming story of a simple garbage man (me) doing my simple job, and meeting the love of my life in the process.

At least she could have been.

One

THE SNOW FELL in lazy flakes, blowing on a light Portland wind on the day I met Adam and Lori Chaser. The temperature was hovering at freezing, but it didn't feel cold out. The snow wasn't sticking. Twenty days before Christmas and the people of Portland were celebrating the snow in the air as a sign the season was really upon them. They could do that because Portland seldom got snow that actually became a problem.

The meeting was casual, in the elevator on our way up to our respective condos. We nodded, I refrained from looking at Lori.

I had been given my assignment to dispose of Adam five days before while living in a rented condo in Phoenix. I always rented under an assumed name while on a job and never stayed long in any one place.

That name was now gone.

I have no permanent home and my real name and history have long since vanished from any database. I always became the person I needed to be in the city I live in for the job at hand.

In Portland, I became Dan Garton.

I wore my now dark-brown hair short and stylish to match a look of extreme money. I usually wore expensive sweatshirts and expensive jeans, with five hundred dollar loafers around the building, but I also had a closet of silk suits and everything needed to pull that look off as well. Nothing about me said "fake money." I made sure of that.

The condo I rented was located in an upscale fourteen-story building in a Portland district called The Pearl District. The building had high ceilings, a doorman, and stone and wood and art everywhere. It was first class all the way and comfortable in brown and gold tones that only can be found in the Northwest part of the United States.

The neighborhood had lots of coffee shops, high-end decorator stores, and bookstores. It was a district where most everyone walked or took the electric streetcars that crisscrossed the area. I had hired a limo service to take me anywhere I needed to go at any time of the day or night. A limo and driver remained on duty within one minute of my building's front door.

I seldom used them.

Adam and Lori had a condo in the same building three stories below mine. Adam worked in his family business of investing, and he forced Lori to remain at home at his beck and call.

I had many cameras in every area of their condo so that I could watch their every move.

He forced her to do all the cleaning and demanded that the huge three-bedroom condo be spotless at all times. He forced her to cook a major meal for him every evening, but seldom came home to eat it. Instead he spent many evenings with high-end hookers in a bondage club.

As far as in business, Adam had been the force and money behind two major projects that had caused two hundred families to suddenly become homeless in three major cities. His company had also bought up and closed down five family businesses in the last five months, forcing almost six hundred people to lose their jobs.

He loved causing that kind of pain while making more money than he needed.

I could track his business dealings easily by hacking his company's computer network. They seemed to think no one would be interested in them, thus had taken few precautions. I read every e-mail he sent from work and listened in on every meeting through someone's computer in the room.

I was a master at all things electronic and digital.

I stood exactly six-foot tall and worked out every day. Adam was one inch shorter and weighed one hundred pounds more than I did. In the ten years since he had graduated college, he had become a fat slob who thought himself untouchable and enjoyed inflicting pain on others, including his wife.

Somehow, even with all the abuse from her husband, Lori had maintained her looks and weight since she had married him. She managed to exercise two hours a day. She said on her driver's license that she was five seven, but I would say it was closer to five-five. She had a tiny and perfectly-proportioned body and long black hair that when released reached her butt.

She also spent almost two hours per day on her computer, but I could not follow most of what she did on that computer and could not seem to find the connection into it. It seemed she was not online at all. More than likely Adam didn't let her, so she only played games.

But that was what made me understand her and finally figure out who she really was. What gave her away was my inability to get to her computer.

The exercise and the computer and private time in the bathroom were her only time for herself every day.

She seemed to have some Asian descent in her, while Adam seemed pure white slob.

I had also set up surveillance cameras in the hallways, near the front entrance, in the parking garage, along with every room in their condo. The cameras I used were so tiny that they looked more like the point of a pen than a camera.

Imagine a camera and battery the shape of a small finishing nail with no head. I just had to drill a tiny hole into a wall and insert the camera, usually at a height that no one could touch. And in most cases, the tiny shell of the camera matched the paint color.

And if touched by anyone but me, they generated so much heat from their tiny batteries that they melted and fused into the wall.

He loved causing that kind of pain while making more money than he needed.

They transmitted only to my computer, which only I could access.

For the entire month of December and then most of January, I followed Adam and Lori's routines, their habits, everything about both of them. During that time Adam beat Lori five times, never hitting her in the face.

Clearly she was a strong woman, and she took the beatings almost coldly, which often did nothing more than make Adam even madder. He lived to see the pain on his victims.

After almost two months, it became clear that Adam had no sense that anyone might want him dead, and he took no precautions at all. He was as stupid as he was brutal.

He would be an easy target, which bothered me a great deal. Lori could have cleared him from her life easily with her skills. So before I moved to clear his odor from the human race, I needed to know more about Adam's will and who would take over his company and what Lori would end up with after her husband's sudden demise.

So I dug.

I am an expert on all things electronic and am constantly updating both my knowledge and my equipment.

A garbage man like me has an ability to dig and we don't mind the smell of rot that we often find. And with Adam, I found a great deal of rot.

And I discovered, as I suspected, that Lori would end up with nothing from the company or even the condo if he died.

Not one dime.

It was clear she wanted none of it.

I went in search of why she stayed with him through all the abuse. I discovered that her cover story was that both her parents were dead, but she had a brother who had broken his back in a car accident and his only care was what Adam provided the money for.

Otherwise, she had no assets. Nothing.

Of course, she had assets and it took me some careful digging to find them. She was extremely rich.

And the kid with the broken back wasn't her brother. Her family was as long gone as mine.

She supposedly had stayed with Adam, the monster, because of her brother's care. Not an uncommon story. I had seen similar stories many times in my years working as a disposal artist, so it played.

Over the month of February, without leaving a trace in any record, I fixed all that. By March first, Lori would inherit everything. At least the Lori of her cover story.

That inheritance would anchor her something awful. She would not like that one bit.

And I set up a trust fund that would fund on Adam's death for Lori's pretend brother. It all looked as if Adam had done

it over a year's time. And all from his own work computer.

Lori would be so angry when she discovered that. But I knew she never would because she had no idea I knew who she really was.

Or why she was putting up with the false life with Adam.

She was good and I had come to like and admire the small, strong woman.

Emotions were often a bad thing for a garbage collector such as myself. I knew that.

I accepted that risk.

But I had to admit, I was enjoying this just a little.

And I really enjoyed watching her in the shower. Especially since she knew I was watching.

Two

MARCH TENTH, Adam Chaser took a long sip of a cup of mocha his assistant had brought for him. His young female assistant lived in the same fear of Adam as Lori pretended she did.

Exactly fourteen minutes after drinking the coffee, Adam Chaser grabbed his chest while in the middle of a meeting. He fell forward onto a big conference table shouting "Heart! "Heart!"

What I had laced in his coffee was untraceable and forced the heart to shut down just as any normal heart attack.

I returned to my apartment before he collapsed so I could watch the show.

They rushed him to an emergency room at a nearby hospital and called Lori to tell her that her husband was there and more than likely wouldn't make it. She smiled as she slowly gathered up her things and headed for the elevator.

I made sure from my computer that the elevator came up to my floor so I could ride down with her.

"Nice day?" I said.

She smiled at me. "It is now. Thanks."

I assumed she meant to thank me about my comment about the weather since I doubted she would blow her cover just yet. And I was only slightly surprised at her calmness. Usually abused wives are upset when the abuser is taken from them and she needed to be playing that part.

I was wrong.

I held the door for her at the lobby and as she walked past she said, "Would you like to take a drive with me? I have to go play the grieving widow. Or you could call your limo service if you would rather do that."

I stood there holding the door to the elevator open, acting slightly surprised. She was showing herself to me before her job was finished.

That could be a fatal mistake.

She stopped two steps out of the elevator and smiled back at me. "Mr. Dan Garton, or whatever your real name is, you aren't the only smart person on the planet. And you are not the only one who works for Clean Sweep."

In all my life I had never exposed my cover to a target. I knew I was her target. I had known it almost from the beginning. I was the garbage that Clean Sweep needed removed. I knew that day would come some day. More than likely this was her play.

After a moment she laughed. "Close your mouth and call your limo. We have some planning to do."

With that she turned and started across the lobby at a fast walk, nodding to the doorman.

I pretended to pull it together and got the limo out front in less than one minute.

I didn't like this play on her part.

After we got into the back of the limo, she flicked a switch to block all listening devices. I had one on me, but clearly she wasn't trusting me at this moment and I wasn't trusting myself, to be honest, because this play on her part made no sense.

"I want to thank you for setting me up with Adam's business," she said, smiling a smile at me that I had not seen before. "I discovered it yesterday, although like you, I assure you I don't need the money. And the paralyzed kid who's going to get the trust fund really isn't my brother. It just gave me a good cover story."

I said nothing, as she would expect.

"After I get through the grieving widow part and the funeral," she said, "I'll explain everything if you feel like staying around. I hope you do, since Clean Sweep and I went through a lot of trouble to set this up."

We were almost at the hospital.

"Check with them if you don't believe me. They want us to work together on a very special case coming up."

I nodded.

Now I got her cover story. And her actions made sense.

The limo dumped her out at the front of the hospital and then took me back to my condo.

I had known for months that each room had at least three of the tiny black dots that were Clean Sweep cameras.

Adam Chaser died at three-ten of massive heart failure, his grieving widow was at his side.

At four I sent the coded message that the garbage was taken out.

A coded message came back telling me to stay in place.

As I expected.

I wanted to contact them directly, but I stayed with what I had been trained.

I stayed in place and waited and watched Lori.

And she watched me.

And for almost a month we both pretended that we were not being watched.

At times, that was very, very difficult. I did not want to hurt her.

I knew for a fact she was looking for a weakness to kill me. Clean Sweep operatives never retired.

We got retired and taken out to the garbage.

Three

APRIL 12TH she made her first and only move.

I knew she had been watching me in the shower as much as I had watched her in her shower. I tried to vary my morning routine, but I always knew she was there watching me.

And I tried to keep her entertained.

And she did the same for me as well.

This morning, as I started to step into the shower, I could smell the simple poison. It was a slow-acting type that absorbed painlessly through the skin and killed in twelve hours. She had more than likely planted the poison in my showerhead when I had left for lunch yesterday.

I had known she had accessed the apartment. I had put my own cameras in my apartment that she did not know about. I did not have one in the bathroom, however.

I tapped a button under a towel rack.

My special cell phone rang.

She would be able to hear that.

I left the shower running and went to

answer the phone I had triggered, wrapping myself in a towel as I went.

I had put a scrambled message to be played to me over my phone in standard Clean Sweep instruction format so she could quickly take the code apart.

The code said I had new garbage to take out in Boston.

I went in and shut off the shower, even though I knew the poison was now long flushed through, I didn't feel safe in there. I dressed quickly in my standard travel clothes.

I quickly packed a suitcase, my computer, and then turned and smiled at one of her cameras.

I slowly mouthed the words "It's been fun."

I went out into the hallway, pressed the elevator button, then stood there waiting.

I knew for a moment she would watch me.

When the elevator dinged only a moment later and opened empty, I knew I had her. Her best bet would have been to get on the elevator first.

I stepped onto the elevator, put my suitcase and briefcase with my computer in the elevator, turned and punched the button for the lobby as if I was about to ride the elevator down. Then as the doors started to close, I triggered a camera loop override showing the door closing to her camera.

I ducked out and into the stairwell.

I silently beat the elevator down the three floors.

She was standing there, gun drawn. She was in her blue nightgown, the one that anyone could see through, facing the elevator as the door opened.

She had her legs spread, gun with sound suppressor aimed at the elevator.

She put four shots into the elevator as the door opened before I put three in her. Two center mass, one in the head.

I doubted anyone heard anything, since both of our suppressors were top rate.

She went down into a pile, showing me clearly that she had no underwear on.

I took my briefcase and suitcase off the elevator.

Then I rolled her onto the elevator and tossed my gun with her. It would never be traceable and I had left no prints on it in any fashion.

I had disabled the cameras on this floor near the elevator and in the stairwell, running them into a loop.

I let the door close and the elevator head for the lobby. Lori was going to expose some of her most private parts to those in the lobby when she reached there. She really should have put on some panties this morning.

I went back up to my apartment and opened my computer back up. Then I sent a virus to her computer that would wipe it clean of everything but standard games.

I also sent a self-destruct to all my cameras, melting them into the walls. And her cameras in my apartment as well. Even if someone dug one out, they would never know what it was.

Then I carefully left tracks on her bank accounts that would let anyone decent with a computer track that she had killed her husband for his money and some of her husband's associates wanted the money back.

I left some videos on her computer of her showing her body to some lover who was not seen behind the camera.

I left threatening e-mails from these made-up associates and love notes from her lover. All dated and untraceable to me.

I unpacked my suitcase and hung up my clothes.

Then I spent one full hour checking every detail of my condo for any traps left by the now very dead Mrs. Adam Chaser.

As with everyone in the building, I was questioned by the police, but I watched their investigation through their computers. They had no leads.

I planted a couple of false ones to help them out a little.

A week later, I gave notice on my condo and paid my last bills and had the limo service drop me at the airport.

Dan Garton stepped into a men's rest room and vanished. The camera in that area of the airport just happened to be having a glitch.

Now I still take out the human garbage.

But now I work for myself.

As I said, there are a lot of people like me. And yet, not enough.

Not by a long ways.

Maybe I'll work on that.

USA *Today* Bestselling Writer

DEAN WESLEY SMITH

THE LIFE AND TIMES OF BUFFALO JIMMY

Chapters 7-9

What came before

Nineteen-year-old Boston native *Jimmy Gray had been traveling with his parents and older brother, Luke, headed west to find a new home and new riches.*

Before even reaching Independence, they were attacked and robbed by Jake Benson and his gang. Jimmy's parents were killed, his brother wounded.

In one of the wildest towns in all of American history, Jimmy Gray, a sheltered, educated son of a banker from Boston suddenly finds himself very, very much alone in a dangerous land.

But then through some luck, he finds other young men about his age and down on their luck who might be able to help him.

If he can just decide what to do next.

THE LIFE AND TIMES OF BUFFALO JIMMY

Part Seven
GETTING HELP

JIMMY DISMOUNTED near where the others were still eating and tied up the horse on a tree limb. Luke had agreed that he should tell his friends about the wagon and have them help.

"How's your brother doing?" Zach asked.

Jimmy was surprised. It seemed that Zach actually cared.

"Very tired," Jimmy said. "We're moving him into a hotel room tomorrow so the Doc can look in on him every day and have the bed in the back free for other sick folk."

Zach and the rest nodded.

"You've got some money," C. J. said, more as a statement than a question.

"Not much," Jimmy said, telling them the truth. "Just what Benson didn't find in my parent's wagon. But enough to buy some provisions and take care of my brother until we decide what to do next."

"So, what's this idea we're going to like?" Truitt asked. "I love surprises, in case no one's told you that yet."

"I might have guessed," Jimmy said, smiling. "I've got a wagon about a mile outside of town. The people who have been watching the wagon and my stock during the day are pulling out tomorrow and I need help."

"You want us to be guards?" Zach asked, looking puzzled.

Truitt just laughed. "We take things, remember?"

Jimmy ignored him. "Actually, I was thinking you could all move out there with me. We can take turns staying with the wagon and stock and I'll pay for all the food and supplies for as long as my money lasts. No more stealing and safer than here or in that alley."

There was silence around the small campfire for a moment. From the distance, you could hear the sounds of pianos and shouting coming from the saloons, getting louder as evening got closer.

"Count me in," Zach said. "On one condition."

"What's the condition?" Jimmy asked, afraid of what it might be. He looked into the blue eyes of a guy he had really come to like over the last few days.

"If you and your brother head west, you take me with you. I promised my dad I'd head west, and this seems to be a good shot at doing just that."

"Me too," C. J. said. "I'm in with that condition."

"Oh, I so love stealing food just to survive, why would I want to join this craziness?" Truitt asked. Then he laughed. "Of course I'm in if you take me with you as well."

They all looked at Long, who just nodded. "I'll join as well. But I have one

question. Are you headed for Oregon or California?"

"California," Jimmy said.

Long nodded that he liked that.

Jimmy looked around at the four friends and decided to tell them the about the gold mine that Benson had taken.

"A gold mine?" C. J. asked, stunned when Jimmy had finished.

Truitt laughed. "I love surprises and you are sure made of them."

Jimmy smiled. "A real gold mine with a real deed that my father thought might be worth a lot of money. And my father had been a banker, so he would know."

"It seems we have an adventure ahead of us," Truitt said, clapping his hands together in sheer glee.

"You mean better than rolling a drum?" Jimmy asked.

"Far, far better," Truitt said. "Who could ask for more fun? The bunch of us heading west."

Jimmy glanced at Zach, who was smiling wider than Jimmy could imagine him ever smiling.

"Thanks," Zach said.

"Don't thank me," Jimmy said. "It's a long ways from here to Sacramento. And first we have to find Benson and somehow, without getting killed, get that mine deed back."

"If anyone can find him," C. J. said, smiling at Truitt, "we can."

Part Eight
THE SEARCH BEGINS

WHILE THE OTHERS had rounded up what few possessions they had from their camps, Jimmy had ridden out and gotten two other horses, then brought all four of his new friends back to the wagon, with Truitt riding behind Zach and C.J. behind Long.

By nightfall, they had had a fire going near the wagon and tents pitched and Truitt was working on what smelled like a wonderful stew. He was clearly a cook, and had gotten excited over all the spices and staples Jimmy's mother had brought along.

Jimmy was surprised at how good a horseman Zach and Long were. Both clearly knew and loved the animals, and how to treat them with respect.

By the time the evening had ended, Jimmy was feeling great about his decision. And he really liked being around them. They were all very different, but all of them were on their own and they all knew that they had a better chance of getting west if they worked together.

The next morning, with Long and Truitt watching the wagon while hundreds of other wagons around it were pulling out, Jimmy and Zach and C. J. headed back into town to help Jimmy move Luke to his room in a three-story hotel that smelled of perfume and baking bread.

Jimmy paid for an entire month of room and food. Twelve dollars. The hotel owner was pleased to see the money upfront and promised to help Luke as much as he could, especially with Doc Davis looking out for him as well.

It turned out that Jimmy had needed the help moving Luke. Luke was so weak, he could barely walk, and climbing the long staircase from the hotel's big lobby to his second floor hotel room tired him so much, he fell asleep almost at once after he got into bed.

"That's normal," Doc Davis told the three of them in the narrow hallway outside of Luke's room. "I have arranged for two meals a day to be sent up to his room, and his bed pan emptied. I doubt he's going to be making it out too much for some time. I'll check him every day as well."

"Thanks, Doc," Jimmy said. "Very much appreciated."

"Just take care of yourself as well," Doc Davis said. "Stay dry and don't go getting chilled. You don't want to be in there on a cot with your brother, do you?"

"Not a chance, sir," Jimmy said.

After Doc left, Zach asked Jimmy, "You want to sit with your brother a while?"

Jimmy shook his head. He didn't need to do that. Luke was as well taken care of as anyone could be at this point. He just had to rest and get better.

"Then let's go see if we can find Benson," Zach said. "We have a gold mine deed to get back."

For the first time in what seemed like a long time, Jimmy felt as if his life was actually moving forward. And even though it was starting to rain slightly again, he was smiling.

They had no luck that day finding Benson, and after checking in with Luke, they headed back to the wagon, where Truitt had cooked an amazing meal of bread and stew.

Long, in the meantime, had brushed the two horses left there and checked them over for any problems. He had also fixed part of the tongue on the wagon that had cracked while crossing the last stream outside of Independence. He had also helped the Taskers with a repair before they pulled out.

It seemed to Jimmy that every one of them had a special skill that fit well with the other's skills. And Jimmy had no doubt he was just beginning to see all their special talents.

Part Nine
A PLAN

IT WAS FINALLY, on the fourth afternoon that the five of them were together, that Zach came back with news about Benson from a small hotel and saloon on the edge of town.

And it wasn't good news.

It seemed that Benson had been there for a week or so, camping out west of town and drinking every night with three or four friends.

"Is he still there?" C. J. asked.

"Nope," Zach said. "The sheriff chased Benson and his friends out of town. It seems they robbed an elderly couple."

"Any idea where he might be heading?" Jimmy asked.

Somehow, in the days since reaching Independence, Jimmy realized he had gone from being the scared kid hiding out from the killer of his parents to a person who wanted to track the killer and make him pay. He wasn't sure when that change had happened, but it sure had. And now, after getting this close to the killer, Jimmy didn't want to lose him now.

"From what the bartender I talked to told me," Zach said, "Benson was bragging that he had a gold mine deed in California and was headed there to work it."

"My father's mine," Jimmy said. He could feel his anger boiling, and right now all he wanted to do was hit something. But instead he forced himself to take a deep breath and try to think.

"I'm afraid it probably is," Zach said.

"How far of a head start does he have on us?" C. J. asked, clearly puzzling out what to do next as well.

"Three days," Zach said. "He left at the same time as those two big trains."

"More people to rob and kill along the way," Jimmy said.

The others just nodded to that.

"I'll meet you all back at camp," Jimmy said, feeling just about as low as he had felt in a week. "I need to tell Luke what we found out. We'll talk about what to do tonight over dinner."

A few minutes later, Jimmy turned into Doc Davis's office.

"Everything all right with Luke?" Doc asked

"Far as I know," Jimmy said. "I'm just headed there now, but I have a question to ask you. How long you think it will be until Luke will be able to travel?"

"West?" Doc Davis asked.

Jimmy nodded.

"At least two months, maybe more to be really safe," Doc said. "Or maybe not this year at all. It depends on how fast he recovers."

"Thanks, Doc," Jimmy said and left without another word. He had known that, but he needed the Doc to confirm it. Now he had no idea what they were going to do.

He was feeling sick to his stomach, not because he was now safe from the man who had killed his parents, but because it looked like that man was never going to pay for what he did.

By the middle of the summer, who knew where Benson would be. It had been hard enough finding him in a town the size of Independence. With the entire west to search, it would be impossible.

Luke was sitting up in bed, sipping on some soup, and he seemed to be stronger.

"Hi, little brother."

Jimmy didn't say anything, just pulled a chair over closer to Luke's bed and sat down.

Luke stared at him, frowning, then said, "You found Benson, didn't you? I'm ready to talk to the sheriff."

"Not really," Jimmy said. "He and his gang of killers were chased out of town three days ago, heading west, bragging that they had a mine to work in California."

Luke sighed and put the soup on the nightstand. "I was afraid of that. I've been laying here the last few days thinking about what to do if you did find him, or if he had left. I've got a plan."

Jimmy felt a sense of relief. His mother always said that Luke was the thinker between the two of them. Jimmy was the one who rushed in for the adventure.

"Do you trust the boys you met here?" Luke asked.

"I trust them," Jimmy said, nodding. "They've been helping me guard the wagon and it was Zach who found out where Benson went."

"Do they all want to go west?" Luke asked.

Jimmy nodded. "All of them do."

"Sell the wagon and all the equipment," Luke said, his voice firm and in control. "You'll never catch him with a wagon."

"Catch him!" Jimmy shouted. "I'm not leaving you!"

He pushed his chair back and stood. His stomach was clamped into a knot. No way could he leave Luke.

Luke held up his hand and kept talking, his voice level. "Let me finish. You need to buy three more horses and leave me one in the stable here. And leave me enough money to pay for a year of this room and board and Doc Davis and a little extra. The other two horses will carry supplies for you. Then the five of you head out to track Benson."

"No," Jimmy said firmly. "That's not a plan. I'm not leaving you."

"Jimmy, you know Doc Davis won't let me travel. And if I try, I'm going to be dead in two weeks. You just keep track of him, don't show yourself, and I'll meet

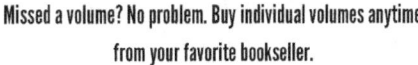

you in Sacramento next July 4th. Then we'll deal with that killer together. It's the only way we can make him pay for what he did to Mother and Father."

Jimmy just shook his head and said nothing. He hated this idea.

"You can't help me by sitting here, you know that?" Luke said, staring at Jimmy. "You did a great job getting me to Doc Davis on your own. You also have to know I believe in you to even suggest that my little brother travel clear out west without me?"

Jimmy nodded. "But I can't lose you."

Luke laughed and patted the bed. "I'll be right here. We'll only be apart until next summer."

Jimmy said nothing. The idea of going west alone terrified him more than he wanted to admit.

More than facing Benson, actually.

"Besides," Luke said, smiling, "You've got your friends to help out, and I've got Doc Davis's daughter to keep me company. Better than your ugly face."

"I can't argue with that," Jimmy said, managing a smile.

"Think about it," Luke said. "But you know I'm right. You have to go, at least to keep track of Benson until I can help you get that killer to justice."

Luke scooted down in the bed and closed his eyes with a sigh. "I envy you the adventure, little brother."

"When you're well, we'll have adventures together," Jimmy said.

"You have a deal," Luke said. "Now get out of here so I can get some sleep. And get a good price for the wagon and the equipment. Make Father proud."

Jimmy left, pulling the door tight behind him.

By the time he had finished a very slow ride out to the wagon, he knew that Luke was right.

There was no choice.

To stop Benson, or even keep track of him, Jimmy and his new frieds had to go and go soon.

They had to chase Benson into the wilderness.

Continued next month…

Stout, the owner of the Garden Lounge always thought he could control the time machine disguised as a jukebox by keeping it unplugged.

Then one day the jukebox started up without power and a visitor from the future asked a very important favor.

A favor that would not only save lives, but maybe everyone.

Now available in audio, paperback and electronic editions from your favorite bookseller.

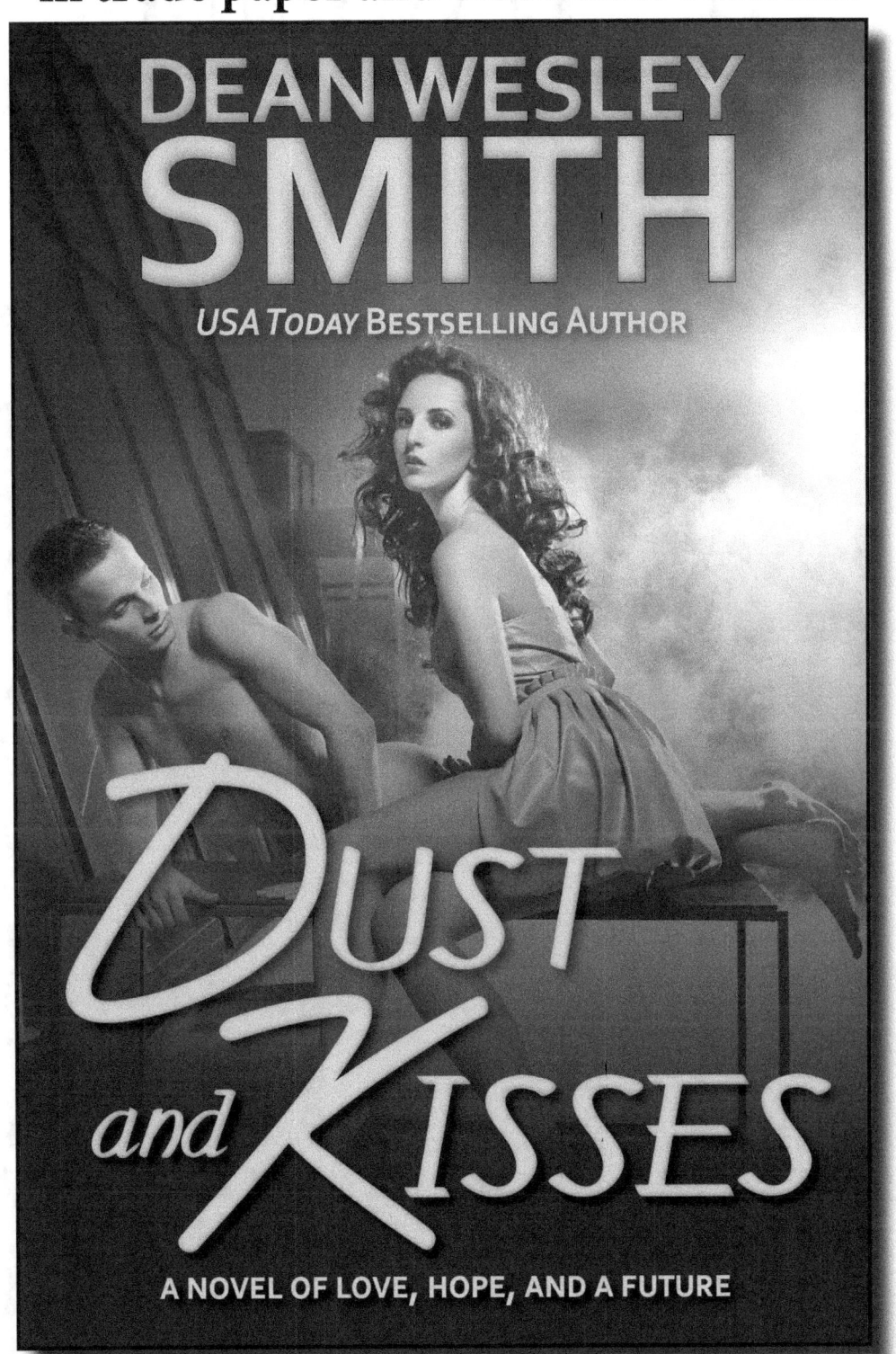

USA *Today* Bestselling Writer

DEAN WESLEY
SMITH

THE CASE OF
THE PLEASANT HILLS MURDER

A Cold Poker Gang Story

USA Today *bestselling writer Dean Wesley Smith mentioned the Cold Poker Gang in his acclaimed thriller* Dead Money.

Now he introduces us for the first time to Retired-Detective Lott and the rest of the retired Las Vegas detectives who play poker, solve cold cases, and call themselves the Cold Poker Gang.

They solve cases every week, but this case becomes very personal for Retired-Detective Lott. More so than any cold case he and the Gang ever tackled before. And as with most cold cases, solutions do not come easy. And answers tend not to be what anyone hoped.

THE CASE OF
THE PLEASANT HILLS MURDER
A Cold Poker Gang Story

One

January, 1992
Pleasant Hills
Las Vegas, Nevada

THE AFTERNOON FELT DARK and gloomy, the wind kicking a chill through Nesto Poretz's gloved hands and light jacket as he expertly dug at the soft soil along the ridgeline with his backhoe, taking large shovelfuls of dirt quickly to one side and dumping them on a pile, then returning the big shovel for another in almost a seamless movement.

The sound of the engine a constant rumbling to him, something he was used to after all the years. Something that he sometimes missed at night, when his apartment was quiet, the kids asleep.

He loved the simple noise of a working machine. There was nothing better.

The sky was cloudy and threatening, coloring everything in the normally brown desert a dull gunmetal gray. Nesto's job, before it got dark, was to get as much of the foundation dug out for this new house as he could. He wouldn't get it all done, but enough to keep his boss happy.

Danny, a tall thin white kid stood beside the hole Nesto was digging, leaning against his shovel. Danny had far too much attitude and thought himself too good to be working this kind of job. He considered himself a real catch for any woman and loved to brag about his conquests, most of which Nesto was sure were completely made up.

For some reason the boss had hired the idiot and had assigned him to Nesto three days ago. As far as Nesto was concerned, letting Danny stand and lean on his shovel was the best place for the kid. That way he didn't screw anything up.

Nesto dumped a shovelful and swung the shovel back over the hole when suddenly Danny shouted "Stop!"

Danny ignored the hand-signals Nesto had taught him and jumped down off the edge into the hole.

Nesto got the bucket stopped just in time, shaking his head and wondering if he would have just done the world a favor not getting the bucket stopped in time. But then he would have had to live with Danny's death and that kid just wasn't worth it.

Most of the time the kid wasn't worth the air he was breathing.

The hole was only about four feet deep where Danny had jumped down and then bent over, so Nesto couldn't see him.

Suddenly Danny scrambled up the bank and out of the hole faster than if some woman was chasing him for child support. He ran about ten steps, then bent over and threw up.

Nesto watched him for a moment from his seat on the rumbling backhoe, then put the machine in reverse and backed away from the edge and shut the engine down.

The silence swarmed over him like a blanket as he climbed down. The cold wind tried to push him back from the foundation hole he had been digging, but he moved over and around to get a better look at what had caused Danny to lose his far-too-expensive lunch.

In his ten years working backhoe, Nesto had dug up a lot of things. Some not so pleasant.

From the looks of how Danny stood, his hands on his knees, shaking his head, this was going to be one of those times.

Nesto moved around and then finally, with a deep breath of the cold afternoon air, he looked down into the hole.

A man's head and left arm were there, sticking out of the dirt.

Most of the guy's skin was gone, his eyes blank sockets, but the guy's brown hair still clung in place.

And on the wrist was a fairly new watch.

Gold watch.

Nesto had just found his third body. The two before had been old settler's skeletons. This one was far from that.

He turned for his truck to call in to dispatch to get the police coming. There was no chance he was finishing this job tomorrow.

More than likely not even next week.

The boss was not going to be happy.

Two

May 2014
Pleasant Hills
Las Vegas, Nevada

AT SIX-THIRTY, I took two bowls of Lays chips down the half flight of stairs to my poker room. I had had the poker table custom built a year ago and sized it perfectly for the area to the left side of the staircase. It could seat eight, with eight matching brown leather chairs around the table. There was a place at each seat to hold chips and a drink and a comfortable light over the table.

I loved that table and felt at home sitting at it.

I already had the chips in place and an unopened deck of cards sitting on the wet bar beside the table. It was Tuesday night and I was flat excited for another fun night of poker with the gang.

I had decorated the rest of the room in framed posters of different Las Vegas events from the past, including one classic showing Sinatra and Martin. A large couch and two recliners filled one end of the room facing a large screen television.

I had to admit, I had spent far, far too much time in this room since my wife, Connie, died two years ago. That's why last year I had decided to completely remodel it and make it the perfect place for me to spend time.

I had made the room all mine, and Annie, my daughter, thought that was a great idea. Upstairs, for me, Connie was still there. I didn't mind that. I thought about her every day and still can't believe I managed to keep going after she died, But somehow I had, thanks to a lot of help from Annie. Now this basement was my space.

Three of the gang said they would be here tonight for the game. Sometimes we had six or seven on a Tuesday night. Most of the time we ended up with only four.

We called ourselves the "Cold Poker Gang" since we were all retired detectives and every Tuesday we played poker while we sat around and talked about cold cases.

I loved poker and I loved being a detective, so Tuesday night didn't come fast enough for me every week.

During the week, each of us would take a case and run down leads and bring the results back to the gang. Just as when we were on the force, one would take the lead on each case.

I just couldn't believe how much I looked forward to the game every week, and especially this week since the case I had lead on for the last month I had finally solved. Together, the gang had solved ten cold cases in just under a year and since we were working for free, that record of closures sure made Benson, the Chief of Detectives, happy.

There was a loud knock at the door just as I sat the chips down on the bar. I glanced at the time.

Someone was very early.

I headed back up and got to the front door as the knock came again.

Retired Detective Andor Williams stood there, a file folder in his hand and a frown on his face. It was Williams' turn to get a new case from the city for tonight, for me to take lead on. The tradition was Williams would present the case to everyone during the game.

Williams looked the oldest of all of us, with almost no hair, wrinkled face, and sloppy clothes like an old man would wear. At seventy, he was still very spry and walked like he was always late for something.

Just like what had happened to me, Williams had lost his wife two years ago, and at times it seemed to me that the gang and solving cold cases was the only thing Williams went on living for. Both of Williams' kids lived in California and he seldom talked about them. He spent far more time than anyone working on his assigned case as well as helping others with their cases.

Williams said, "Lott, good seeing you." Then he handed the file to me, and pushed past. "Figured you needed to see this before we open it to the gang."

I stared at the file in my hand. It was an official homicide folder of the Las Vegas police, with the words "copy" stamped on both sides.

Normal.

I pushed the door closed and followed Williams to the staircase and back down into the poker room. Williams took his normal seat with his back to the staircase and I took the file and went to the wet bar and opened it, spreading it out on the marble top.

It took a moment for me to finally see what I needed to see and why Williams had brought the case to me early. A murder victim had been found in January 1992 and the case never solved.

"Holy shit!" I said.

"My opinion exactly," Williams said.

I was so stunned, I didn't know what else to say.

I just kept staring at the address where they had dug up the vic, not really believing it wasn't a joke or something. The body in this cold case had been found right here.

"That's why I brought it over early," Williams said. "They found the body when they were digging this very basement twenty-two years ago. Go figure, huh? And I can tell by the look on your face no one told you when you bought the house."

I had nothing I could say.

I had had no idea. And I was pretty darned certain Connie would have never agreed to buy the place if she had known.

This was now one of the strangest cold cases I had ever seen.

Three

May 2014
Henderson
Outside of Las Vegas, Nevada

I BANGED ON the weathered screen door on the small house, knocking some paint flecks loose. Beside me Williams stood, looking stern and official. Or at least as much as he could with his rumpled suit and unshaven face.

The weather was headed toward the warm side for the day, a promise of the hot summer to come. We were about two blocks off the old Boulder Highway, in a Henderson neighborhood that had seen a far better time in the past. The houses here were small and the yards tiny, built to house casino workers coming in during the first boom in the late 1960s.

The house we were at hadn't seen a coat of paint in a decade or more and the lawn had long since turned to weeds, only slightly green now because of the wet spring we had had.

I had no idea what we would find, but this was the address we got for the dead guy's daughter.

"Yeah," a woman's voice came from inside the house, then some rustling around and the door opened.

Both of us had our guns unstrapped and ready, just in case. If there was nothing else we had learned over the years, we didn't go knocking on a door without being ready for anything to come at us.

As the big, paint-peeling door swung open, the stench of uncleaned cat boxes and stale beer hit me, turning my stomach. It was a toxic mix and I hoped like hell she wasn't going to invite us inside.

Beside me, Williams short of shook his head at the odor, giving a slight cough.

Through the dirty screen on the door, I could see an extremely obese woman in what had been a blue bathrobe that had more stains than color. She had short hair that looked greasy and a tattoo on her neck that was as faded as her bathrobe.

"Detectives Bayard Lott and Andor Williams," I said. "We're looking for Karen Rafferty."

"You found her," the woman said. She sounded like she had smoked far, far too many cigarettes in her lifetime as well as eating far, far too much.

The Chief didn't mind us introducing ourselves as detectives as long as he didn't hear about it. With our track record of closing cold cases, he was willing to let us drop the "retired" part at times.

Williams and I both flashed our old badges as well to the woman who just looked dazed, more than likely on something even this early in the morning.

"What do you want?" she asked. "That kid of mine get into trouble again?"

"No," I said, "we're here about your father, Nixon Rafferty."

She actually seemed to take a step back from the door and her face twisted up into something so ugly, I couldn't imagine being around her for more than a few seconds.

She pulled her poor, abused robe even tighter across her large bulk and said in a very cold voice. "I don't want to ever think of that bastard again. Not ever. He ruined my life and killed my mother and my baby sister."

With that she slammed the door in our faces, sending paint chips flying into the air around us.

I looked at Williams, who just shrugged.

"More than we expected," Williams said as we turned away.

I could only smile as we headed back toward my brand new Jeep Grand Cherokee, a Christmas gift from Annie.

That response had been a lot more than I had expected. We had solved a lot of cases on a lot less.

Now at least we had something to go on.

Four

June 2014
Pleasant Hills
Las Vegas, Nevada

I TOSSED my ten-jack offsuit into the muck as a response to Williams' three-dollar raise and sat back in my leather chair. Williams usually played tight and when he raised, it was either a stone cold bluff, or he had decent cards. Ten-jack wasn't a good enough hand to test the bluff theory.

The Tuesday night game of the Cold Poker Gang had four retired detectives around the table in my basement game room. The game we always played was pure Texas Hold'em. The stakes were one-dollar small blind and two-dollar big blind with a max bet of five bucks. The worst I had gotten hurt one week was two hundred and my best night winnings had been around one hundred and fifty.

All four of us tonight were good poker players, but not professional level like my daughter, Annie, and her boyfriend, Doc Hill. They both made more money from the game than I ever wanted to think about.

All the players tonight had no real worry about money, so the stakes were good, but not enough to hurt any of us.

To my right sat Ben "The Sarge" Carson. He was a year younger than I was at sixty-two and was in the best shape of all of us since he spent so much time in a gym every day. He told us it was a great place to meet women. I tended to believe him.

He had gray hair cut perfectly, a smile that he said had cost him a fortune, and more money than any one person should have. He was the only heir to a major fortune. Except for a new sports car, he still lived as he had when on the force.

He got his nickname from being a Sergeant in the Army before retiring and becoming a cop. Over the years that I had known Sarge, the guy had gone through three wives and yet managed to have no children. Now we all kidded him about looking for wife four, but he always said no, he had too much money to risk another wife.

Outside of the game or working on a case, I never saw Sarge without a younger woman on his arm. Always a different one as well, so Sarge's plan of avoiding another commitment seemed to be working.

The fourth member of the night was Conklin. I wasn't even sure of his first name since in thirty years I had never heard Conklin called by any other name.

Conklin was the only one of us here tonight with a wife. She supported his poker and cold case hobby because "It got him out of her hair." He had a badly broken nose that hadn't healed right and looked smashed on his face, and he never seemed to smile, although he had a dry and biting sense of humor.

He was also the only one of us with an advanced college degree. He had gotten a night-class MBA years back when he had considered quitting the force to start a business. Conklin always amazed me with his ability with numbers.

Conklin called Williams' raise and, since he was dealing the hand, burnt a card and put three up on the board, face up. My ten-jack would have been even weaker since the flop had come king, five, four, all off-suit.

Williams bet three dollars again and Conklin just shook his head and folded, passing the deck of cards to Sarge for the next deal.

"So, where does the Rafferty case stand?" Conklin asked, sitting back. Every night he was the one to sort of do an inventory of the cases we were working on.

"It's just laying there like a dead, stinking fish," I said, feeling disgusted.

Beside me Williams nodded.

"The daughter said that the vic had killed her mother and her sister," I said, "but the mother and younger sister both died a few years after Rafferty went missing, both from drug overdoses."

"We got no idea what she was talking about," Williams said.

I felt slightly angry that I had to agree with Williams. This case just seemed to be going nowhere.

We had looked through all of Rafferty's bills and debts and he seemed like a poor working slob that no one had paid any attention to.

"So no luck there," Conklin said. "But when I was coming in here tonight I noticed your view, Lott."

I glanced at my flat-nosed friend. "Yeah, one of the reasons Connie and I bought this place."

Conklin nodded. "Back when Rafferty was buried up here, why would someone bury a guy they had just shot on a hill with a view?"

I glanced over at Williams. "That's a question I never thought about. Why kill a guy and then give him a view like you care about him?"

"Family," Williams said, nodding. "Rafferty was a slight drinker, but had no gambling problems and no mob connections or any other crime record. So it goes back to family or a mistress."

"We need more on the wife and younger daughter," I said, nodding. Now I suddenly felt like I had a direction with the case again.

Sarge dealt, then as he put the deck down, he said simply. "Family. If it's not sex that gets a guy killed, it's family."

"Spoken like a guy with far too much experience in both," Williams said.

"You can never have too much experience in sex," Conklin said flatly, picking up his cards and studying them as we all laughed and agreed.

But I knew there was a lot of truth in what Sarge had said. And chances are if we were going to solve the murder of the guy who had been buried right were we were playing cards, I was going to have to dig deeper into the mother and younger daughter.

I tossed away my seven-ten offsuit and sat back, sipping on my Diet Coke and thinking about the next step in the case as the others all called the blind and waited for the flop.

It didn't get any better for me than Tuesday night.

Five

June 2014
Martin Luther King Blvd
Las Vegas, Nevada

I HAD DONE ALL the searching I could online of records about the wife and the younger daughter of Rafferty.

But some of the older records hadn't been loaded up to the online services, so I found myself once again downtown in the Clark County Records building, the smell of dust and cleaning solution filling the air like a musty perfume.

It felt like old home week. I couldn't begin to remember how many hours over the years before computers I had spent in this building digging through records.

I had called Williams and got him to join me, since I knew Williams loved the musty paper files and didn't trust the information on the computers. He was as old-school as they came. And sometimes that had paid off for us.

It took us about twenty minutes, but we eventually found the death certificates for both the daughter and the wife of Rafferty. Both had died of prescription drug overdoses, way before that problem was even considered a problem.

"Take a look at this," Williams said, pointing to a name of the doctor who prescribed the drug for the daughter.

I glanced at the name and then the credentials. It was a psychiatrist.

I quickly glanced at the wife's file, then nodded and slipped it over to Williams.

"Same doctor," I said, pulling out my iPad, another gift from Annie, and doing a quick search to see if the Doctor Harriet Bert was still alive. It was always a problem with cold cases, especially really old ones like this. People had a way of dying or moving out of state and making it damn hard to track.

"Alive, but retired," I said, feeling relieved as I jotted down her address. It was a house address off the strip near the university.

"A visit?" Williams asked, smiling and standing.

"A visit," I said, glancing at my watch. It was almost noon. We might actually have a chance of catching her.

It turned out she wasn't home, but had started teaching part time at the University, so we tracked her to her office on campus in one of the older buildings.

The day was growing hot and both of us were sweating when we reached the red-brick building from the parking lot.

I felt very much out of place walking down the narrow hallway toward her office as students passed us, giving us both odd looks.

"Guess not many old farts take classes here," Williams said.

"No, they think we are professors," I said.

"Yeah, us professors," Williams said, and laughed.

"Why not?" I asked, laughing as well. "We could teach kids a thing or two."

"And both of the things would be wrong and outdated," Williams said as we reached Harriet Bert's office door.

Shaking my head and trying not to laugh, I knocked and a woman's voice said we should come in.

I went in first to be met with a room full of books, floor-to-ceiling, with a matronly woman sitting behind a big, wooden desk. The place was fairly large and smelled of flowers and tea. Or a very flowery tea.

We introduced ourselves and Harriet Bert switched glasses and offered us the only two chairs facing her desk.

"We are investigating the murder of a man by the name of Nixon Rafferty," I said.

Bert looked puzzled for a moment, then said, "Excuse me for a moment."

She switched her glasses again, leaving the other pair hanging from a chain around her neck and turned to her computer. After a moment she finally nodded.

"Sorry, just had to refresh a failing memory," she said, turning back to us and again changing her glasses. "I didn't know Nixon Rafferty was killed. All I knew was that he vanished suddenly leaving his family behind. I treated all three of his family for a time."

"That's why we are here," Williams said. "Rafferty's body was dug up in 1992. He had been shot. The case was never solved."

"So you are trying to solve the cold case now?" she asked, nodding. "I like that. What can I do to help?"

"As you mentioned," I said, "you treated the entire family after the disappearance. Could you tell us when your treatment stopped?"

She nodded, switched out the glasses again and went back to her computer. Then she looked over her glasses at them. "I treated all three for over a year, working to help them get past his disappearance, but all three quit at the same time in January of 1992."

I glanced at Williams. I knew that couldn't be a coincidence. That was when the body was found.

"We would never ask you to break client confidentiality, doctor," I said, knowing I had to be very careful and walk a fine line. "But both the younger daughter and the mother died later that year from drug overdoses. The younger daughter first, then the mother. The older daughter is still alive. But on the two that are dead, is there anything you would feel comfortable telling us about."

Doctor Bert frowned and went back to studying her records. Then without looking at us she said, "I remember when they died. They had used a prescription

I had given them while I was still treating them. It was no longer valid since they were no longer in my care, but they somehow made copies and altered it and filled it at a dozen different places. Police ended up shutting a few of those places down after that."

I said nothing.

She studied the record for a short time on her computer screen, then switching glasses, she turned back to us. "I can tell you that Nixon Rafferty was a pedophile. He abused his youngest daughter and the mother had huge guilt feelings about letting him do that because she discovered it and let it go on. I was doing my best to help the two that died get past that. Clearly I failed."

I nodded and stood. I knew we would get nothing more from Doctor Bert. But now some pieces were starting to fall into place.

We thanked the doctor for her time and headed through the crowds of young students to get to my car.

"Think the family did it?" Williams asked as we climbed in and I got the car started and the air conditioning going.

I nodded. "One of them did it, and I have a hunch which one."

"Youngest?" Williams asked.

"Youngest," I said, nodding. "Now, let's just figure out how to prove it."

Six

June 2014
Pleasant Hills
Las Vegas, Nevada

I SAT WATCHING the rest of the Cold Poker Gang battle over a hand. All three of them were in and Williams ended up taking it when he hit a third king on the river.

That clearly disgusted both Sarge and Conklin.

"Okay," Conklin said turning to me, "after that stupidity, how does the Rafferty murder case go?"

"Solved and closed," I said. I bowed slightly as the other three applauded.

"Williams had a lot to do with this as well," I said.

"So lay it out," Conklin said as Sarge gathered the cards and started to shuffle.

I explained how Williams and I had tracked down the psychologist on the prescriptions. She had given us the information that Rafferty had been a pedophile.

"Family?" Conklin asked.

I nodded, "But we both figured the younger daughter killed Rafferty in the act. She would have been twelve when he died and was fourteen when his body was found when they dug this basement in 1992."

"Why in the act?" Sarge asked.

"The bullet went into his mouth," Williams said, "in an upward direction and exited out of the back of his head."

"So he was on his back," I said.

"So she shot him," Sarge said. "Then the fourteen-year-old sister and mother helped bury him up here on the hill."

Conklin nodded. "Thus the view."

"Exactly," I said.

"Just ugly," Sarge said, shaking his head. "A tragedy all the way around."

"That it was," I said. "A twelve year old girl killing her own father. Doesn't get much worse than that."

"Didn't the detectives back when they found the body in 1992 make a run at the family?" Sarge asked as he started to deal out the next hand.

"They did, but had no luck," I said. "The three family members all held to their story that he had just vanished one night walking to the store for smokes. They were a complete dead end and the detectives then had nothing at all to point to them, or anyone else for that matter."

"So how did you get the older live sister to come clean now, after all this time?" Conklin asked.

"Good old-fashioned blackmail," I said, smiling.

"She has a son who's in and out of jail," Williams said.

"We got dealt some perfect cards," I said, laughing. "At the moment the son was in jail for a minor drug bust, so when they hauled the older sister, his mother, in for questioning, the detectives told her that her son would serve twenty years on the drug charge unless she told them the truth about what happened to her father."

"And the chief went for that?" Sarge asked.

I had to admit, I had been stunned when I suggested the idea and he had agreed.

"He did," I said. "The kid would have been released in a day or so, but she didn't know that. It was a pure bluff."

"And she caved to that?"

"She did," I said. "Spilled every last detail like she had been waiting twenty-four years to tell someone."

"She had," Conklin said.

"So her younger sister killed her father for what he was doing to her," Sarge said, nodding.

"And when the body was found, the guilt just overwhelmed the poor young thing," Williams said. "She could make herself believe that her father was just gone without the body and the investigation. But not after a funeral."

"Killed herself a month after the body was found," I said, "and the mother did the same the next month."

"Wow," Sarge said as he finished dealing out the cards. "What kind of deal did the older sister get?"

I shrugged. "She'll spend some time in jail for a number of charges. Chances are it won't be many since she was a minor when it all happened. And maybe she can now get some real help."

"Always an optimist," Williams said, laughing at me.

I glanced down at a pair of jacks and nodded. "Sometimes I am."

I raised three dollars and only Williams called.

"Now who's an optimist?" I asked.

"Trust me," Williams said, "these cards have a thousand percent better chance of winning this hand then that poor woman has in coming out of that family mess even slightly healthy."

And with that, I sadly had to agree. Sometimes solving old cases had their downsides.

But I still felt like a cop and it was my job, and this poker group's job, to dig up the past and solve the cases.

And even when what we found showed a true dark side of human culture, solving the case felt great.

I sat back slightly and watched Sarge put a third jack on the flop.

And somehow I managed to not smile.

It didn't get any better for me than Tuesday night with the Cold Poker Gang.

41

USA *Today* Bestselling Writer

DEAN WESLEY SMITH

Chapters 7-9

THE ADVENTURES OF

HAWK

WHAT CAME BEFORE...

Nineteen-year-old Danny Hawk, his uncle, and his best friend Craig, were in Cairo to look for his missing father. Danny had witnessed the death of his only contact in Cairo, Professor Davis, because the professor had Danny's father's journals.

Danny knows that the men who had killed the professor were now after him and the journals. Danny finds the journals and gets his uncle and friend to safety in an airport hotel where he tells them what happened. They decide to keep searching for Danny's father and try to rescue him.

But their only problem. They need help.

THE ADVENTURES OF HAWK

SOME HISTORICAL BACKGROUND

In 1970, the world was in great turmoil, and the United States most of all. Protests to the Vietnam War raged throughout the country, and more violent factions of organizations bombed places on campuses and in the cities regularly. So many, in fact, that nothing but the local news reported them.

The mandatory draft was in place, and most high school boys of the time worried about turning eighteen and having to sign up. If a young man could go to college to avoid the draft, he did. Thousands were being killed every month in Vietnam. The Beatles had just released their last album ever, and Richard Nixon was still four years from being impeached and forced to resign.

The cold war still raged between the U.S. and the Soviet Union. China was still an unknown country, for the most part.

In Egypt, the man who had been ruling the country since 1952 had just died, and a man named Sadat had just taken over, but the country was in great turmoil, and no one was sure if it could hold together. The next war with Israel was still two years away.

Cairo, the largest city in Africa, was just starting to undergo a modernization process, but much of the city still looked like it had for thousands of years.

South Africa, the home of the twins, was still governed by a white government, holding the majority black population under control by a brutal policy called Apartheid.

CHAPTER SEVEN

August 19, 1970
Khan Al-Khalili bazaar, Cairo, Egypt.

STEPPING OUT of the modern city of Cairo and into the bazaar was like stepping through time back centuries, much like turning off a modern boulevard in New Orleans and going into the French Quarter. The narrow streets were jammed with everything imaginable being sold on both sides, and the noise level was intense, with people bargaining for everything, often at the tops of their lungs.

Ancient two story buildings and many cloth overhangs and tents kept out the early morning sunlight, making the long, crowded market seem like a carnival without any lights turned on. From what Danny understood, it was this crowded all morning and into the early afternoon every day. At least for now, the shade kept the temperature down. Later this afternoon, with the sun directly overhead, this street would be almost too hot to walk on.

"Oh, wow, does that smell good," Craig said, walking past a booth where a woman was cooking something in a large pot.

It did smell wonderful, like a combination of beef stew and baking bread, but Danny wasn't sure if he was up to eating from a street vender just yet, even though he was starting to get a little hungry.

They passed one booth after another, all cooking something different. And the cooking smells mixed with the smells of incense and new rugs hanging from almost everything.

The booth and the crowds stretched as far as Danny could see, and the moment they got into the crowds, he became separated from Craig for a moment. After they got back together, they agreed that if they did get separated, they would meet back on the corner where the cab had just let them off.

"So, where do we start?" Craig asked.

Danny looked at the crowds and booths selling food, incense, rugs, lamps, and just about everything else. "I don't have a clue. Let's just walk and see what we see."

They were looking for help with languages reading the journals, and Uncle Steve had suggested that the best place to find help, and maybe a guide to the city, was at the famous bazaar. So it was the first thing Danny and Craig were going to try.

They had walked the crowded street for most of an hour, not even beginning to see all of the bazaar yet, when a short, young Arab man approached them and motioned that they should move to the edge of the street, near a building, so they could talk.

The guy was short, no more than five-three, and both Danny and Craig towered over him. He looked to be about their age, maybe younger, and had a robe on that clearly had seen better days. He wore the traditional sandals of the city, and nothing on his thick, unruly black hair.

As they got to a place near a building wall where the crowd wouldn't bang at them like a river trying to go around a rock, the guy said, "American tourists?" He spoke in clear English with a slight British accent that seemed really odd coming from a short Arab boy in ragged robes.

Danny nodded.

The guy introduced himself, rattling off a name that was long, complex, and that Danny had no chance of following. Then he smiled and said, "But my American friends all call me 'Bud'."

"Nice meeting you, Bud," Danny said without giving him their names.

Bud looked at each of them, then shrugged. "You looked like you were looking for something since you entered the bazaar. I just thought I'd offer my services in finding what you are searching after."

Danny felt a shock of fear hit him, and clearly Craig wasn't happy with the sound of that either. This guy named Bud had been following them since they entered the bazaar and they *hadn't* noticed. And Danny had been watching for anyone following them.

"You were following us?" Craig asked, sounding as worried as Danny felt.

Bud shrugged, his tattered robe moving like waves on a calm sea. "Sure. You looked like you needed help. That's what I do, I offer my help."

"For a fee," Craig said.

Bud smiled. "Of course. But it is a very *small* fee."

"I'll bet," Craig said.

"Was anyone else following us?" Danny asked.

"No," Bud said. "I would have seen them. We're you expecting someone to be?"

"We're hoping not," Danny said. "But for all we know, you were paid by the people looking for us to follow us."

Bud laughed. "Oh, trust me, anyone could have followed you. They would not have needed to hire me."

Danny had to agree the short guy was right. He was starting to think that his guy might be able to help them, or at least, for a small fee, point them in the right direction.

"Do you know the city well?" Danny asked.

Bud laughed. "I have survived on these streets since I was ten. Of course I do. The streets are my home."

"Can you read other languages besides Arabic and English?" Craig asked.

"Some Italian, some French," Bud said, now looking puzzled. It was clearly not a question that he had been expecting.

Danny glanced at Craig, who nodded.

"Can you find us someone who also can read Latin and knows some hieroglyphs?"

Bud again shrugged. "Of course."

"Can you wait here for a moment," Danny asked Bud. "I need to talk to my friend."

Danny and Craig stepped a half dozen steps away. "He might be exactly what we're looking for to start with," Danny said.

"As long as you keep an eye on your wallet at all times," Craig said, "I agree."

Then he smiled the devious smile that Danny had come to know over the years. It was a smile that tended to get them into trouble more than anything else.

"How about we make up some sort of treasure?" Craig said. "Tell him that we're searching for it, and offer to let him join us. That way he's got a stake in it as well and won't charge us when he helps us."

"You mean like the Hydra Journals and the Fountain of Youth?" Danny asked, smiling.

"Yeah, that treasure," Craig said, laughing. "I guess we really are after a treasure, aren't we?"

Danny nodded. "I have a hunch we find those Hydra Journals, we find my father."

"I bet you're right," Craig said. "And let's just hope the fountain of youth is real as well."

"So," Danny said, "let's hire this Bud to help us find someone else to do languages, tell him we're in danger and ask him what he suggests for places to live and hide, and then if we like him, we'll tell him everything."

"A good plan," Craig said.

Together, they returned to Bud, who had been leaning against a building, waiting and watching things around them. He seemed almost invisible, he blended in so well. And his eyes didn't seem to miss anything. Danny didn't know why, exactly, but he trusted this guy. He just hoped he and Craig wouldn't pay later for that trust.

"We'll talk money in a few minutes," Danny said to Bud, "but we first need to know if you can get us to someone who can read Latin and hieroglyphs."

"Sure," Bud said. "The twins. They're staying in a small apartment near here."

"Twins?" Danny asked.

"Ernie and Ed," Bud said, shrugging. "That's more than likely not their real names, but that's what they go by here. They're from South Africa and have skin as black as the night. They say they're traveling the world searching for treasures, but I think they're trying to escape something."

"How old are they?" Craig asked.

You two look about twenty," Bud said. "The twins are about your ages I'd say, but they've never told me."

Danny was shocked at how smart this short guy was.

"How old are you?" Craig asked.

The guy shrugged. "I am close to your age, but I have lived a long time in those short years."

Danny didn't doubt that at all. "How do you know these twins can read Latin?"

"Because I watched them one day in an old palace underground near here. They're the smartest two people I've ever met."

Danny looked at Craig, who nodded.

Danny turned back to Bud. "Can you help us find a place to live that will be hidden from those chasing us?"

"Sure," Bud said. "Where are you living now?"

"A hotel," Danny said, not wanting to give him the actual name just yet.

"Real tourists," Bud said. He looked at Danny, then at Craig. "But you're here alone?"

Danny nodded.

"And someone might be following you and you need a place to live and hide while you translate some sort of language problem. Right?"

"Right," Danny said, knowing exactly what Bud was doing. He was starting to bargain for a rate to help them. "Twenty LE's for the day for you to help us."

"Fifty," Bud said. "And if you don't like the twins, I'll find you someone else."

"Thirty," Danny said, "and not a penny more."

"Thirty-five or you find yourself another guide. And you have to show me you have that much on you."

"Deal," Danny said, flashing a fifty Egyptian Pound note. "And if you do us a good job today, we may have another offer for you after we're finished."

Bud smiled. "I like the sounds of that. What first? A safe place to live or meet the twins?"

"The twins," Danny said and Craig nodded.

"Follow me," Bud said and turned, almost vanishing into the crowds of shoppers at once.

Danny quickly checked his wallet. It was still there. He had a hunch that with Bud, he would be checking for his wallet all the time.

CHAPTER EIGHT

August 19, 1970
Khan Al-Khalili bazaar, Cairo, Egypt.

BUD HAD TO WAIT for them a number of times in the short two blocks through the bazaar to an ancient stone building on the right of the street. The heat of the day was increasing by the minute and Danny not only found himself even more hungry than he had been earlier, but also sweating.

Craig was sweating as well. They needed to get out of the heat pretty soon and get something to drink. The Pacific Northwest just didn't have this kind of dry heat.

When Bud finally stopped and waited for them one last time, he said as Danny stopped in front of him. "We're going to have to get you both some better clothes for this heat and not being followed. You stand out like a fire on a dark night."

Danny nodded. He had thought of that, but hadn't expected Bud to.

"Wait here," Bud said, indicating a place still in the shade against a building. "I'll see if they are home and if they are interested in seeing you."

With that, Bud turned and disappeared through an archway that led somewhere into the shadows of the buildings.

"We're going to need food and water pretty soon," Craig said.

Danny nodded. "Bud can tell us which booth is safe to eat at."

"If you buy him lunch," Craig said, laughing.

Danny had no doubt he was going to have to do that. Luckily for them, the exchange rate made staying here very cheap. The thirty-five Egyptian Pounds he had offered Bud for his services was less than five U.S. dollars.

Less than a minute later, Bud appeared near Danny silently, startling both Danny and Craig.

"You two seem very jumpy, even for Americans," Bud said.

"It's been a long few days," Danny said.

"How bad are these people you are hiding from? Bud asked.

"Bad," Craig said and Danny nodded.

Bud frowned, then said, "The twins will talk with you if you bring us all some lunch." He pointed to a cart making some sort of wrap of meat and bread. "Five of those, five bottles of Coke-a-Cola."

"Heaven," Craig said, as all three headed toward the booth where a woman worked and two children sat in the shade on the ground behind her. The entire lunch cost Danny two LE's, including five warm small bottles of Coke, and the woman seemed very happy with that much.

As they walked away, Bud said in a disgusted voice, "You should have only given her one. You two Americans really do need my help."

Danny was starting to believe him.

The twin's apartment, as Bud had called it, was no more than a room not much larger than an average bedroom. It had two sleeping pads against the back walls, one window that was open, and one table with two chairs. If there was a bathroom, it was down the hall or outside.

The place actually felt slightly cooler than out on the street, but Danny wasn't sure if that was because they were out of the sun or if it actually was cooler.

Bud had been right about the twins being Danny's age. They actually looked a little younger, with startling-dark black skin, short-cropped hair, and smiles that seemed to light up the room.

They were clearly identical twins and Danny could see no difference at all, not even a mannerism that separated Ernie from Ed. Thankfully, Ernie had a small silver stud earring in his right ear, while Ed had the same earring in his left. Otherwise they were completely identical twins, so much so that they even finished each other's sentences and wore the same color brown robe.

Bud handed them the food and drink, and Ernie thanked Danny in a polite British accent.

No one sat at the table, since it was covered in papers and books, so all five of them ended up sitting on the floor with their backs against the bare, paint-pealing walls, eating.

Danny was stunned at how good the bread and meat tasted. Almost like a Sloppy Joe back home, only with a much sweeter spice and a very thin, dry bread. And he was so thirsty that even the warm Coke tasted great.

Danny thought he ate the food fast, but when he finished and looked up, Ernie, Ed, and Bud were sitting watching him, clearly waiting. Craig was still eating.

Ed looked at Danny, then at Craig. "We thought all young Americans your age were killing women and children in Vietnam."

Danny was stunned at the directness. He had spent the last few years worrying about being drafted and going to Vietnam. He hadn't realized that the rest of the world paid attention as well.

"College deferments," Craig said, staring back at Ed.

"I must apologize for my brother," Ernie said. "We just do not believe in what your country is doing."

"Half of our country doesn't either," Danny said. "It's why our cities and college campasses are being destroyed by bombs and people are marching in the streets."

Ed nodded. "I am sorry."

"Not a problem," Danny said, waving it off.

"So, what can we do to help you?" Ernie asked.

Danny didn't know where to start, so he figured a little background might ease him into what they needed. He introduced himself and Craig, using first names only, and told them where they were from in general.

"My father is an archeologist. He went missing a few weeks back and we're here looking for him."

"Professor Kenneth Hawk?" Ernie asked, suddenly sitting forward, clearly excited and very interested.

"You're his son?" Ed asked, also excited.

"You have his notebooks, don't you?" Ernie asked.

"And you need help reading them," Ed said. "Oh, this is so amazing."

Bud stared at the twins, then at Danny.

Danny didn't know what to say. Or do for that matter. He just sat there stunned.

Beside him, Craig's mouth was open.

"We would be honored to help you find your father," Ernie said.

Ed nodded. "Very honored. I hope my rude comment about your country's stupid war did not upset you too much. We have already been doing what we can to find your father."

"Without success," Ernie said.

"Sadly," Ed said.

"Yes, your father was a brilliant scientist and archeologist," Ernie said.

"He was onto something very large when he was taken," Ed said.

"Very large. Very important," Ernie said.

Danny held up his hand and stopped the constant talk of the twins. He was suddenly very worried that they had come to the wrong place. "How did you know my father?"

"We met him many times, and worked with him some on his latest dig." Ernie said.

"Only as brushes," Ed said.

"And dirt haulers," Ernie said.

"But we were still honored," Ed said.

Ernie only nodded in agreement.

"Oh, I knew these two could help you," Bud said, smiling. "I'm so good."

Danny glanced at Craig, then back at the twins, trying to clear his head. Finally he managed in the silence of the room to get back to what they had come here for. "Can you read Latin, Italian, or hieroglyphs?"

"Yes," both twins said at once.

Danny glanced at Craig, who was nodding. "Might as well tell them everything."

Danny shrugged. He had no choice. He was going to have to trust some people. Not everyone could be on the other side. His uncle wasn't even a few hours away from Egypt and they were making better progress in getting help than Danny could have hoped for in weeks. Assuming these two were not members of the Hydra League.

"My Uncle Steve, Craig, and I arrived in Cairo two days ago," Danny said, "to start a search for my father, since the authorities and U.S. Embassy seem to have had no luck."

"They wouldn't either," Bud said. "Not with everything that's going on with the new government."

"And your father was taken by forces far more powerful and older than any government," Ernie said.

Ed nodded.

Danny didn't like the sounds of that at all, but he went on. "Professor Davis at the American University had been given my father's notebooks to keep, since clearly my father was worried something would happen to him.

Ernie and Ed both nodded. "Yes, Professor Davis, a good man."

Danny took a deep breath. "I was in his back office when two men burst in and threatened him to get the notebooks. I ended up hiding on the ledge outside his back office window and they didn't see me."

"Oh, no," Ernie said.

> *He had no choice. He was going to have to trust some people. Not everyone could be on the other side.*

"Professor Davis refused to tell them that he even knew what they were talking about," Danny said, going on. "So they killed him and searched his office. Then they cleaned up his office and took his body away, saying they would dump it in the desert."

Now it was Ernie and Ed's turn to look shocked. And Bud didn't look very happy now about even being with them.

"I also overheard them say that they would come looking for my uncle, Craig, and me, since we had just arrived and must have the notebooks."

"That's who you were afraid of following you in the bazaar?" Bud asked.

Danny nodded. "We managed to escape without them seeing us and found another hotel where we registered under false names. Then we bought three tickets back home to lead them in the wrong direction, but only my uncle used his ticket to go home and get my mother to safety. We stayed to continue the search."

"Very smart thinking," Ernie said.

"Yes, very," Ed said.

"So these killers may not know you are even still in Cairo," Bud said.

"That's what we're hoping," Craig said.

"So, you don't have your father's notebooks?" Ernie asked.

"No, I have them," Danny said. "They are very safely hidden. But we could only read a part of them, since my father alternated between English, Latin, Italian, and hieroglyphs."

"Do you have training in archaeology?" Ernie asked.

"Some," Danny said, "but not officially. Just from being around my father growing up, and listening to his stories when he came home."

"So," said Ed, "even if you could read it all, you might not understand it."

Danny nodded. He had considered that as well.

"So what was your father looking for that got him kidnapped and this Professor Davis killed?" Bud asked.

"The fountain of youth," Danny said.

Bud laughed, but Ernie and Ed both nodded.

"It is very real, and has been known about for centuries," Ernie said. "Your father had become the leading expert on it."

"But it is not a fountain," Ed said, just as seriously as Ernie. "Your father, of course, knew that."

"Actually, no one knows exactly what it is," Ernie said.

"But it is the world's most protected secret coming down through the centuries," Ed said.

"It is believed that many people have lived thousands of years because of what is called the Fountain," Ernie said.

"Who protects it?" Danny asked, worried that he already knew the answer. "Men in red hoods?"

Ernie and Ed looked stunned, but slowly both nodded.

"The Hydra League," they said together.

Craig shook his head and stared at the floor. "We are so screwed."

CHAPTER NINE

August 19, 1970
An apartment near the Khan Al-Khalili bazaar, Cairo, Egypt.

THEY TALKED for another hour or so, and the more they talked, the more Danny came to trust all three of their new friends. He learned that the Hydra Journals his father was searching for wasn't really a journal in a traditional sense, but a series of clues that when put together would lead to the secret of the Fountain.

The Hydra League had supposedly been formed six centuries ago to protect the secret, and the journals' clues had been placed in varied places around the globe. Taccola searched for one of them, as did Napoleon and his people.

"Both are said to have found one part of the Hydra Journals," Ed said.

"Do you think my father was close to finding another piece?" Danny asked.

The twins shrugged. "There was a reason he was taken. It was rumored he found the key to finding them all."

"So he's been killed," Danny said, very much afraid of the answer the twins might give him.

"I don't think so," Ed said.

"I think he was taken to the Fountain," Ernie said, and Ed nodded.

"What?" Danny said, surprised. "Why would a group that killed Professor Davis spare my father?"

"Even the Hydra League is rumored to have rules," Ed said. "Very old rules."

"You father cracked their secret code, we're sure," Ernie said. "And thus he would have earned the right to go to the Fountain, the world's greatest archeological treasure."

"But he's being held?"

"Of course," Ed said. "How else would the Hydra League protect its secret?"

"Sure," Ernie said. "They would only have to hold him for a hundred years or so. All of his family and friends would be dead, and who would he tell, and if he tried, who would believe him then?"

Danny felt all the energy drain out of his body. If these two were right, the chances of seeing his father again didn't exist.

"So, we crack the Hydra Journals and go rescue him," Craig said.

"Oh, sure, nothing to it," Bud said. Then he seemed to realize something and brightened. "If we did find this Fountain, it would be worth a great deal of money, wouldn't it? Count me in."

Ernie and Ed both shook their heads with looks of identical disgust.

Danny closed his eyes and leaned back, banging his head slightly on the wall. His father's only hope was him and these guys with him in this tiny Cairo apartment. But at least, as long as they were still alive and looking, trying to find him, there was still hope. No one else was going to go looking for his father, that was for sure.

The image of his father, tall, lean, hungry eyes, boarding the plane for Egypt the last time came to Danny's mind. His work had always consumed him, often more than his family. And Danny had always thought it somewhat stupid, digging in the ground for old things to put in museums.

But it seemed that the past held secrets that were deadly even to the present, and those secrets could change the world if they were exposed. Maybe it was time to tell the world that the Fountain of Youth was real.

The only chance of ever seeing his father again was to find the Fountain. They all needed to pick up the quest where his father had left off. And somehow not get taken by the Hydra League.

He had to actually follow the Hydra Journal, find all of its clues, and go to the Fountain and rescue his father. More than likely the quest would kill him, but he had no choice.

He had to try to save his father.

Danny sat forward and opened his eyes. "Ed, Ernie, would you help Craig and me search for my father?"

"Of course," both said at the same time.

"I will pay all expenses," Danny said, "including food and travel if we have to change cities."

Both nodded in agreement to the terms.

"And if we do find treasure, we divide the value evenly."

"I agree," Ed said, "but I would argue for the archeological treasure we might find be sold to museums."

"Of course," Danny said.

"Then I agree as well," Ernie said.

"How about a five-way split?" Bud asked. "You're going to need someone like me along on this adventure. I know how to find things. I got you four together, didn't I?"

Danny smiled at the short guy. "I was hoping you would want to join us. You're right, we are going to need you."

"You know," Craig said, "we all may get killed going after this."

"It's highly likely," Ernie said.

"But it is a great treasure," Ed said. "And great treasures are worth great risk. Danny, your father believed as much."

"I like that part," Bud said. "Great treasure."

Danny looked at them. "I have no choice. My father needs me. I'm his only hope."

Then he smiled. "But finding the fountain of youth wouldn't be all that bad either."

Continued next month...

Available in January
from all your favorite booksellers in trade paper and electronic editions.

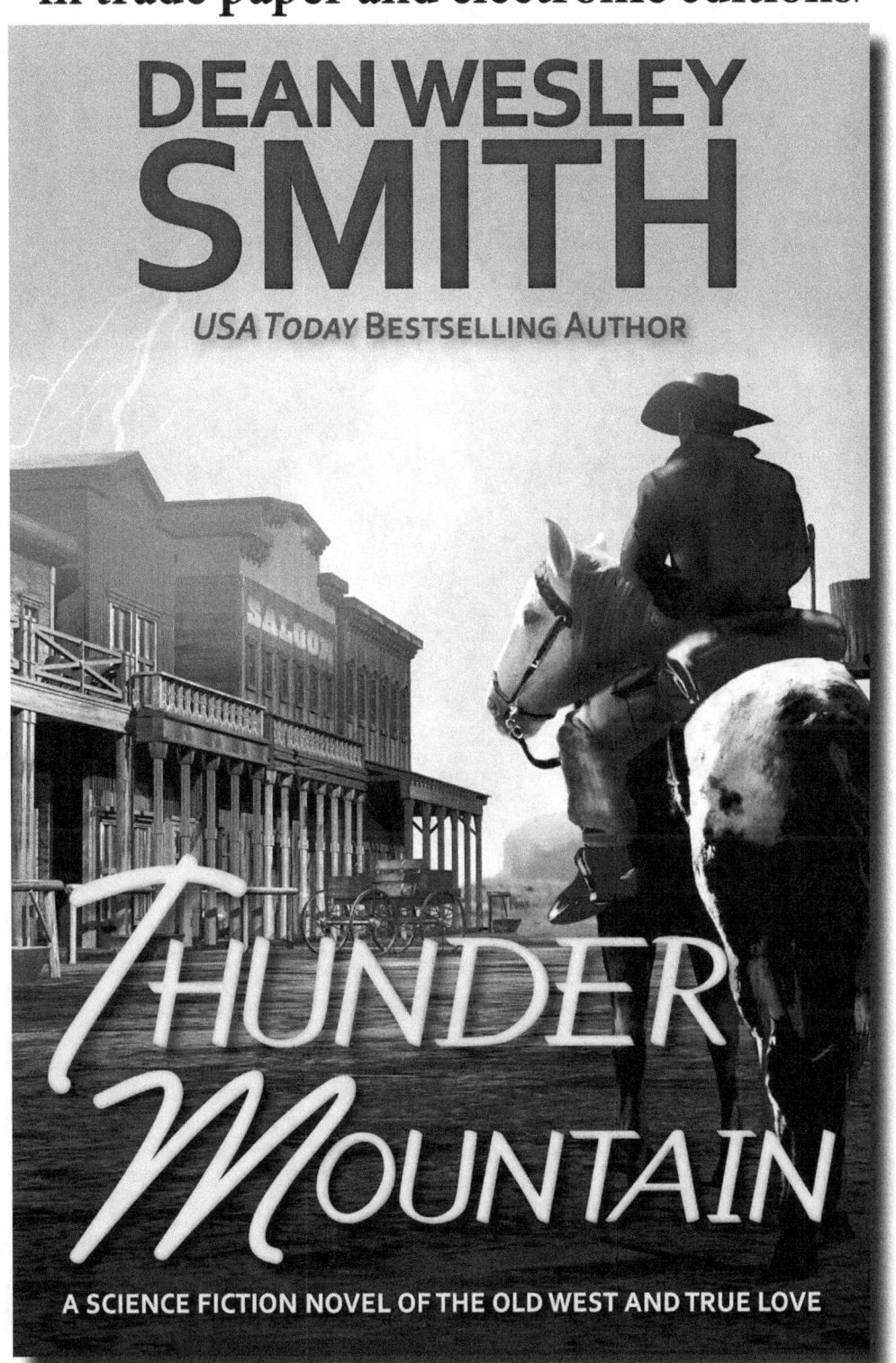

DEAN WESLEY SMITH

USA Today BESTSELLING AUTHOR

THUNDER MOUNTAIN

A SCIENCE FICTION NOVEL OF THE OLD WEST AND TRUE LOVE

USA *Today* Bestselling Writer

DEAN WESLEY SMITH

When Life
Becomes Art...

OUT OF COFFEE EXPERIENCE

USA Today *bestselling writer Dean Wesley Smith enjoys playing against the limitations set up by time travel.*

In "Out of Coffee Experience," an artist works in a moment of time to set up a perfect piece of art.

Just hope you are not in his next work of art. But, of course, how would any of us ever know if someone from the future thought of us as nothing more than props?

OUT OF COFFEE EXPERIENCE

AS A TIME TRAVELER, I quickly came to hate the smell of burnt coffee far more than I used to as a child. And trust me, I really hated it back then. My parents drank the stuff constantly, day and night, and Mom could never remember to turn off the burner under the coffee pot. I lost count of how many times I would come home from school with the house filled with the burnt smell of coffee.

Not once have I ever been able to even taste coffee because of that.

Now, as an adult with a thousand trips back in time to capture different aspects of life in the year 2004, the very idea of drinking coffee turned my stomach. There's an old expression about great art coming from great emotion. When I realized just how repulsed I was by coffee, I knew it would make great art, if I could just capture my repulsion.

My name is Arrington, and in case you haven't heard of me, which I suppose most have not yet but will at some point, I am a time-artist, one of the new and struggling breed of people who capture moments in the past in artistic fashions. Today I planned to travel to the year 2004 and capture the true nature of coffee in metaphor, using a group of people frozen in time in a diner.

After I entered the small, crowded diner called Henry's Place, the first thing I did was move through the people frozen in their places and around behind the counter. Walking through groups of people stuck in the moment used to make me feel creepy, like being in a forest of mannequins. Now it was part of my art.

I took the three coffee pots off their burners, and waited until the machine making another pot of coffee stopped and then removed it from the burner. Since I was going to be in this diner for at least a few hours my time, the last thing I needed was the smell of burnt coffee in the picture too soon.

I poured the coffee out into a sink and rinsed the sink just to get rid of the smell. Because of the law of conservation of time, matter, and space, the people stopped in time around me would never miss it. The coffee would be back, smelling like coffee, tasting like coffee, the very next instant in time.

But for this instant, for this moment, for this piece of art, I wanted that awful coffee smell out of here.

I stepped away from the sink and took a deep breath, taking in the texture of the air in the diner. Getting rid of the coffee had left the place smelling of bacon, and toast. Perfect.

I next went around into the kitchen and scraped everything the two chefs had cooking off the grill, then turned off every burner. Lastly, I made sure no toast could burn.

It wasn't that doing this was because time traveling had made me sensitive to smells. I just had learned that to keep an environment perfect for my art, I needed to take care to make sure no food burnt. I didn't need that problem today, at least until I was ready for

it. This project was going to take long enough as it was.

I stopped in the kitchen door and studied the place, a classic diner for the year 2004, decorated in a throw-back fashion to the 1950s. Everything was a bright red or polished black or shiny white. The contrasts would make for a great piece.

There were over thirty people in the diner, most sitting in booths, others at the counter, plus two waitresses and two cooks, all posed in what they were doing or saying at this instant in time.

It was a perfect frozen picture of a diner just outside of Seattle, Washington in the year 2004.

Sometimes I was amazed at how time travel had given mankind the ability to understand that old saying of "living in the moment." The frozen people around me were in a moment, passing through, I was in another moment sixty years in the future, passing through it. Time travel had allowed me to live in my moment while visiting other moments.

Who would have thought that right along with the law of conservation of energy, there was a law that governed the conservation of time. So when you traveled back in time, you landed in one instant, and stayed inside that same instant until you went back to your own time frame.

This rule of the conservation of time stopped all paradoxes and made time travel completely safe. Nothing anyone could do in a moment could hurt the time line. If you went back to an instant in time and killed your father, due to the law of conservation of time and energy and matter, he would still be alive in the next instant.

Of course I had heard of really insane people going back thousands and thousands of times to kill a parent, just because their anger was so great. And counselors a few years back in my time line had started using the kill-the-parent technique to help get people past their problems from childhood.

Matter and energy reset every instant of time. So far no one had figured out a way to measure just how small an instant of time was.

I moved over to the spot by the front door that I had figured would be my viewpoint location, the place where the viewers of my art back in my own time would stand and view my work. Everything I did today would focus on this one spot. With any time-art, the most important thing was the viewpoint.

As I stood there, I noticed a few details about how things had moved since I had come in. Mechanical things only. I was sure that the first few time travelers who had had to smell burning coffee were the ones who had come up with the theory of "The Observer Effect on an Instant in Time."

Basically, that effect was that the coffee would not burn on hot burners inside every instant of time in every restaurant unless there was an energy field from a future time moving it forward inside the instant of time.

Humans were energy fields, thus when I entered the restaurant, all inanimate objects continued to move, as if the objects were functioning in my time period. The food on the grill continued to cook, the coffee continued to pour, electricity and lights continued to burn, and so on, as long as I was within observational range.

A waitress had been pouring a cup of coffee for a woman in the second booth from the back. When I became an observer in this instant, the coffee continued to pour out of the pot, overflowing the cup and running down the woman's arm, even though neither the waitress nor the woman moved. I would have to clean that up.

Of course, the woman would never know that during one fraction of a fraction of a fraction of a billionth of a second, the coffee had poured over her arm, then in the next fraction of a fraction of a fraction of a billionth of a second, it hadn't.

Interestingly enough, the observer rule had no effect at all on the thirty plus people around me. Or anything else living. They just stood there in their own instant of time like warm statues.

Besides allowing me to become a time-artist, the good side of all this time travel was control of population. With the advent of cheap and easy time travel, billions of people over the last twenty years had simply moved to different instants of time in the past, setting up a thousand different societies, living off the supplies that existed in that one instant, hurting nothing because time reset everything the next instant.

Just last year a report stated that there were more people alive at that moment who lived in the past than did in their own time frame.

Sometimes I was amazed at how time travel had given mankind the ability to understand that old saying of "living in the moment."

My art was for those who lived in my present. "Henry's Place," named after the diner, would be my best work yet because of my passion for the subject of coffee. It might even get me famous, make my name, allow me to move to a better apartment, sell some of my older work, get me a better agent. Hate often brought out the best in an artist and I hoped my hate of coffee would do so for me this time. I was so broke that anything would help at this point.

I studied the diner for another minute from my viewpoint position, then started with the people sitting at the long counter.

Six men, two women. The two women were together at the far end near the entrance to the rest rooms. The men were scattered along the counter and clearly didn't seem to be together. Both women had their mouths open as if talking at the same point. One looked to be in her mid-thirties, the other might have been her mother.

One thing that always surprised me was how warm human skin frozen in an instant felt. I usually tried not to touch anyone, but for this work, I was going to have to touch everyone in the diner.

I worked quickly, stripping the man closest to me, taking off his suit jacket, his shirt, his pants and shoes, leaving him only in his underwear and socks, the same way I planned on leaving everyone in the diner.

Then I took the man's right hand and used his thumb and index finger to pinch together his nose. In his other hand I put a coffee cup and put him into a position that looked like he was drinking.

I tipped his head back slightly and then pushed the skin around his eyes together a little to make him look like he was squinting, like he really hated the taste of the coffee he was trying to drink.

I stood back and studied him, making sure every detail was right.

It was.

I tossed his clothes in the kitchen out of the way of the image I was building, and went to the next man at the counter. The younger woman at the end of the counter caused me the most problems. She hadn't been wearing any underwear under her business suit, and she was going to be very clear in the final setting.

I didn't want nudity in my work, since so many people had already done that. I wanted everything about this work to be original and focused on the coffee. So I had to go to the woman in the back booth who had her back to where my viewpoint shot would be taken and take her underwear and put it on the woman at the counter. That was a lot more work than I had planned on doing for one person.

By the time I had finished undressing and posing everyone at the counter, I was sweating and needed a break.

And I needed some food. Another good thing about time travel was that the food was free for the taking.

I moved into the kitchen, poured myself a glass of orange juice, and took a couple of doughnuts from a tray in the back. Then I moved to my viewpoint position near the front door and stared at the work so far. It was as good as I had hoped it would be when I came up with the idea.

Excited at the progress I had made, I quickly downed the snack and went back to work, only taking off the clothing of the people in the booths that would be seen from my viewpoint position. And each person I posed in the same fashion, with the same type of coffee cup.

A room full of patrons in their underwear downing a cup of coffee they clearly hated. This was turning out better than I had hoped.

Finally, I moved to the two waitresses, the crowning touch on this image.

One waitress was short and attractive. She stood near a booth where she had been pouring the coffee, and I left her right there.

The other was near the cash register and I moved her a little so that she was in the foreground of the shot more, yet not blocking any other line-of-sight from the viewpoint to another person.

I undressed them both, glad that both had on the standard white underwear and bras of the time. Then instead of putting coffee cups in their hands, I posed both of them drinking right out of an empty coffee pot, only with their other hands on their hips.

They looked like super-coffee-drinkers.

Only in their underwear.

A dozen times I went back to my viewpoint to make sure everything was perfect, every detail in its right place, nothing but underwear and coffee cups and sour expressions showing.

The image I was about to record for all time would have two major parts to it. It would appear life-sized and three dimensional to the observer from the viewpoint, reproduced exactly at this real size in my gallery, an instant in this time caught in symbolism for all to see. The second aspect would be that it would have a sensory impact.

I planned on having the lights dimmed as the observer approached, then bring them up to the brightness of color and intensity of the diner, just like the observer had come in from the dark outside. Of course all of this would depend on selling it to a gallery who could do those sorts of things. But I had no doubt this would be my best, so I would sell it.

As the viewer approached, the smell would also grow stronger. At first it would be the smell of regular coffee, bacon and eggs, then as the observer reached the viewpoint, the smell would turn to one of burnt coffee.

After every detail was right and I had double- and triple-checked everything, I was ready for the final smell touch. That was the critical factor, and to make it right

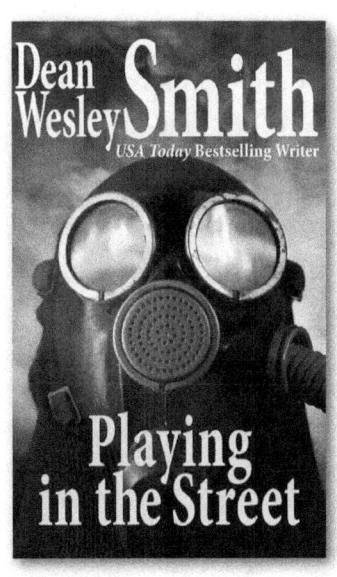

it had to be recorded at the exact moment of capture of sight. It was my attention to those kind of details that I knew would someday make me famous.

I moved around behind the counter and studied the old coffee machines. I had planned on having all four of the coffee makers pouring out coffee onto hot burners with no coffee pots. But I quickly discovered I had a few problems.

First off, I had no idea how to make coffee. I hated the stuff so much, I had no idea how it was made. I know my mother had put some sort of coffee bean in some part of the machine, but I had no idea how or where, especially in the bigger restaurant machines.

The second problem was that I couldn't find any fresh coffee. There was an empty sack beside one coffee maker, but it looked like that the restaurant had run out. I went back and searched the kitchen and the store room, but still couldn't find any.

I ended up standing there by the coffee machine and staring at the scene I had spent hours creating. The smell of burnt coffee, the image of the coffee pouring out of the coffee machines onto hot burners without pots, was the main impact of the image. Without it this work of art would say nothing. It would be just like all the other time-art pieces I had done, and everyone else did.

Yet there was no coffee, and even if there was, I had no idea how to make the big machines make the stuff into liquid form.

What a waste of a day of work.

I couldn't go home and figure out how coffee was made, because time travel would never bring me back to this exact instant again. It would be close, but I would have to do all the work I had al-

ready done in the undressing and posing. No exact instant could ever be returned to after going to the present. An instant in time in the past was just too small a unit to hit.

I dropped down onto one of the stools at the café counter and just sat there, staring at all the work I had done, and that was now wasted. I had had other pieces of art go bad before, but never this bad.

There didn't seem to even be much reason to take the image at all. The statement wouldn't be enough without the coffee pouring from the machines and the burnt smell. The piece would have no impact. I was better off just calling it a day, going home, and maybe trying it again at some point later.

But I knew that would never happen. Once I had lost interest and excitement in a project, it never came back. Ever.

I sighed and stood. How could some place like this be out of coffee?

Suddenly that question hit me, and I realized how I could make an even stronger statement about the stuff I hated so much.

I went back to work, my excitement even higher than before, changing each person's pose from one of disgust at the drink, to one of surprise alternating every third person with anger.

I turned the cup in each person's hand over, and moved the position of the cup up above each person's head, as if they were looking up into the empty container.

Then I opened about half of the people's mouths, as if they were trying to catch the last drop from each cup.

I posed two of the customers at the counter licking out their cups.

I posed each waitress with the empty coffee pot upside down, clearly empty, with a look of panic on each of their faces.

Then I stood back at my viewpoint position, checking every detail. It took me another fifteen minutes to get a few expressions right, a few arm angles in the right place.

The empty coffee machines would be perfect in the picture and I took the other two empty coffee pots and placed them on their sides beside the machines.

But there still felt as if something was missing.

Actually two things. I would need a title as well.

I stared and stared at the scene I had built until finally inspiration hit me like a glass of cold water. I knew exactly what was missing.

I took three people out of the booths and moved them into positions around the waitress in the back, empty coffee cups held over the heads like weapons. Each person I posed with an angry expression on their face and in a posture as if they were about to beat the waitress for not having coffee.

I put an expression of fear on her face, and on the other waitress's face.

Then I stood back and again studied the work. Now it was perfect.

But I still needed a title. Maybe a title would come after I took the image? It sometimes worked that way.

I took my hand-held recorder and got it into the exact right position, where the empty coffee machine was clear, where the attack on the waitress was clear, where all the people out of coffee were clear. This one didn't need smells after all. It would do just as it was.

I quickly captured the scene and then stood and stared at the image I had recorded. If this didn't sell, nothing would. I just had to have a title.

Then suddenly it came to me. Coffee, it seemed, was an addiction for the ages, and everyone would understood my work because I tapped in on that.

I quickly titled the work in my scene recorder.

"Seattle Addiction."

And no matter how famous this made me, I would never tell a soul that it had all come about because I couldn't make even a single cup of coffee.

———

DEAN WESLEY SMITH

USA Today Bestselling Author

the First Tee Panic

AND OTHER VERY REAL GOLF STORIES

Former PGA Golf Professional and USA Today *bestselling writer Dean Wesley Smith walks you step-by-step, club-by-club from your car to the first tee and beyond in a laugh-out-loud style that not only teaches, but entertains.*

In the first six parts, Dean got you from the parking lot, through the pro shop, on and off the driving range and practice putting green. Now comes the big problem: How to deal with all the issues of the first tee and getting that first shot away.

THE FIRST TEE PANIC
And Other Very Real Golf Stories

PART SEVEN:
HELP! THE STARTER HAS JUST CALLED OUR GROUP AND I'M FROZEN STIFF

METAPHORICALLY, OF COURSE. Actually, more than likely, you have already shed your morning coat and are down to just a sweater and your golf attire. But that echoing call over the practice putting green sends a wave of excitement and fear through you.

"Smith foursome on the tee, Jones group on deck."

You jump in your cart and follow the small signs toward the first tee. Interestingly enough, on many of these big courses, the first tee is a good distance away. Don't get lost. Trust the signs. They will be much bigger than those warning you away from the dining room in the clubhouse.

A man or woman with a big smile, scorecards, and a quick lecture on the day's local rules will greet you at the first tee. Pay attention to those rules as well, since they may mean the difference between a good day and a bad one. And hope it isn't a "path only" day. If it is, that means you have to leave the golf cart on the path no matter where your shot ends up. By the sixteenth hole on days like that, you tend to aim toward the side of the fairway with the golf cart path. Trust me, it can be a long, long walk from a cart on one side of the fairway to deep in the desert or trees on the other side. Especially if you get to your ball and discover you need a different club.

But assume it's a great day, you can take the cart anywhere, and the local rules are about things like not damaging any cactus.

So how do you make yourself relax enough to hit the ball somewhere down the first fairway? The answer is, simply, you won't relax. But that doesn't mean you can't hit a great shot.

Joke with your playing partners, and make sure you get enough strokes on the bets. I used to make sure I didn't get enough strokes from better players for two reasons. First, it made me play better, or so I thought. Second, I had more money then sense.

Don't do as I did on this topic of setting bets on the first tee. Get the strokes. As far as your friends are concerned, on the bets for drinks and dinner, you are the worst player to ever walk on a golf course and it still wouldn't be fair if they gave you a stroke a hole to make up for your defects.

Of course, they're going to be trying to get the best deal as well, so the compromise ends up taking some first tee time.

When that's all done, and the starter says, "Play away, folks," it's again time to get serious.

Remember that great last drive on the range? Remember how it felt? Now's the time to start thinking about it.

Then follow the very easy steps in the next part that will help you stay calm

enough to make contact with the ball and get started into a fun day of golf. Note, I didn't say stay calm completely. I'm not a miracle worker here.

But if you do remember that great shot on the driving range where your drive sailed perfectly on target, you have managed step one.

PART EIGHT:
EASING THE TENSION

FIRST, TAKE A DEEP BREATH. Giving birth to this first round isn't going to be as painful as delivering a baby, but breathing really does help if you don't want it to be as messy. The last thing you need to be is light-headed walking up there between the tee markers. Fainting on your golf ball really is the stuff of jokes and legends, although I will have to admit, I have only heard of golfers passing out on the first tee, and one guy going to his knees with a heart attack. I have never actually seen it happen.

And thankfully, it hasn't happened to me.

But it does happen. I thought I might pass out once on the first tee at Olympic Club outside of San Francisco. They had the tee markers backed up so close to a giant window in the old clubhouse, I swore my back-swing was going to break the window between me and a hundred or so people in the bar. The fairway snaked down the hill away from me, with trees on the edge so tall, it looked like I was staring down a tunnel instead of a fairway. I managed to keep breathing, but I have no memory of where that drive went. I do remember sort of coming to as I walked past the woman's tee markers.

So breathe, slowly and deeply while you do the second step, which is to get your driver out of your bag. Toss the head-cover either into the cart's basket behind the clubs, or on the seat of your cart where you will see it when you go to sit down.

Don't take it onto the tee with you. Doing so is just asking for trouble and having to drive back down the first fairway to get it after you remember where you left it. So leave it where you are going to sit on it, or put it in the basket where it can just ride along until you come to your senses.

Third step, no matter how many jokes are flying among your friends and the starter, remember to get your golf ball. I can't tell you how many times it was my turn to go to the first tee and I didn't have a ball ready. For some reason, for some of us, that little fact just slips our minds in this preparation routine.

Breathe.

Get your ball, and put a second one in your pocket just in case. Don't think about why. Just put it there and forget it.

Breathe.

I said don't think about why that second ball is with you. So stop it and breathe.

Now, get at least two tees, one for the ball in your hand, one for a spare in your pocket.

Breathe.

You're ready, so climb onto the first tee.

It doesn't matter if it's flat from the cart path to the tee, or downhill. It's still climbing onto the tee like a prizefighter climbs into a ring in a fight. This is the area you're going to battle.

This is the start of the round.

It's you against yourself and the acreage stretched out in front of you.

Gaze down the fairway at your opponent.

Yeah, I know, it looks impossibly narrow.

And really nasty.

And those looming sand traps could swallow your entire house and not even burp.

Breathe.

Hitting the fairway doesn't matter. Remember that.

Repeat after me... "Hitting the fairway doesn't matter."

The goal now is to just get off this tee box alive and with some dignity intact.

So, instead of staring at the fairway of doom, spend this moment picking a target, more than likely a tree or cactus or rock on a mountain in the distance.

Don't look at those traps unless you are using the edge of a distant one as a target. Just pick a target and ignore the rest of the fairway. Ignore the trees, ignore the deep rough and all the problems that lurk on both sides of the fairway. Just like on the driving range, you're going to put a slow, paced swing on your ball and watch it sail toward your target just like it did on the range.

Got that?

Target. Critical.

Don't think about the problems ahead or the width of the fairway. Chances are, the landing area is much, much wider than it looks anyway. The evil golf course designers can do amazing things with perspectives and visual distractions on golf courses. Ignore them. Don't let those pencil pushers beat you.

Pick a target and nothing else matters.

Now, let me end this chapter with a little story about a first tee.

I wasn't playing, so I was very calm and clear-headed when this all happened.

A Little Side Story

I WAS THE STARTER for all the "rabbits" on the PGA Tour in the winter of 1973 in Palm Springs, California. Back then, they didn't have tour schools or anything else like that. You could play on a PGA Tour event by simply signing up for a Monday morning qualifier and scoring well enough to get one of the top spots that day, which allowed you to play in the tournament.

In 1973, the Monday qualifier for the Bob Hope Desert Classic was at a club called Westward Ho Country Club. I was the assistant professional there under an old-time pro named Zell Eaton. So my job was to sit on the first tee box, check in the young professional players and when the group in front of them was clear, say, "Play away, gentlemen."

Now, understand, in my entire life up to that point, I had never seen such a large bunch of idiots trying to play a game that takes thinking and brains to play well. The first hole that year at Westward Ho Country Club was about 320 yards long, with the last 100 yards of the fairway in front of the green being no more than about ten paces wide between an out-of-bounds on the left and a lake on the right.

No landing area, lots of punishment for anything but a perfect shot.

And no reward for hitting a perfect shot, either.

Any smart person would take one look at the maps we gave them, the yardage booklet, and simply hit a three iron back into the wide part of the fairway, where there was no lake or out of bounds, then take a wedge into the green. Safe.

That kind of play made the hole an easy birdie hole.

But safe and smart didn't seem to be words these want-to-be touring professionals had in their vocabulary. Man after man stood up there with driver and either hit it out of bounds or into the water. At least nine out of ten of them.

I was stunned and I learned a great lesson from that day as well. When you are standing on every tee box, pay attention to the hole in front of you for a moment. If there is a lake out there in the middle of the fairway about 200 yards, don't hit your driver.

Again, golf is a mental game. And sometimes that means you have to actually think and plan how to play a hole. Startling concept, I know, but something to think about.

However, I must admit, in my later days of playing the game, I tended to forget this basic rule as well, as many of my golfing friends will tell you in stupidly-funny stories.

So, look at the hole. If the driver is still the right play, pick your target. It's almost time.

PART NINE: GETTING THE TEE INTO THE GROUND

BACK TO BREATHING.

At this point, this is critical because, as your turn to hit comes and you have to walk forward and put your tee into the ground, you are going to have to bend over. Now breathing and bending over do not go well together. If, for some reason, you don't believe me on this important point, try it at home, next to your bed, with a phone nearby. Hold your breath for as long as you can, then without breathing bend over facing your bed and pretend to put a tee into the carpet.

Make sure you fall onto your bed and not the cat.

Now, imagine falling over your ball, kicking it as you try to get your balance, and landing on the wooden tee marker. Number one, that has got to hurt. Number two, it's just not the way to get a round started.

So, you are fine with the breathing thing, but your hands are shaking. What I'm about to tell you next is critical.

Put the ball on the tee in your hand.

The ball and the tee are now one unit, not to be parted until you force the separation with a mighty swing.

Sure, on television, you see the pros putting the tee in the ground with the ball, then picking up the ball, looking at it, then putting it down on the tee so that the logo on the ball is where they want it to be.

You can do that for the next seventeen holes as well. But for this first hole, just leave the ball and the tee as one unit in your hand.

Then, from about five steps away, pick a spot where you are going to put the tee and ball. There is a critical second point to this. Make sure the spot is behind and between the tee markers. Your golfing buddies and the starter tend to frown on you playing either ahead or outside the markers. And besides, it's against the rules and can cost you strokes.

An aside right here. If you don't own a Rules of Golf book, go buy one and spend a few nights reading it at home. There are other books with examples, written in an interesting manner, to explain each rule, but start with the little Rules of Golf booklet and keep it in your bag.

But at the first tee, the most important rule is to get the ball teed within an imaginary rectangle that has the leading edge between the two tee markers and extends backward two club lengths.

Pick your teeing spot with a couple things in mind.

Is your swing clear of any overhanging tree limbs and too-close benches? And can you stand normally if you put the ball in that one spot, without having to stand straddling one of the tee markers?

On the first tee, it's just safer to pick a spot right square in the middle of the markers, back about two feet. Very safe there.

Now, with your focus on that spot in the grass, and your breathing under control, make the motion of putting the tee in the ground one movement. Don't hesitate, don't get down on one knee, don't bend over like a stork wanting to put your head into the ground. Simply, at the end of a stride, bend forward and just get the teen into the ground, then stand up.

Ninety-nine percent of the time, this will be good enough with standard tees. That one percent of the time the ball falls off, just pick up the tee and the ball again, put them together in your hand, and get them into the ground again.

Then pretend like that never happened. No jokes, nothing. And for heaven's sake, never say that lame sentence, "Well, that's one."

It's not, everyone knows that, so don't say it. Just makes you look like an idiot and no one will laugh.

So, with the ball teed up, you are focused on your target and that's all that matters.

Stop looking at those big fairway bunkers.

Target. Just think target.

You should be like the Dustan Hoffman character in the movie *Little Big Man* right before he fires a gun. Remember how he went "snake-eyed?" Don't go snake-eyed, actually, because you have to still see the ball enough to hit it, but do the same kind of focus on your target as the Hoffman character does.

Nothing else matters but the target.

Block out all other things.

And don't forget to breathe.

Going "snake-eyed" and fainting could really worry your golfing buddies. And might just get you life-flighted to the nearest hospital.

PART TEN:
TAKING A DEEP BREATH, MAYBE TWO

DON'T SKIP THIS SECTION just because you think I've already pounded the breathing thing home. This is different.

Right now, you have your ball teed up, you've stepped back directly behind the ball, you have your driver in your hand, and you're about to step to the ball and address it.

Your golfing buddies are silent, watching.

The group on deck has arrived and are sitting in the carts, watching.

The starter is watching.

It's the nightmare come to play itself out in real life.

No, not hardly. Not with all the things that have gone right to get you to this point this morning.

So, standing there, staring at your target and nothing else, the ball two steps in front of you, it's time for the final few details of the preparation.

Take two, long, very deep breaths. This will get you enough oxygen to get you through the shot without problems. But two deep breaths like that also relax muscles. It's like a signal to your body to let the stress go.

Just like Jack or Tiger or any of the big guns on the tours, while you are doing these breathing exercises, focus on your target. If you haven't noticed them doing this, watch the next time they show a professional player tee off on television. They are not just staring lamely down the first fairway hoping to have their ball land out there somewhere. No, they are staring intently, snake-eyed at a single target.

And they are taking in and letting out long, deep breaths.

Do the same.

This single-minded focus tends to block out all the problems that could happen as a result of a poor shot. This focus tends to bring in only the aspects of a good shot.

And if you do this focus while taking the two deep breaths, it somehow puts that single focus down into the part of the brain that steers the golf swing. I don't think there have really been studies on why this happens, but trust me again, it does.

And if you don't trust me, pay attention during the next tournament on television, especially to the big ones like the Masters or US Open that show the leaders teeing off on the first tee.

You will see an amazing amount of deep breathing and snake-eyed focus. If the camera angle is good on Tiger on a first tee, you will see him acknowledge the applause when his name is called, then you will see in his eyes that he actually just closes out everything around him but his target. It's an amazing skill to be able to do that. Us mortals can't do that completely, but we must try.

You must try.

Focus on the target and take two deep breaths.

This will take about three seconds. If you take any longer than that, your playing buddies might say something and break the mood.

Besides, you don't want to take any longer than a few seconds standing behind your ball staring forward. There's just too much chance you might freeze up.

So breathe twice, focus on the target, and then step toward the ball.

PART ELEVEN:
VISUALIZING THE PATH OF THE BALL

YOU'RE STEPPING TOWARD the ball, the target is solid in your mind.

Now, remember that final great shot you made on the driving range?

Remember the feel of it?

Remember how the ball went right toward the target?

That's what you need to be doing now.

Remembering and visualizing how the ball sitting in front of you is going to go sailing toward the target.

Take your quick practice swing, thinking about how that perfect drive on the driving range felt.

But more importantly, that practice swing is done to make sure you have the memory of that good shot in your mind. Look up at your target as you finish the swing.

See it?

See the imaginary ball floating right out there, right at the target?

Okay, okay, don't take very long on this. Maybe a fraction of a second is all. You stand there posing with your practice swing and your golfing buddies will really, really start making jokes.

Nasty jokes, like calling you "poser boy" after David Caruso in that television show *Miami: CSI.* Trust me, if you haven't seen that show, watch it once and you will know exactly why you can only take a few moments on this.

But it doesn't take long to visualize a perfect golf shot, to get the memory back into your mind.

Do it.

Then step to the ball, look once more at your target with the memory of that perfect shot. You are there.

You are ready to start your round.

From bag drop through the golf shop, from driving range to the practice green, through an early morning snack to walking onto the first tee, it has all come to this moment.

You are ready.

For heaven's sake, don't whiff it.

Just kidding.

Take one last deep breath and then...

PART TWELVE:
...JUST HIT THE STUPID THING

A COUPLE OF QUICK THINGS for you to do correctly in this fraction of a second you are swinging. And it is amazing how many thoughts can go through a golfer's mind during a swing. Sometimes it feels I could write entire novels in a back-swing.

But one final thought is important, besides visualizing the path of the ball toward your well-focused target.

Keep your attention on the ball.

Actually, keep your direct gaze on a dimple on the back of the ball, and if your eyesight isn't good enough to see a dimple from a standing position, what are you doing on a golf course anyway?

Keep your gaze on that spot until the ball vanishes from your sight and there is nothing but grass. Not one moment earlier.

It will take a fraction of a second after impact for your brain to make note that the ball has vanished, and this will be enough time to allow you to keep your head steady enough to make a good swing.

Why this advice now? Simple. You have intense focus on the target, intense visualization of the path of the ball, intense memory of the good shot on the driving range. Right? All that will make your brain excited to see the outcome of this shot. And thus, you might look up before the swing is finished.

Looking up has the effect of pulling up your shoulders with your head and chin. And when you pull up your shoulders in the middle of your swing, only three ugly things can happen.

One, you manage to make contact and get the ball into the air, but it goes way to the right, way fast.

Second, you make contact with the top of the ball and it does the bounce-bounce thing off the front of the tee box, through the woman's tees, and often doesn't even make it to the mowed part of the fairway.

Or third, you pull your head and shoulders up enough to miss the ball completely.

Whiff.

Nightmare of sweating sheets and laughter from friends.

So, keep your gaze focused intently on the dimple on the back of the ball and then don't look to see where the shot went until the ball has vanished.

Congratulations, you now have made it off the first tee. Go have fun, enjoy the day, beat your friends out of dinner and drinks, and mount the score card on a plaque when you get home.

Then, practice your putting. Your score could have been ten shots lower if you had just made a few more putts.

A TRUE STORY FROM THE FRONT LINES

FEAR AND THE ART OF PUTTING FROM THE MIDDLE OF THE FAIRWAY

FAST FORWARD A FEW YEARS from those first two stories. For me, it's now the summer of 1976 in Northern Idaho. I am a second-year architecture student in the little town called Moscow, the home of the University of Idaho. I still loved golf, but I had decided I hated traveling as much as it took to be a rabbit on the professional tour during those days.

You don't think that's a good reason to stop working toward something you love? Trust me, just spend a few months alone in a hotel room, with nothing to think about but golf, nothing to look forward to but more and more weeks in hotel rooms. And I was good. Darned good, after the years with Zell, so I could see making it on the tour and maybe doing nothing but spending the rest of my life in hotel rooms.

You think touring professionals have it easy, think again. It's a hard, nasty life out there on the road, and it takes a real special kind of person to do it. I clearly liked books, reading, and other things far more than I liked living out of the trunk of my car.

So one fine day, while I was the head professional of my own course in Palm Springs, getting ready to go play some mini-tours or maybe some stops on the Canadian Tour, I got thinking about the long road ahead. And the linked hotel rooms, year-after-year, and the thought just made me shudder.

I just quit, sold everything, and went back to finish a college degree I had started in the late sixties.

So, when I got to college, what did I decide would be a good job for me while attending college? Golf Professional, of course.

I seemed to have a little experience at it at that time. So the nice head professional at the Elks Golf and Country Club hired me to be his assistant, starting in the early spring, through the summer, and ending early fall. And he promised he would work with my school schedule.

He also wanted me to play in tournaments, both as a professional in regional events representing the course, and as the club pro going with members to tournaments called pro-ams.

I agreed. At the time, after a long winter of doing nothing but studying, it sounded like fun.

But during the years since I had first turned professional, and that spring of 1976, the PGA had changed some rules for its members. One of the rules they added was a playing test. In other words, you had to be good enough playing the game before they would let you into their tournaments.

I heard that and just laughed, if I remember right. Good enough to the PGA during those days was something like playing 36 holes of golf in less than ten over par. My thinking was I could do that in my sleep.

One cold March day in the spring of 1976, the section of the PGA decided to test its young professionals.

The test course was a very easy golf course in Spokane, Washington that sat on a bluff overlooking a river. That

Monday morning, twenty-eight of the Pacific Northwest Section's PGA young golfers gathered, including me.

I had skipped a few classes to be there, got up at three in the morning to make the drive, and hadn't even touched my golf clubs for six months of a long Northern Idaho winter. But I had no worries at all that I would pass the silly test. My memories of the lessons from Zell just years before were still fresh, and during my last days of working full time in the game of golf, I seldom had a round of golf near par, let alone over par.

Ten over par in thirty six holes would be a joke.

The joke was on me.

None of us made it.

Not one of us.

I was fifteen over, low score out of all of us, and felt darned happy about that score. The wind was blowing at a constant thirty miles per hour, the rain couldn't decide if it wanted to be sleet or snow. And it never let up. Not for one minute. It was the longest, most miserable day in my golfing life.

We all figured the PGA section would adjust the test for the conditions of the day, but nope, ten over was the score and that was that.

They did, however, quickly decide to schedule another test because no PGA section up to that point had had everyone fail.

Not one assistant in all the Pacific Northwest and a few head pros taking the test could play in a tournament and that was the last thing any section of the PGA needed at that point in publicity. So the retake of the test would be on the same course in two weeks.

By the time I had made the two-hour drive back to Moscow, I was so angry, I

could have bitten through the shaft of my driver. I could just hear Zell's voice in my head.

"Conditions don't matter. Only the score matters."

And in this case, I had failed. Sure, I had the best score of anyone there that day, but so what? I had made more mistakes than I could ever imagine, including the big one of going in unprepared and not thinking correctly about the goal ahead.

Now understand, I was still very cocky about golf, and I hadn't failed a test in golf in a long, long time. I wouldn't fail a second time.

Every day, between classes, snow, wind, or rain, I went out to the course and hit golf balls, practiced putting, worked the winter kinks out of the Palm Springs golf swing.

By the time that second test came around, I was behind in school and mad about that.

And really, really mad I had failed the qualifier the first time.

I went up to Spokane the night before this time and stayed in a hotel to get the rest needed for the next day's 36 holes of play. I worked over the map of the course, planning a game plan, making notes as to which holes to play safe, which holes to attack.

In other words, I did the same thing I used to do for golf tournaments before going back to school.

The morning of the second test broke clear and cold. The weather this time would not be much of a factor.

By the time I had made it through my warm-up routine on the range and putting green, I was even angrier that I was even there. I was in the third group to tee off. All I remember on that first shot was that I swung as hard as I could because there was just no trouble on either side of the fairway to get into. Turned out, I hit one of the longest drives of the day there among all the professionals.

I birdied the first hole with a tap-in putt.

I birdied the second hole with a three foot putt.

I chipped in for an eagle on the par five third hole.

I birdied the fourth hole with a ten foot putt.

Five shots under par in four holes.

Now that was the player I remembered myself being from Palm Springs. Zell would have been proud of me.

But what now?

I knew I couldn't keep playing out of the anger. I had to play smart, stay focused on the only reason I was there, which was to pass the stupid ten-over-par test.

So, on the tee of the fifth hole, I changed style. From that moment on, I played safe. I had 32 holes left to play and fifteen shots over par to spend to make the test score.

I made pars on the rest of the holes on the first nine, for a 30 on the par 35, rimming out a birdie putt on the 9th hole for what would have been only 29 in my life.

I was two over par on the next nine. Still three under for the first eighteen holes.

Two over par on the next nine, playing safe all the way.

Then, still even par for the tournament since my little splash of birdies right off, I came to the really nasty sixteenth hole of the second time around, actually my 33rd hole of play that day.

It was a short par four with out-of-bounds the entire right side of the fairway and out-of-bounds about ten feet behind the green. I had already played it once

and it was one of the holes I had worked out the night before that was a real danger to a score.

"Play safe. Stay away from that out-of-bounds."

I remember thinking that as I stood on that tee.

So, much to the laughter of the rest of the pros in my group, I turned and aimed my drive over the bench and clear out into the bordering fairway. In fact, I hit it so far in that direction, I hit it clear across the neighboring fairway and into the rough on the other side.

Safe.

The rest of my group sort of waved goodbye to me as they started down the hole we were playing and I started off at an angle.

My second shot now had another problem. Instead of just having the out-of-bounds on the right and behind the green, I was so far left, I had to aim directly at the out-of-bounds just to aim at the green.

And the green sloped off the back toward that out-of-bounds behind it.

All I could think about was bouncing my shot out of the rough over the green and then standing there in a neighboring fairway and doing what I called a "McLean Stevenson" meaning a replay of that ten I took in Palm Springs in my first professional tournament.

So I played safe with my second shot, took a good two clubs too little for the distance, and aimed my shot toward the front of the green, into a wide spot in the fairway. My plan was that I could then chip up and make the putt for another par. I had learned the lesson well of it didn't matter how, it was just how many that counted.

My ball stopped in front of the green, a good fifty paces short.

As I stood over the third shot, all I could think about was blading the ball over the green and out-of-bounds. I just couldn't shake that nasty thought, which meant more than likely, that was exactly what was going to happen.

I stepped back and looked at the situation. I only had two holes to play after this. What difference would a bogey make at this point? I was still even par and the cut line was ten over. Bogey didn't matter, but numbers higher than that did.

So I put my wedge back into my bag and took out the club I had the most confidence with.

My putter.

Now, understand, there was a good fifty paces to the front of the green, and another twenty paces to the pin. All downhill. All over rough, late-winter ground.

In other words, I had no idea where this ball was going to go. The correct shot was to chip it into the air.

I didn't care what was correct.

At that moment, I just wanted to bang my ball down by the green, maybe on the front edge, two putt and go to the next hole.

The other three professionals started laughing at my club choice as I walked up to the front of the green to get a sense of the distance. But they had no right to laugh and they knew it. I was a good six shots ahead of my nearest playing companion. I just wanted to get off this stupid golf course and get home to see how far behind I was with my classes.

So, pretending I was standing on a really, really big green with a really, really long putt, I hit the shot.

I remember my ball bounced a good ten feet into the air fairly soon after I hit it.

Putts aren't supposed to bounce like that.

Then still bouncing, my ball kept rolling and bouncing, right onto the front of the green.

Then it broke right, then broke back left, hit the pin, and went into the hole.

Birdie three on the scorecard.

It wasn't pretty, it wasn't done by the book, and the entire hole was played out of sheer fear and common sense.

And it sure was fun.

I passed the test with a par-par finish on the last two holes. Actually, I was eight shots ahead of the second-place finisher.

That summer, due to summer school classes, I ended up never playing in any other tournaments. The following year I didn't renew my PGA membership status and a few years later I applied to the USGA and got my amateur standing back. That was my last tournament as a professional golfer.

But that hole was a way for me to see everything Zell had taught me and what I hope many will get from this book. Fear is a part of the game of golf, as well as in life. Learn how to play with fear, and how to use it.

Don't panic.

Just learn the routines, keep your head and wits about you, keep your breathing regular, and think.

And always remember, it doesn't matter how pretty a golf shot is. All that matters is the final score.

That, and having a great time.

Available in March
from all your favorite booksellers
in trade paper and electronic editions.

Coming Next Issue in Smith's Monthly

DEAN WESLEY SMITH

USA TODAY BESTSELLING AUTHOR

AGAINST TIME

SOMETIMES TRUE LOVE GROWS FROM THE RUINS LIGHT YEARS FROM HOME

USA Today *bestselling writer Dean Wesley Smith returns with a second novel to the world of* Dust and Kisses *from the first issue of* Smith's Monthly.

Paleontologist Callie Sheridan spent a few days deep in the Oregon Caves on a dig with three students from the University of Oregon. When she emerged, they found almost everyone in the world dead. Survival now became her only thought.

Mathematician and galactic explorer Vardas Fisher dropped into orbit over a planet where almost all of the human life had been recently killed for no obvious reason. Suddenly hundreds of other ships, all human, appear in orbit and start working to save the remaining population of the planet.

Together, Callie and Fisher work to discover the secrets of a galaxy that have been hidden in plain sight, even from the powerful humans who had rescued millions. And in the process, they just might change everything.

AGAINST TIME
A Science Fiction Novel of True Love

PART ONE

CHAPTER ONE

CALLIE SHERIDAN felt a sense of relief that she could finally see the light ahead. More than she imagined she would feel, considering she had enjoyed the three days down in the Oregon Caves. A real change and a relief from her normal grind of research and teaching undergrad classes in Paleontology at the University of Oregon in Eugene.

But after three days completely in the dark and damp of the cave, she was ready to see some natural light once again, even if it was just a rainy Oregon day.

She and the two graduate students with her had gotten permission from the Forest Service to go into a special area of the Oregon Caves complex, far off the normal tourist trails. It had taken them almost four of hours of hiking just to get to the tiny room. There they had been allowed to dig for signs of fish skeletons preserved in the rocks of the cave.

One of the students, Jim Williams, was in his final year, working on his thesis, married, with a child in Eugene. He stood no more than five six, shorter than Callie by a couple of inches, and had bright red hair. From the pictures Callie had seen of his new child, the red hair had moved on a generation.

Barb Hillcrest still had over a year in school to get to her thesis. Barb was a solid woman and towered over Callie at over six feet. Barb lived alone with three cats and was worried about getting back to them.

Callie liked them both, and both had turned out to be hard, hard workers during the entire time in the cave. Both had focused their studies in vertebrate paleontology, which was Callie's specialty.

The Oregon Caves had been formed out of granite instead of normal limestone and was a gold mine for fossils from various times in history. It had taken her almost a year to get the permission from the Forest Service for the short surface dig. A cave specialist and park ranger named Dave had gone with them to make sure that they wouldn't disturb anything in the cave with their dig except around one small area tucked in the back of a small cave.

Dave was a middle-aged guy with a gut and gray hair and had a fantastic sense of humor that kept them laughing, even though he must have been bored to tears with their conversations at times and the excitements over finds of tiny fossils.

On the way in he had kept them entertained with his stories of the cave and the names of the different rooms and how they had been named. For a pretty long distance into the cave the path had been covered with asphalt and was an easy walk, with some stair climbing and one bridge over a stream called The River Styx.

Now they were all carrying out some great samples in their backpacks that would keep them busy for months at school. The trip was a great success and she honestly had no idea what they might have found.

Dave had decided that instead of having them climb out the tourist exit where the tours left, he'd have them just backtrack to the way they had come in. As they neared the front entrance to the cave, Dave suddenly shouted "Karen!" and ran forward.

He had been leading the group up the incline on the asphalt trail that wound through some rock fall, so Callie couldn't see what he had seen.

The light from the small cave opening was bright, even though it had an airlock on it. So someone must have left the door open.

Callie shielded her eyes, carefully watching her step as she went forward to make sure she stayed on the asphalt.

Suddenly both Barb and Jim ran up behind Dave, who was now kneeling over a woman who looked to be Dave's age. She also wore a park ranger uniform like Dave's. Her gray hair had been cut short and she looked like she had been beautiful in her day.

But now she was sprawled on the ground in the middle of the asphalt trail and to Callie she looked very dead.

And smelled dead as well.

Behind Karen, scattered along the trail were a dozen more people, all sprawled in various positions and all very dead. Clearly this Karen had been leading a walking tour into the cave with a bunch of tourists when something really awful happened.

Callie quickly checked out a couple of other bodies, an older couple wearing heavy coats. There were no obvious marks on them and no blood.

Callie stepped back and just stood, staring at the bodies, trying to make sense of what she was seeing.

He stomach was twisted into a knot and she wanted to just get sick. Never had she seen so much death in one place. Seeing something like this on television was something, standing here staring at the dead bodies and smelling the rot starting to take over was another matter completely.

Was this some sort of elaborate practical joke?

She looked around the rocks scattered through the cave mouth, but saw nothing that looked out of place.

Could someone have been this sick to do this sort of joke?

She moved back a few more steps closer to her two students and Dave where he now held Karen in his lap and was sobbing.

Callie had been around dead animals and a couple dead humans in her time, and this smell was very, very real and going to get worse, much worse, very soon. These people had been laying here dead for at least a day, maybe slightly longer.

> ***Behind Karen, scattered along the trail were a dozen more people, all sprawled in various positions and all very dead.***

How was that even possible, in the middle of a tourist attraction during a busy season?

As Callie looked along the group of dead, eleven men, women and one teenage boy, she could tell a few animals had worked at ones closest to the cave entrance, since it was braced open by the body of a man laying face down on the asphalt.

More than anything she wanted to be sick. This was not a pretty sight. But she had to stay clear in her thoughts for the moment. There would be time for reacting later.

She just couldn't imagine what might have caused this and why no one had come for these people and bodies.

This made no sense at all.

None.

She covered her nose with her sleeve and tried to think.

Then suddenly one very ugly word popped into her head.

Gas.

"We need to get out of here now!" she shouted to her students and Dave. "Move past the bodies quickly, don't look at them. Get up the trail to the parking lot."

"What do you think caused this?" Barb asked, clearly stunned, but moving.

"Might be gas," Callie said. "Jim, help me with Dave."

They both went to pull Dave away from the body of a woman named Karen, but he brushed them aside, angry.

"No, I'm staying with her."

"Dave," Callie said, "there's nothing you can do for her."

"I don't care," he said, looking up at Callie, his eyes full of tears. "She's my wife. I'm staying."

"We'll send help," Jim said.

Callie nodded, but doubted that they would find help as quickly as Jim made it sound. Something here was very, very wrong.

Callie motioned for Jim to follow Barb up the trail and past the bodies.

Without a look back at the man holding his very dead wife or at the bodies she passed, Callie followed her two graduate students up and into the light.

Outside the big trees looked normal, the day was beautiful, a slight breeze blowing among the pine.

It felt normal.

And that scared Callie even more.

All three of them took off running up the paved path through the trees, following the signs that said "Parking Lot."

It took them only a minute at full run for the three of them to reach the wide, paved parking lot.

Callie expected police and everything else to be there, but instead the lot felt deserted.

Two bodies lay sprawled near one car.

Around them the towering mountains stretched upwards, leaving most of the parking lot tucked into the side of the hill in shadow.

Callie made herself stop, take a deep breath to clear her mind, and then look around for anything that seemed wrong or out of place.

Nothing.

A beautiful afternoon in the Oregon Mountains.

Except for the two bodies sprawled in the parking lot.

"What happened?" Barb asked, her voice shaking.

It was clear Barb was barely holding it together. But Callie had no answers for her. All Callie could do was stand there on the edge of the parking lot, staring at the bodies and shaking her head.

She had no idea what had happened.

But she had no doubt now that this was a lot bigger than some poison gas in the mouth of a cave.

A lot bigger.

Chapter Two

VARDAS FISHER sat in his big black inertia chair, holding on for dear life as his ship, *The Lady*, came from deep space way too hot and directly into orbit insertion around a big, green-and-blue planet they had named N-21-7.

He had no doubt his fingers were going to have to be pried from the soft foam of the armrests and it tasted like his stomach might revolt from the sharp garlic on artichoke pizza he had baked them for lunch.

Doc, sitting to his right in his inertia chair, had them braking like crazy to hold the orbit as the features of the planet flashed by far, far too fast for Fisher to even catch a glimpse. You would have thought they had someone with damn big guns on their ass.

Doc was skinny and over six foot, with a wide grin and blue eyes that seemed to almost twinkle at times. Fisher, on the other hand, stood about four inches shorter than Doc with a body one person in a gym called a perfect V-shape. Wide shoulders, narrow waist and he kept his brown hair cut very short and no beard or moustache, while Doc wore a wide moustache that seemed to just be expanding on his skinny face.

Doc's fingers were flying over his control panel. Fisher's job was to watch for anything in front of them in orbit, but as fast as Doc had them braking, their orbital trajectory just kept changing, so Fisher had no clue what was coming up, let alone be able to watch for anything.

They might hit something before they even had time to blink, and if the object they plowed into was too large, their screens might not block it.

This stunt was all his skinny partner's idea. Doc wanted to test out a new theory. He wanted to see how close to a planet they could drop out of a trans-tunnel and still control slowing into an orbit.

He had convinced Fisher to give it a try by saying, "Just never know when it might come in handy in the future."

Fisher was big on being prepared for just damn near anything, and they had been chased more than once in the last few years of roaming around through space. And more than likely it would happen again.

Besides, he figured that if they didn't plow into something large, the worst that would happen was that they would just sling off the orbit like a flea off a dog's back and then have to backtrack.

Doc was convinced that wasn't going to happen, and he tried to show Fisher the math. Fisher had just nodded like he always did when Doc got into the math on anything concerning orbits and trans-tunnel speeds and finally Doc just stopped and said, "You'll see. It will work."

"Just don't hit the damn planet square on."

"No worries, Skip," he had said.

And that always made Fisher worry. Especially when he called him "Skip" which was short for "Skipper." Doc never did that unless he was worried as well. Fisher got called Skip because he owned *The Lady*, as he called this deep space exploration ship.

Most of the time Doc just called her "The Ship."

They had built her in two years in a huge warehouse on Fisher's parent's estate just north of their hometown, right after they both finally finished with far too many advanced degrees in college.

Fisher had family money in a trust, more than enough, actually, to build a couple ships. And he had patents on a dozen devices he had invented that drew energy from dark matter.

Doc had the idea for the gravity drive that allowed them to not only just float out of a gravity well, but jump long distances very quickly in what Doc called "Trans-Tunnel Flight."

Basically Trans-Tunnel Flight was a form of time-bending warp drive, but when they were in it, space looked like it had become a tunnel, so Doc named it the "Trans-Tunnel Drive."

"Better than Warp Drive," he had said.

In the planning stage, they had decided to make the ship really huge and really cool, right out of a 1950's science fiction movie. They even had painted it silver and put fins like a nifty plane and a pointed nose on it so it looked like a cross between a very fast plane and an old rocket ship. The fins were worthless unless in the atmosphere if the drive went out, and the pointed nose housed nothing but sensors.

They each had huge five-room suites on board, since the ship was the size of a hotel that flew. It was so big, there were parts of this ship Fisher hadn't been in for over a year.

It actually didn't need to be this big, but both of them had figured they never knew what they might run into out in space, or how much room they might need, or who might be riding along.

The actual engine itself took up the size of a small closet and a large warehouse area in a lower deck was filled with many, many spare parts. The rest of the ship had a game room, an exercise room, a small gym, a massive kitchen with a dozen freezers, and numbers of spare bedroom suites for a future crew or guests.

So far, those guest suites had not been used.

Before they took off, they had stocked more food than they would be able to eat in five years, even though from darned-near-anywhere in this area of the galaxy, they could jump back to Earth in a matter of a day or two.

Food was Fisher's passion.

Somewhere back in college, after getting his first doctorate, he had allowed himself to get close to three hundred pounds on his five-foot-ten inch frame. Back then people said he and Doc looked like the old comedy team of Laurel and Hardy, but he was larger back then than Hardy ever got.

And Fisher loved cooking.

And eating.

Especially really rich foods. But a couple doctors told him that if he didn't lose some weight, he was going to have to cut down on many of the dishes he loved to cook if he wanted to live much longer.

He had been only twenty-six when they told him that. It had gotten through.

He had gone exercise crazy.

Right before they left on this trip, he had run in his tenth marathon and he had been training for an Iron Man competition. He now weighed just under one-seventy and that was all muscle. And he could eat anything he damn well wanted.

Somehow, Doc ate everything Fisher served him with relish and never gained a pound and spent only a minor amount of time in the gym, usually when he wanted to talk to Fisher about something and knew Fisher was a captive audience while in an exercise routine.

Fisher didn't feel right if he didn't exercise, just as he didn't feel right when he didn't eat decent food.

One of the most enjoyable aspects of this exploring around space was discovering new types of food and ways of cooking it. He was stockpiling the recipes with hopes of doing a number of cookbooks when they got back home.

He could spend two or three hours a day in the kitchen just testing new foods and writing it all down. And often did.

He doubted anyone would give his books any credit, just as they didn't give his energy inventions even a second look. The power for everything on this ship and Doc's drive came from the energy floating around between matter and dark matter.

For some reason Fisher had the ability to understand when something hidden was between two obvious things.

He had perfected the idea of using the energy between the two states of matter while in school and applied for patents, but no professor would let him write it as a thesis. No one really gave his ideas any credit at all, actually, just as they didn't give Doc's trans-tunnel drive and anti-gravity work anything but laughter.

If they could only see them now.

Finally, Doc had them slowed enough that the orbit they had settled into seemed stable, even though they were still braking.

"Told you it would work," Doc said, smiling at Fisher, his thin face twisted into mostly bright white teeth and wide blue eyes.

Fisher just shook his head and worked his fingers off the armrests of his chair. "Only emergencies," he said as his stomach started to settle.

"Exactly," Doc said, nodding and going back to continuing to brake them into a stable orbit. "At some point I hope to figure out how we can come out of a trans-tunnel without forward speed. It should be possible."

"Make that a priority," Fisher said.

Suddenly the warning lights on Fisher's heads-up panel flashed into a display that would do a Christmas tree proud.

The orbit they had dropped into had them hitting a large orbiting object in about five seconds.

Fisher kicked off Doc's controls and cut the braking, which allowed them to move out higher away from the planet. On his screen their orbit around the planet changed from a nice circular pattern into a big egg-shaped elliptical orbit.

They flashed past what looked like an orbiting station far too fast to get a good look at it.

And far too close for Fisher's stomach to be happy. He had long ago lost the desire for near-misses on anything.

If they had hit that station, they would have put a very, very large hole in it. Their screens would have kept them safe, but the station and everyone on it would have been in trouble, if not killed instantly.

"Wow, good catch, Fisher," Doc said. "Looks like we have a space-faring culture on this planet."

"Great, just great," Fisher said. "Someone to chase us again after we almost destroy their space station."

Doc laughed. "Yeah, we have a way of making an entrance, don't we?"

Chapter Three

CALLIE FINALLY DECIDED she couldn't just stand there at the edge of the parking lot any more. She needed to move, to do something, to get more information.

"Let's put our packs in the car and check out the lodge," she said.

"No," Jim said, shaking his head.

He had his cell phone to his ear and was shaking his head. "No one is answering. I've got to get to my wife, my kid."

It was Jim's car they had come up in, so Callie actually had nothing to say about him leaving or not. Even though they were her students, they were all three adults.

"I want to go back too," Barb said, her voice barely holding together. She also had a cell phone to her ear. "My parents in Salem are not answering either."

Callie pulled out her phone and tried to call her office. She got her machine, as expected, so the phones were working. She had no family and no one else to call that she could think of off the top of her head.

The three of them stood there for another two minutes trying everyone they could think to dial.

Phones were working.

No one was answering.

That scared Callie more than she wanted to think about. She was fairly certain she didn't want to know how far whatever had caused this had really spread.

And she had no idea what might have caused it. She did know for certain that those bodies in the cave had died almost instantly and without any sort of trauma.

And it had happened at least a day ago, while they were deep in the cave digging.

And she was certain that it had been the fact that they were deep inside the cave that had saved them.

That cave just might save her again.

She was going to stay, even though she had no idea what was happening.

She had come to trust her gut and her gut told her to stay put.

"You two go," she said.

Then she looked Jim directly in the eye. "You drive carefully. If this is widespread, there will be wrecked cars on the road."

He nodded, his face completely pale.

"And you call me from Cave Junction and tell me what you see."

"I will," he said, nodding. "Be careful."

"You too," Callie said.

Barb just nodded and the two of them turned and almost ran for Jim's car.

Callie stood and watched them drive off down the road.

The silence of the mountain came back in strong around her, like a very, very heavy blanket.

The breeze flowing lightly in the trees was the only sound.

Normally she loved the mountains, the timber, the smells of summer pine, and the silence.

Now the silence just worried her more.

And normally she liked being alone, living alone.

Now being alone scared her far more than she wanted to admit.

Ignoring the two bodies she could see, she started off toward the old lodge down the paved road.

The lodge was a rustic three-story hotel built in the 1930s as part of the construction to put people to work during the Depression. It was a place she found stunning and wonderful.

Everything was wood and a huge river-rock fireplace dominated the two-story main lobby. Huge wooden chandeliers hung in the open areas and a wide staircase next to the big wooden front desk led to the upper floors.

It sat perched on the side of a very deep ravine and on the floor below the lobby was a restaurant and café that looked out over that ravine.

In one part of the restaurant it had formal seating, while in another part it looked like an old counter-diner right out of the 1930s. When the Forest Service remodeled the place, they had kept the early look and décor and she had loved the place the first time she stayed in the old lodge a few years back.

In the lodge she found everyone was dead as well.

She spent the next hour keeping her panic in check and slowly working her way through the building, checking every room with a passkey, knocking on every door and calling out before she opened it.

She counted nineteen people in the entire Lodge on all three floors. A couple of cleaning staff, a front desk clerk, two people downstairs in the kitchen, one person slumped over at the counter, and the rest in their rooms.

All dead.

She went back to the lobby and dropped onto a couch.

She couldn't think.

She couldn't even hardly breathe.

Suddenly her phone rang, making her jump and sending the sound echoing in the large open space of the hotel lobby.

She fished it out of her pocket.

"We're in Cave Junction," Jim said. "We had to move some cars and push others out of the way to get down to here."

"Meet anyone?" she asked.

"Everyone is dead."

"You all right?" she asked, knowing the question was stupid.

"No," he said.

"Any sign of anything moving? Helicopters, planes, anything?"

"No," Jim said. "We're going to keep going."

"Carefully," Callie said. "Call me when you get to Eugene."

"I will," Jim said and hung up.

She doubted that he would. At least not for a very long time after finding his wife and daughter dead.

She just hoped that wouldn't happen and this wasn't that widespread.

But her gut told her it was.

And that meant up here on the mountain, she was alone.

Completely alone.

And she was going to be alone for some time to come.

Chapter Four

AS DOC BROUGHT them around the planet again and worked to match the orbit of the space station, Fisher scanned the planet. It felt a little like scanning his own home world from a low orbit.

Evidence of human activity was everywhere. Large, sprawling cities on all of the major continents. Thousands of roads and smaller cities and towns.

It looked the same, if not almost identical, as many of the Earth-type planets they had visited. Humans had clearly been seeded on every Goldilocks zone planet that they had come to at some point in the distant past. They had run across no aliens, but humans were everywhere.

And he meant everywhere. So many human civilizations, it was startling.

At least in this small area of the Milky Way Galaxy which they had explored.

At last count, they had found over two hundred Earth-like planets and every one of them had either had human life on them at one point, or still did have thriving civilizations.

And not many of them seemed very far beyond or behind Earth's level, as if they had all started at the exact same time in history.

That bothered him a lot and he and Doc had talked about it, but neither one of them could come up with any reason.

Plus even stranger, all the plants on all the planets were the same as well, as were the animals. Dogs, chickens, pigs, cows, deer, everything, all the same. Clearly every planet had had some sort of terraforming in a distant past before the humans were placed there.

Very, very strange and it had been their main topic of conversation over meals for the first fifty or so planets. Fisher didn't know how he felt knowing that humans were alone in the galaxy, just not all on the same planet.

And he really didn't know how he felt thinking of himself as part of a huge galaxy-wide lab experiment, which it seemed they might be.

But finally, after finding so many civilizations and having no obvious answers present themselves, Fisher and Doc started growing used to the idea.

If growing used to something that was flat impossible was even possible. Fisher assumed it was.

He and Doc didn't talk about it much anymore.

The human civilization on the planet below also seemed to be around Earth's level of growth and expansion.

But as they went around the dark side in their orbit, Fisher noticed one major problem: Nothing was moving.

And the planet was slowly dropping silent and dark.

Only basic recorded sounds were coming from the surface.

In very short order the entire planet would be ghostly silent.

And very, very dark.

"Doc, we have a problem," Fisher said.

"They can't be coming after us already," Doc said, not looking up from his board as he brought *The Lady* up slowly on the orbiting space station. "We missed them, didn't we?"

"No one is coming after us," Fisher said.

"That's good," Doc said, still not looking up. "So what's the problem?"

Fisher's fingers were moving as fast as he could get them to move over his controls to confirm what he feared, doing test and reading after reading.

All the readings came up the same.

Just a day or so ago something had completely wiped out almost every human being down there.

Not all of them, but almost all of them.

"They are dead," Fisher said, sitting back in his chair and forcing himself to take deep breaths.

"Who's dead," Doc asked.

"Just about everyone on the planet," Fisher said.

At that, Doc looked up.

Chapter Five

CALLIE SAT ON the big over-stuffed couch in the grand foyer of the old lodge for two hours after talking with Jim, just thinking.

One moment she felt so panicked, she wanted to just run, get into a car and drive. The next moment she would feel calm, working on a plan of survival until someone came.

The survival plan eventually won over the panic. But not by much.

She did a quick calculation.

It had to be Thursday morning, around eleven. From her best calculations of what she saw of the bodies in the cave and in the lodge here, everyone had been dead for just over twenty-four hours.

And if she was right on that, she knew that she was going to have to move fast if she was going to have a sane and comfortable place to stay here in the lodge.

When in college the first time, she had started as pre-med and one of the things they forced the students to do near the end of the first year was actually smell a human body that had been rotting for a couple of days.

It was not an odor anyone could forget. And that day she had taken three showers and still didn't feel like she had the smell off her. That smell, along with a few other events, most notably an old boyfriend also planning on going on to the same medical school, convinced her to move to a major in paleontology, which she ended up loving with far more of a passion than she could have ever imagined.

She loved puzzles, finding clues to history where no one else would think to look. And now she could never imagine herself as a medical doctor.

But she knew, without a doubt, that she needed to deal with the bodies inside the lodge if she hoped to stay here until things started to clear up. And since Jim had reported the deaths were as far as Cave Junction, down in the valley below this lodge, she really had nowhere better to go.

In the basement she had seen a large four-wheeled supply cart for bringing in supplies to the kitchen from the driveway outside. It was low to the ground and on four solid wheels. She decided she would use that.

She borrowed some clothes, including a large yellow maintenance jacket, some gloves, and some snow pants from a maintenance storage area. There she also found two large generators set up to take over when the power went down.

She patted one on the side, very happy to see them.

Then, with a surgical mask on, the heavy coat, the gloves, and the snow pants, she went to work moving the bodies.

She started in the basement kitchen area since she was going to need that area to cook and for supplies. She managed to get one body up and on the cart and wheeled out the supply door and into the driveway before she suddenly questioned what she was going to do with the poor people she was moving.

The day was starting to heat up and that meant that the smell would get worse quickly.

The woman on the cart was about fifty, had a wedding ring on one finger, and a hairnet on graying hair. She wore what looked to be a blue and white restaurant uniform.

Callie had taken her keys, but put the woman's purse and coat with her, in case down the road someone would need to identify the remains.

But now, standing outside in the late afternoon air, Callie realized she had a real problem.

This was more than a body on the cart, this had been a person and Callie just couldn't dump her out onto the road for the animals to tear apart.

She had to treat these people with respect, at least as much as she could under these circumstance. But where could she put everyone that animals couldn't get

into and that she would have enough energy to move them to?

She knew that up near the parking lot was an old dormitory where the park rangers lived, but that would be too far for her to push the cart up that much hill.

She left the woman and the cart near the kitchen entrance and started up the shallow-sloped driveway toward the main road.

About halfway up she saw a medium-sized supply truck parked to one side of the lodge, tucked into a parking spot like it was going to be there for the night.

The back of the truck was mostly empty except for some cases of canned fruits, which Callie quickly unloaded onto the ground in a shady spot beside the building. She would take those inside later.

Then she climbed in behind the steering wheel of the truck.

She had driven her share of large trucks on different archeological digs over the years, especially when she was a graduate student.

She didn't expect the keys to be in the ignition, or on top of the visor, but she checked both places. Then she checked the closed tray beside the driver's seat. The keys were in there, along with a couple of Snicker's Bars.

One bar she put in the jacket pocket, the other she took a big bite out of, realizing she hadn't eaten since an an hour inside the cave. The wonderful nuts and chocolate tasted great, far better than it should have.

She was going to have to be careful to watch her food and when she ate. She often had a habit of forgetting to eat when she was busy.

Or stressed.

She managed to get the truck backed down the loading area and fairly close to

the door into the supply area of the kitchen without hitting anything.

Shutting off the engine, she again noticed the silence of the mountains around her.

She went around to the back of the truck and quickly figured out how to lower the loading lift. She got the cart with the woman on the tailgate lift and up and into the truck.

Callie rolled her off the cart and apologized, then laid her on her back, her hands on her chest, near the back wall.

Then Callie went back for another poor soul who had been caught in whatever had happened to everyone.

In one hour she had everyone out of the basement and kitchen and maintenance area and into the truck.

One floor clear.

She was sweating like crazy and decided to stop for a quick bite of lunch and a large bottle of water.

She stripped off the big orange coat and the gloves and mask, letting the cool evening air take some of the sweat away. She exercised every day and had never been afraid of hard labor, but this was more than she had expected it to be. Dead human bodies were difficult to move around.

And they were all starting to smell.

She washed off her hands and face and blew out her nose, then went to work finding something to eat, even though she was far, far from hungry.

She forced herself to eat a turkey sandwich and an apple while sitting at the old counter in the silence, watching the afternoon slowly pass on the mountains around her through the big windows.

She felt incredibly alone, but she wouldn't let herself think about what she was doing.

Or even try to guess at what had happened.

There would be more than enough time for that later. Right now she just had to act.

She ate the second Snicker's Bar for dessert, then she put her protective clothes back on and took the cart up the elevator like she was a bellman from hell and started to retrieve the dead bodies from the main floor, starting with the poor woman behind the desk.

It was going to be a long, long afternoon and evening.

Chapter Six

THEY DID TEN ORBITS over the next few hours, recording and studying everything they could.

To Fisher there was no doubt the planet below had just gone through something horrible. Actually, the planet was fine, but vast numbers of the humans and a bunch of animal life had died very, very suddenly.

And very recently.

Maybe just a day ago, at most.

There were numbers of smaller animals and some larger ones still alive, and human bodies lay everywhere, in every building, on every street.

Not one corner of the planet had been spared.

There were fires in most every major city, but all were minor. There seemed to have been no violence in the slightest.

Fisher felt really, really bad for the people who had somehow survived. He couldn't imagine what they were going through, finding loved ones dead, walking around among the bodies.

It made his stomach ache just thinking about it.

Something had killed a couple billion people on the planet and had done it quickly, where they stood, as they walked, as they drove cars that looked to Fisher frighteningly like cars from home.

"You got any idea how many are alive down there?" Fisher finally asked Doc.

"Not a clue," Doc said, his voice unnaturally soft. "Not that many compared to how many died."

He looked over, his eyes looking haunted. They had run into a couple of Earth-like planets with no humans and only signs of a civilization in the distant past. That was one thing, almost a scientific curiosity as to what happened.

Humans did have a way of killing each other and a few planets hadn't escaped that.

But it was a different thing when they could see human bodies littering the streets and filling the buildings.

Recently dead human bodies.

Millions and millions and millions of them.

A vastly different thing.

And what worried Fisher more than anything else was that this could happen to their home world. They somehow needed to find out what happened here.

They sat in silence until finally Fisher had an idea.

"The station," Fisher said.

Doc nodded. After this many years together, they often didn't have to finish sentences or thoughts.

They both knew that the instruments there might give them some sort of understanding of what had killed most of the human population of this planet.

Doc's fingers again flew over the control board, bringing them even closer in to match the orbit of the large space station.

Fisher just felt stunned. He was not really looking forward to going into that station. More than likely it was full of dead bodies as well.

They would have to be very, very careful.

Suddenly space around the planet filled with numbers of huge spaceships.

It looked like at least fifty, maybe more from what Fisher could tell.

They just appeared out of nowhere and at a dead stop, spaced evenly around the planet.

From what Fisher could tell, they made *The Lady* look like a kid's ship in a bathtub compared to an aircraft carrier.

"What the…" Fisher said, pushing back in his chair as if he needed to get farther away from those clearly alien monster ships.

Doc glanced up and jerked, also pushing back.

Then suddenly, on the sensors, Fisher started reading humans disappearing from the planet below.

Some alone, some scattered in groups.

But if the big ships were taking them, they weren't missing anyone.

One moment a person was on the planet, the next they were gone.

Fisher did a quick calculation. If those ships were as big as they seemed, there were enough ships to handle all the survivors from below.

Fisher pointed to the readings and tapped Doc who glanced at it and nodded.

"They are transporting humans to the ships," he said. "Looks like we found our seeders."

"We are not the originals," a voice said clearly inside the control room of *The Lady*. Only it wasn't Fisher's voice or Doc's.

And it was in perfect English.

Then everything around them shimmered for a moment and stabilized again.

The Lady was no longer floating in space near an empty space station. It was now seemingly sitting on a huge landing dock inside another ship.

"Oh, man," Fisher said, trying to keep the last bit of control he had. Somehow he managed to not scream and run to the back of the ship, which would have done no good at all, but he was sure it would have felt better than just sitting there.

"Now what are we going to do?" he finally asked his partner as they stared out the viewport at what appeared to be the inside of a huge hanger deck.

Doc shook his head slowly, clearly as shaken as Fisher had ever seen him before.

Then Doc turned and with a half-smile and shrug said, "Go and say hello?"

Fisher preferred the idea of running and screaming much better, but figured Doc was more than likely right.

Chapter Seven

BY EARLY EVENING, Callie had cleared the main floor, taking the bodies down the service elevator and out onto the truck.

After the sun went down, she had started closing the door to the truck just to make sure no animals got in. She was far from used to the smell and it clearly wasn't getting any better.

There were six bodies on the top floor in four rooms. She needed to get them out before she could stop.

Two couples and two single guests. Or at least guests who were alone when the death hit, as she was starting to think of it.

She didn't know what else to call what had happened besides "the death."

Over the next hour she got four of them out, the one couple together. Now she only had one more couple, but she wasn't looking forward to this at all, which was why Callie had left them to last.

The couple had been young, very young, and when the death hit, they had been making love. So both were nude and even though they were dead, Callie felt embarrassed she had to see them and touch them and move them from that position.

When she found them the first time, she had covered them with a blanket.

Now she had no choice. She had to get them out of the hotel.

"Think like a doctor," she said to herself as she opened their door, the rancid smell hitting her solidly. "You've seen naked flesh before. You can do this."

She pushed the cart over beside the bed, then pushed back the blanket.

The young girl, a natural redhead, was slumped on top of the boy who didn't look much older than eighteen.

She pulled the girl over toward the cart. For a moment Callie didn't think the girl was going to let go of her boyfriend.

Then she did and flopped down on the cart, her dead eyes staring up at the ceiling.

Callie then took the boy and rolled him over on top of his girlfriend on the cart.

Again, they looked like they were making love.

Callie quickly threw a blanket over them and somehow managed to get them downstairs and into the truck. She left them together, covered in a blanket and threw a change of clothes and their indentifications in beside them.

Then, as she closed the back of the truck, Callie said simply to all nineteen in there, "Rest in peace."

She moved the truck up to the parking lot and parked it near the two bodies there. Animals had done horrid work to those two and she didn't even want to try to load them into the truck. There was only so much she could do and she was beyond tired.

She took off the orange coat and draped it over the woman on the ground, then took off the ski pants and draped them over the man.

That wouldn't help them, but it was the best she could do.

She could do nothing for those in the cave.

Then suddenly it dawned on her that Dave was still in there with his dead wife.

She had completely and totally forgotten about him.

Suddenly her heart was racing and she was excited again. She had someone to help her survive all this.

How could she have forgotten him?

She took a flashlight she had been carrying and a second one from out of the glove box in the truck, then headed down the path through the dark trees to the mouth of the cave.

The smell in the cave was bad, but she waded in.

"Dave!"

Her words echoed among the rocks.

Dave was still with his wife, her head cradled in his lap.

At first Callie thought he was just sleeping, hunched over her.

But as she got closer, she knew that wasn't the case.

A large knife lay beside Dave and there was a dark pool of dried blood on the asphalt.

Dave had slashed his wrists and died there with his wife, not willing to leave her.

"Damn it all to hell," she said, resisting the urge to just kick his body. "I needed your help you selfish bastard."

Then she managed to get herself a little under control.

"Sorry, Dave," she said, her voice soft. "I've just seen so much death already, I didn't need more."

She stared at the guide she had come to like over the last few days.

"Rest in peace," she said. "All of you."

Then she turned and headed back to the lodge.

She needed the longest, hottest shower she had ever taken with as much soap and shampoo that she could find.

And then she needed some sleep.

And maybe, just maybe, she might wake up from this nightmare.

Chapter Eight

BOTH FISHER AND DOC did some quick checking and the atmosphere outside the ship in the huge space dock was normal, no bad things in it that could kill them. And the gravity seemed to be Earth-normal as well.

Beyond that, they couldn't tell much of anything about the ship around them past what they could see in the huge room. The dock had to be as large as a football stadium and could have easily held three or four ships *The Lady's* size.

They tested, but every control they had was locked down solid and the engines were offline. Something was blocking them. They were going nowhere under their own power.

"You ready, Skip?" Doc asked, pretending to stretch like he was relaxed about meeting the owners of these huge ships.

Fisher just shook his head and stood. "Seems like we have no choice, doesn't it?"

A good minute later they were standing on the deck looking around. The sides of the room seem to vanish in the distance and Fisher had been clearly wrong. This room could hold twenty ships the size of theirs, and have room between them all.

And he thought they had built a large ship when they built *The Lady*. Everything in space was relative it seemed.

Then, just as the first time they were grabbed, everything shimmered and they found themselves in a high-ceilinged meeting room with tables full of meats and vegetables and breads along one wall. It looked like preparations for a huge party, but so far the guests hadn't arrived.

To Fisher, the place had a warm feel and it seemed that someone was pumping in the smell of baking bread as well. Or maybe they actually were baking bread nearby.

He turned slowly around, surveying the large meeting room. There were stacks of blankets and chairs and cots everywhere. One wall was filled with a huge viewport that looked down on the greens and blues and whites of the planet below.

"Looks like we are just in time for the party," Doc said.

"If you had come to this planet a day earlier," a voice said from behind them, "you more than likely would have been as dead as most of those on the planet below."

Fisher and Doc spun around to see a man about Fisher's height and weight walking toward them, smiling. He had gray/silver hair, wore jeans and a green short-sleeved shirt tucked into his pants. He looked as normal and as human as anyone from Earth.

And as far as Fisher could tell, he was speaking perfect English.

They had met a few human cultures that had perfected some sort of translation devices that just made it sound like they were speaking English. But this was even more advanced. His lips seemed to match what he was saying.

Considering the size of this ship they were in, Fisher figured he would have been less stunned if an alien had joined them spouting six arms and a beak and squeaking their national anthem.

The guy extended his hand for Fisher to shake. "I'm Benson."

"Fisher," he said, carefully shaking Benson's hand.

It felt as normal as any human handshake, which bothered Fisher even more.

"Doc," said softly as he shook Benson's hand next.

"So you are the two explorers we've been hearing about," Benson said, smiling. "I understand you have had some adventures."

"A few," Fisher said, even more shocked that anyone had followed them around this area of space. Granted, it was a tiny area in comparison to the entire Milky Way Galaxy, but they had still covered a lot of light years and visited a few hundred Earth-like planets. And tracking them through open trans-tunnel space wasn't like following footprints in the mud. Or at least Fisher didn't think it was.

"So where are you two from?" Benson asked.

"Earth."

Fisher gave him the answer he knew would make the guy smile and at the same time give him no information at all, since most of the human planets they had visited had called their planets Earth. In fact, every one of them had.

He did smile. "I don't blame you for not wanting to tell me. How about I show you around and tell you what we are doing and then maybe you'll feel more like talking. And maybe you can help us a little with what's coming. We're going to need all the help we can get for a few hours." He waved at the room that was prepared for visitors.

"I find it fascinating," he said as he started to lead them toward a door, "that a human culture in this area has advanced as far as you have."

Fisher almost told him that the rest of their planet hadn't just yet, but instead just nodded and said, "Hold on a second. Can you tell us what happened down there? And what's happening now? How come all those people are vanishing off the surface?"

Fisher pointed at the planet that could be seen out of a large viewport on one side of the room.

Benson tapped something on his wrist and in the air near them an image of the Milky Way Galaxy came into being, spinning in the air.

Impressive three-dimensional image.

Then like focusing in, the view shifted down to this spiral arm of the galaxy and then to this small section of space. There had to be five hundred suns represented by nothing more than bright colored lights floating in the air.

One light was suddenly circled in the air by a red ring.

"An explosion in this sun caused rays of extreme electro-magnetic energy to be sent out into space."

From the circled star a number of white rays seemed to expand outward.

Benson went on. "By the time we noticed the explosion and calculated the frequency of the energy and then traced its path, we were too late to get here to save all the people of this planet. We couldn't mount a big enough rescue force to even attempt it."

Fisher was watching and it was clear Benson was very, very upset at that fact.

"EMP blast killed them where they stood," Doc said, nodding. "That makes sense now. The right frequency would short-circuit human brains like that."

Benson nodded. "About two million of the population survived by accidentally being in different forms of shelters or underground or inside something that shielded them. They didn't know it was coming."

Then Fisher finally understood what we had seen and why they were taking people off the planet. "But there is a second blast of energy following the first."

Benson nodded. "You guessed it. We got here ahead of that with a large enough fleet to get all the survivors out of the way. What you are witnessing is my people taking them off the planet during the night hours in each area of the planet. This ship should start loading in an hour. We will move out of the way of the wave for a few hours, then come back and return everyone."

"We arrived between the waves?" Doc asked.

"About one day after the first one," Benson said. "And about ten hours ahead of the second. Your shielding might have sheltered you from the second one since it's not as powerful, but it might not have either. Before you leave we will help you strengthen that shielding some for the future."

Fisher looked at Benson and then nodded. "Thanks."

"So you go around rescuing planets full of humans?" Doc asked.

Benson shook his head sadly. "First time. But after this we will be more vigilant. Billions died down there before we got here."

He seemed actually deeply affected by that, so Fisher tried to change the subject.

"So you know who seeded humans on so many planets in this area of the galaxy?" he asked.

"In every area of the galaxy," Benson said so matter-of-factly that it bothered Fisher. "There are hundreds and hundreds of thousands of human civilizations in different stages of development in this galaxy. And no one knows much about the people or race who did it except that it took them over fifty thousand years to complete the task for the entire galaxy."

"Your planet was seeded as well?" Doc asked. "How come you are more advanced than any culture we have seen?"

"We were all seeded," Benson said, nodding. Again the floating map of the Milky Way Galaxy came into being in the air beside them. "My home planet is there, also called Earth."

A circle appeared around a dot a third of the way around the galaxy. Then another appeared around a dot Fisher knew to be the sun they were orbiting.

"We are here at the moment," Benson said. "My area of the galaxy was seemingly seeded first, so civilizations that survived in that area are the most advanced. This arm of the galaxy was next, and as you move around in a clockwise direction, each human civilization gets more primitive."

"Wow," was all Fisher could think to say. Stunned didn't begin to describe how he felt.

Benson went on. "Our area of the galaxy has formed a large organization of aligned planets and about fifty worlds work together. That's why we could mount such a large fleet on such short notice."

"And no alien life at all?" Doc asked.

"Nothing above basic animal level," Benson said. "The Seeders, as we call them, not only seeded humans, but all the plant and animal life it would take to sustain human civilizations in the growth years."

"All the same on every planet?" Doc asked.

"All the same," Benson said. "Exactly."

Fisher stood there shaking his head and just staring at the image of the galaxy floating in the empty meeting room air. He remembered how stunned he had felt every time they came across another human civilization during their first year exploring. But after a while he had just come to expect it.

Now he was feeling that same feeling again. It was just too much to grasp.

Humans always thought they were alone in the galaxy. It seemed they were. But not in the way people back home might think.

Finally he shook his head and glanced at Benson, who looked almost haunted as he stared out the viewport at the planet below. For some reason he clearly felt responsible for all those deaths.

Fisher decided that their only hope in learning even more from Benson and his people was to confide in him.

"Could you focus this image in again to this area of space?" Fisher asked, pointing to the floating galaxy.

Benson nodded and the floating image focused down and Fisher pointed to a yellow star about sixty light years from this sun. "That's our Earth. And we are the only two that have this kind of technology at the moment."

Benson nodded. "I figured as much," he said. "On a couple of the planets in our area single explorers were the first out between the stars as well."

"So we are the first in this area of space?" Doc asked.

Benson nodded. "But after some of your visits to a few of the planets, I have a hunch those won't be far behind now that they know it's possible."

How in the world had he traced us? Fisher was about to ask, but Doc got a question in first.

95

"So is your drive the same technology as ours?" Doc asked as Fisher turned to stare back out at the damaged planet below.

Out of the corner of his eye he saw Benson shrug. "Just more advanced, but the same principles. If you want, I'll get some of our scientists to explain some of it to you."

"You'd do that?" Fisher asked, turning to Benson. Fisher was again as stunned as Doc looked.

"Why not?" Benson asked. "We're all out here together. If we can't help other human civilizations, what's the point?"

Doc opened his mouth, but nothing came out. He was like a kid that had just been offered everything for free in a candy store.

Fisher just shook his head and turned back to the viewport. "So how do we help all those people still down there?"

"When they get here, we just keep them comfortable and calmed down as much as possible," Benson said. "After we put them back, we can't do much. At least not right now. Not until they get through the rebuilding stage, which the experts tell me is going to take a few hundred years at least."

"They have enough population to survive?" Fisher asked, surprised.

Benson nodded. "More than enough. The Seeders only put a hundred and forty-four thousand humans on every planet and all but a few populations managed to keep going. There's almost two million alive down there still."

That exact number the Seeders used bothered Fisher, but now was not the time to ask. A lot about this was bothering him, but he knew he was in such shock, nothing was fitting together.

"You are saving millions of humans," Doc said. "That's impressive."

"And we didn't save many millions and millions more," Benson said, his voice soft. "But the one thing we know about humans, we survive. And the people of this planet will as well. The Seeders made sure we all had that trait."

Chapter Nine

CALLIE MADE IT BACK to the lodge and turned on lights in the big lobby, then locked all the doors to the place. She wasn't sure exactly who she was locking doors to stay safe from, but she felt better doing that.

At this point, she was too tired to question anything she was doing. She just had to keep moving, stumbling forward.

The only clothes she had were the ones she wore in the cave and they were all muddy. So she headed back up to the room where the young couple had stayed and borrowed the woman's suitcase that had been tucked off in a corner of a second room, so the smell had not yet got to it. The young woman had seemed to be about the same size as Callie.

Callie went down to the main floor, found the biggest suite on the floor. The suite had been made up for some future guest that would now clearly not arrive.

Callie left the clothes that she had been wearing out in the hall near another door, then went back, locked the suite door and turned on the shower.

She could feel that she was completely numb. She had just been moving, not thinking, and now she was so tired, she didn't dare allow herself to think about anything.

After a long hot shower, she got her hair dry with the blow dryer, then went through the girl's suitcase.

Callie found a nice pair of sweat pants and some new underwear that the girl had never worn that fit Callie fine.

She also had a green and white University of Oregon sweatshirt, so Callie put that on as well, along with some nice new socks. Clearly, this trip with her boyfriend to this lodge had been something special for the young girl.

Then in the sweatshirt and sweatpants and socks, Callie crawled into the big featherbed.

She almost shut off the light, but then on second thought decided she wasn't ready to face darkness at the moment.

She curled up under the large comforter on the soft old bed and was instantly asleep.

What seemed like only a moment later she was awakened by the strangest feeling of floating.

Then a moment later she found herself in a bright room with hundreds of other people.

She wasn't laying down, but instead standing.

All of the people she faced looked shocked.

As shocked as she was feeling.

If this was a dream, it was the strangest and most real dream she had ever had.

Some of the people around her started crying, some dropped to the floor and huddled with their heads down.

Everyone looked like they had been through a very, very hard day.

Some were dressed, some were naked and others were moving to cover the naked ones in blankets.

And the distinct smell of human death seemed to suddenly be everywhere again.

Callie looked around. Huge tables of food filled one wall, medical staff seemed to be working their way through the people,

while still other rescuers were helping others toward what looked like showers.

She scanned the room until suddenly what was behind her caught her eye.

She spun around, only to be faced with the most incredible sight she had ever seen.

An entire wall that looked like a window and seemed like a lot of movies she had seen shot from orbit.

Below her the Earth was slowly spinning past.

Not possible.

That view was too much for her to take.

She could feel the room growing faint and she started to slump to the ground, but strong hands caught her.

She mumbled "Thanks" before everything went black.

Chapter Ten

FISHER STOOD AND WATCHED the people appear in the big room.

It was just creepy. One moment there would be an empty spot, the next moment a person would be standing there. No shimmering, no sound, nothing. Just sort of "blink" and a person appeared.

Creepy.

Benson had left them almost an hour before to tend to other duties, so Fisher and Doc had stayed in the room, gotten a quick sandwich, then helped the crew get ready for survivors to come in.

A guy by the name of Glove explained to them what was going to happen. It seemed they were going to bring in about two hundred survivors to this room, give them medical attention, let them get cleaned up and eat something and try to just keep them calm for a number of hours until they could be returned to the exact spot where they were taken.

"Will the rescued people remember any of this?" Doc had asked.

Grove had shaken his head. "Very few of them will, and those few who do will think they just had a very strange dream."

Grove had stationed all the help around the room to assist people as they appeared. He told Fisher and Doc that when the room was full, all the survivors that were coming to this room were here, Benson would come and give an explanation of what was happening.

Then it would be up to the staff of the room to keep the people calm and fed until they could be sent back.

Fisher had been assigned an area near the big window looking over the city.

At first he was stunned at the smell of a few people as they arrived. The worst-smelling were taken out of the room almost at once, which Fisher appreciated. He had been around dead animal bodies before, but never anything like this.

After fifteen minutes, most of the people had arrived. He had helped a couple people find chairs and reassured a couple others that a full explanation would be coming.

Then, when he thought the room couldn't hold any more, about ten feet to his left a beautiful woman appeared, looking as stunned as everyone else.

Fisher had to step back. The attraction to her was so intense, he could feel it instantly.

She was the most beautiful woman he could remember seeing.

Ever.

And he wasn't honestly the type that noticed attractive women. He had been so wrapped up in his work and studies

for years and years, a relationship hadn't even crossed his mind.

It just seemed like it would have been too much work and taken too much time.

And back when he was fat, no woman would look at him anyway.

So the fact that he had a reaction to a woman was very different for him.

Very, very different.

His heart was racing, he felt short of breath, and all he could do was stare at her.

She looked to be just slightly shorter than he was and about the same age. She had short brown hair that was messed up so that it looked like she had been sleeping when brought up to the ship.

She wore a green and yellow sweatshirt that looked like it was from a university somewhere and dark sweatpants. She didn't have shoes on, only green socks.

And she looked to be in great shape, as if she exercised.

She stood there, alone, sort of staring around, taking in the big room and clearly trying to get her balance and bearings.

And then suddenly she caught sight of the view out the big window behind her.

She spun around to stare at it.

Fisher somehow got himself to move and just in time as she stared at the planet below and then just sort of slowly started to slump.

He managed to catch her before she hit the floor.

She mumbled something and then passed out.

He picked her up, savoring the feel of her in his arms. He quickly moved her over to an empty chair where he eased her down into place.

Fisher got her situated and motioned for one of the big ship's medical staff.

An older woman in a white smock came quickly over and knelt in front of the woman he had caught.

The medical person did a quick check with a small medical device and scanner and nodded. "Exhaustion, hunger, and shock," she said. "She'll be fine. Stay with her. I'll have someone bring some food and something to drink."

Fisher nodded and pulled another chair over facing the woman he found so attractive.

A juice drink and a few cookies were brought over from the food table by another staff member and handed to Fisher just as the woman started to come around.

"You're going to be all right," Fisher said softly.

He wanted to lean in and touch her hand, but instead stayed back.

The woman opened her eyes and seemed to take a moment before she focused on Fisher's smiling face.

At least he was doing his best to smile. His stomach was twisting and he was scared to death even trying to take care of this woman.

When her eyes focused, she jerked back in her chair.

"Sorry," he said, still smiling. "I'm really not a monster. Honest. A scientist, yes, but not a monster."

She didn't respond to his lame attempt at a joke, but he kept smiling. Damned if he could think of anything else to do.

"I…" she tried to say, but nothing came out.

"Here, drink a little of this," he said, indicating the glass. "I have no idea what it is, but more than likely some sort of apple juice."

She nodded and tried to take the glass in her shaking hands.

Fisher just held onto it and she closed her hands around his to guide it to her mouth.

He thought his heart was going to leap out of his body.

Her touch was wonderful, her skin slightly rough, but still electrical.

She just kept staring at him, into his eyes, and he helped her take a drink.

After a little sip she nodded. "Apple."

"Good to know," he said, still smiling like he was a fool in a carnival.

He pulled the glass away, suddenly very disappointed he was not touching her hands again.

He then offered her a cookie.

"Again, I have no idea what kind, but the medical people said you should eat them. They said that more than likely you were hungry and in shock."

She nodded, took the cookie and pretty much devoured it.

"Peanut butter," she said as he handed her another.

"Good to know."

She glanced back at the view of the planet below, then back at Fisher.

"Is that real?"

Fisher nodded. "You are in orbit above the planet. A very nice man is going to show up in a few minutes and try to explain this all."

"Were you down there as well?" she asked.

He shook his head. "I just arrived above your planet about four hours ago."

"Arrived?" she asked. "Where exactly are you from?"

Fisher had no way to not tell this incredibly attractive woman anything but the truth.

He pointed off to his right. "About sixty some light years in that direction."

All she could do was nod as she worked on the other cookie and alternated her attention from looking into his eyes to staring at the planet below.

Chapter Eleven

CALLIE SLOWLY CAME BACK from the darkness.

Before she opened her eyes she heard the sounds of a large room of people, some crying, some talking, but all the voices sort of merging into one loud sound.

She had spun around and looked out from what seemed to be a position in orbit. The moment before, she had been asleep in a lodge in Oregon after cleaning out more dead bodies than she wanted to think about.

The quick turn had made her dizzy, more than likely made worse by being suddenly woken up.

That lodge had been a nightmare she hoped she would wake up from.

But she didn't expect to wake up in yet another unexplained nightmare and then just pass out like a real baby. That was not like her at all.

She was now sitting in a chair and she slowly eased her eyes open.

Someone was sitting across from her, but she let the last of the dizziness fade a little more before she tried to focus on that person.

When her eyes did focus, she jerked back.

She was facing the most handsome man she had ever seen, with the most beautiful, if not strained smile on his face.

He had short brown hair, bright green eyes, was clean-shaven, and had shoulders like an athlete. She guessed him to be about her age.

He made a lame sort of joke about not being a monster and not meaning to scare her.

He hadn't scared her. She just hadn't expected to wake up to her perfect man. Now if the guy had a brain, she would be in heaven.

Then she looked around, realizing she actually hadn't dreamed being on a ship in orbit.

Mr. Handsome offered her a juice he thought might be apple juice and then had to help her drink it.

His hands felt wonderful.

Hers were shaking.

He said something about her being in shock, being exhausted, and being hungry.

Of course. She really needed to learn to pay attention to her eating. She had only had a sandwich six or so hours before crawling in bed after doing all that physical work moving the bodies.

No wonder she passed out.

The apple juice tasted wonderful and then he gave her a peanut butter cookie she managed to not completely inhale.

She could feel her nerves starting to calm as the juice and cookie hit her system.

She just kept staring into the guy's wonderful green eyes, not at all really wanting to look away. But then finally she did, turning to look out at the planet below them.

Then she asked him if he had been down there and he had said he hadn't been, that he had just arrived, and was from a planet about sixty light years away.

Okay, she was still dreaming.

But at least now instead of dreaming about moving dead people, she was dreaming about the most handsome man she had ever met.

Then, as Mr. Handsome had promised, a man came out of a back room and got up onto a stage.

Somehow he managed to get everyone's attention. Mr. Handsome moved his chair around so that he would also face the guy talking. She felt disappointed because she couldn't look into his eyes anymore.

She finished off the second cookie, downed the last of the apple juice, and he gave her a third cookie.

She was feeling a lot better.

"My name is Benson," the man said, smiling at the room that Callie guessed had at least two or three hundred people in it, if not more.

"And this is my ship you are on. We are in orbit around your planet. There are just under one hundred other ships similar in size and shape to this one also here representing almost fifty different planets in this rescue operation."

There was a lot of murmuring and Callie understood why. That simple information was almost too much for anyone to swallow.

Benson held up his hand. "All of us are as human as all of you, I can promise you that. And we are here to help."

The sounds in the room slowly settled away and she glanced at Mr. Handsome, who seemed to be very intently interested in what Benson was saying, as if he had never heard it before.

"About a day ago your planet was hit by an intense wave of electromagnetic energy."

On a large screen behind him the image of this area of the galaxy appeared and showed one star sending out an intense white beam of light and it intersected another sun.

"The electromagnetic pulse basically short-circuited the human brain. You were all saved in one way or another because you were either inside something that sheltered you, or underground. Just over two million survived the first pulse."

"First pulse?" someone shouted.

Callie didn't much like the idea of a second pulse either.

"That's right, a weaker but still deadly second pulse will be hitting your planet in just under five hours. We will have everyone off the planet when that happens and a safe distance away."

"Then what happens?" someone shouted.

"Then we bring you back to your home and let you begin the process of rebuilding your world. The trip away and back will take a very short amount of time, so rest, eat, and let our staff help you in any way they can. The crew in this room came a long ways for this moment to help you all survive."

"You are actually going to rescue all two million survivors?" someone shouted from the other side of the room before Benson had a chance to turn away from the microphone.

"Every last person," Benson said, with an intensity that surprised Callie.

Then he turned and left the stage and the room.

Around her the noise exploded as everyone tried to talk at once.

Mr. Handsome scooted his chair around so he could again face her.

All she could do was stare into those fantastic green eyes and try, try, try to get one simple thought together.

Nothing.

Chapter Twelve

CALLIE FINALLY FELT like she was getting some of her brain back.

"Would you like something more to eat?" the handsome man across from her asked. He didn't seem to be inclined to leave her and for that she felt very grateful.

"I would," she said. "Thank you."

He stood and started to turn toward the food when she asked, "What's your name?"

"Fisher," he said, smiling at her. "And yours?"

"Callie," she said.

"Right back with some food. I could use some myself."

She sat and watched him walk away. She liked his name and was stunned at how attracted she was to him in these strange circumstances.

But she was. And she couldn't stop staring at his butt. Clearly he had the walk of someone who knew how to carry himself. An athlete.

And he filled out those jeans perfectly.

And his broad shoulders moved with an ease she had not seen before.

When he vanished in the crowd, she turned and let herself just stare out at the planet below, not wanting to pay any attention to the others in the room. Interestingly enough, the view of the planet below calmed her.

She forced herself to take deep breaths and relax some.

What seemed like only a moment later he brought her back a plastic plate with a sandwich made on white bread, an apple, and five more cookies.

He had a plate as well that had a matching sandwich and cookies.

He also had two plastic bottles of what looked to be some sort of juice that looked like what she had before.

"They tell me this is apple juice again," he said, handing her a bottle. "And the sandwich is turkey."

Callie just looked at her plate, shaking her head. "How is it that alien people from other planets can get this kind of food?"

"You wouldn't believe me if I told you," he said, shaking his head and taking a bite of the cookie first.

"Try me," she said. "At this point I'll believe darned near anything."

He laughed and she loved the sound of his laugh. "I hear you there," he said. "I can't believe I'm sitting here either."

Then he waved his hand. "Sorry, got way off track with that. Let me try to answer your question, but remember I warned you that you wouldn't believe me."

She laughed and motioned for him to go ahead as she took a bite of the wonderful-tasting turkey sandwich on the soft white bread. It was salted just perfectly and had some sort of light sauce that gave it just the right flavor.

"Well," he said, "from what I have seen, and have been told, a race called The Seeders terra-formed every possible planet in the galaxy and planted the exact same plants and humans. So every planet has human civilizations and eat basically the same things."

Callie just looked at him. She could tell he was serious.

She shook her head. "You are right, I don't believe you."

He laughed. "Oh, trust me, unless I had seen all this for myself, I wouldn't have believed it either. I sometimes still don't."

"So exactly what are you doing here?" she asked.

He pointed to a tall, thin, nerdy-looking guy standing talking with a group of people near the viewport. "That's my friend, Doc. We're both from the same place and we invented a ship that could take us out into interstellar space."

"Something like this ship?" she asked.

He laughed. "Oh, heavens no. Our ship, *The Lady*, is sitting like a tiny flea in this ship's docking port. We thought our ship was huge when we built it. Guess not, huh?"

She nodded, so he went on.

"We had visited a few hundred planets like yours, almost all with thriving human civilizations at about the same level as yours and mine. Not kidding. We just got to this system about five hours ago and were trying to figure out what had happened when all these big ships suddenly arrived and started pulling off survivors from below."

"So they rescued you as well?" she asked.

"Sort of," he said. "They tell us our shields on *The Lady* might have saved us from the second wave. But they wanted the extra help here and we were more than glad enough to help. Seems these people are really into helping other races and sharing information."

"Sure seems that way," Callie said. "Where are they from?"

"From what I'm told, about fifty planets in a sector of the galaxy that was seeded earlier, so they are more advanced than this area of space, than your people and mine."

She just shook her head. "So if we're all from different planets, how come we can all speak the same language?"

"Now that's something that's been bothering me as well," he said. "I just haven't had the chance to ask anyone how that works."

She took another bite of the sandwich and then opened the juice.

"I hope I'm not being too personal," he said, looking worried, "but did you have family down there and how did you survive?"

"No family," she said. "And I'm a paleontologist and a professor. I was on a dig in a regional cave."

"Your students survive as well?" he asked.

Suddenly her brain clicked in even more. "They did, at least as long as they were with me. We didn't come out of the cave until this morning to discover what had happened. They had family and went in search of them."

She started to scan the people she could see, looking for the two of them.

"Well, Benson told me they were taking survivors from the same general areas for each room, so they might be here. Although there are hundreds of rooms on this ship alone and I doubt they will let us go wondering from one to another. You want me to help you look in this room?"

"In a minute," she said, working on another cookie. "I think I need to get some more food in me. I was moving bodies out of a lodge near the cave and when I finished I just took a shower and climbed into bed. I flat forgot to eat."

"I never seem to have that issue," he said, laughing. "I love to cook, actually."

"Seriously?" she asked.

She flat couldn't believe this guy sitting in front of her. More than likely he was married or gay or something. That had been her luck with the very few men she had been attracted to.

He nodded. "As we've been traveling, I've collected all kinds of recipes from different worlds. On our ship I have a gourmet kitchen."

She smiled because he seemed to be extremely proud of that fact.

"Family or significant other at home?"

"Mother and father," he said. "No one else."

Again those green eyes of his bored through her and she just couldn't look away.

"So you are an inventor?" she asked, finally letting herself think of something besides how incredible this man was.

"Sort of," he said. "A couple doctorate degrees in mathematics and physics tends to shove a person in that direction."

"I suppose it would," she said.

Now she *really* couldn't believe this guy. Not only was he fantastic looking, but he was as smart as they came.

"We're moving," he said, pointing at the window.

The big room slowly went silent as everyone turned to watch as the planet seemed to suddenly get smaller. Then for a brief instant the stars blurred.

Then without even a sense of movement the stars came back and the planet and sun were completely gone.

Callie just sort of shook her head, not having a clue as to what had just happened.

Around them the room burst into noise.

A few people started crying.

The skinny guy who Fisher had called Doc came running over all excited.

"Did you see that?" he asked Fisher. "No sense of movement, instant trans-tunnel jump. Amazing."

"I saw it," Fisher said. "Can you get *The Lady* to do the same thing?"

"I'm going to stay here until we can," he said, laughing like a little kid.

Then he moved away, going back to talk to some of the crew.

"My friend gets excited easily about space drives," Fisher said, again turning and smiling at her.

"I can see that," she said, smiling. "Where do you think we are now?"

Fisher shrugged. "A safe distance away from that second wave. Maybe a light year or so outside your system."

Callie just looked at him, stunned to her core. He said that so casually.

All in one day she had experienced more death than she wanted to ever see again and taken a ride into deep space on an alien space ship.

And in doing so met a man of her dreams.

When she woke up finally, she was going to have to write all this down.

Chapter Thirteen

FISHER COULD NOT BELIEVE that he was managing a conversation with this beautiful and very smart woman. More than likely it was because she was in such shock from all the events that she was even paying him the slightest bit of attention.

Yet she seemed interested.

He honestly didn't know when a woman was interested or not in him. He had been blind to relationships for so long, he now found himself completely unprepared when he found someone interesting.

Yet she had been through so much, he couldn't imagine how she was dealing with everything. Her basic core beliefs were no doubt being shattered, not counting the fact that billions of people had died on her planet.

"I think I'm ready to see if I can find my students," she said to Fisher after finishing her sandwich and all but one of the cookies he had brought her. "Would you mind helping me?"

"I would love to," he said, smiling.

He wanted to help her to her feet, but refrained. She seemed to be fine and had power now in her movements and walk.

Side-by-side, they stared around the outside of the room. She gave him a quick description of what they looked like, and it took them almost thirty minutes to wind through the groups of people standing and sitting.

With some survivors, the smell of death was very strong. Other survivors just lay on blankets or sat in chairs with their eyes closed.

When he and Callie had made it three quarters of the way around the big space, it was clear to him that her students were not there.

"Ahh, well," she said. "I hope they are all right."

"I'm sure they are," Fisher said, leading her back over to the two chairs they had left.

They sat and talked for a while about her teaching and where the cave was in comparison to where she taught and so on. He loved to hear her talk and he could tell that the love for her profession was amazing.

"So what were you doing clearing out a lodge by yourself?" he asked.

She took a small bite of the last cookie on her plate. "This lodge and cave is a long ways up in the mountains. My students left, going in search of family. When they called me from about fifty miles away to tell me the death was everywhere and they were continuing on, I knew I was going to have to take care of

myself for some time to come. So with no other place to go, I figured the lodge would do fine since it had heat and food to last me for some time."

He nodded. "So you had to clear out bodies to make the lodge livable? How many?"

"Nineteen," she said softly.

"Oh, my, how did you do that?" He couldn't believe she had managed that. He doubted he would have been able to.

She shrugged.

"You don't look big enough to manhandle human bodies."

"A big food cart," she said. "And protective clothing. I did what I had to do. But when I was finished, I locked up the lodge and took a shower and crawled into bed. Completely forgot to eat."

"You think you can survive in that lodge for some time?"

"Maybe a half year or more," she said. "At least through the coming fall and winter."

Then she looked at Fisher and her wonderful brown eyes were wide and she looked like she was about to panic.

"They are going to put us back, aren't they?"

Fisher nodded. He didn't know what else to say.

"And we're not going to remember any of this, are we?"

"They tell me no," he said.

She actually shuddered.

He reached over and put his hand on her hand.

Her skin felt wonderful, but her hand was shaking.

"Tell you what? Let me ask if you can stay with Doc and me. We have a lot of extra room on *The Lady*, entire suites, actually, and maybe we can find a way from up here to help out your planet even more."

"You would do that for me?" she asked.

He squeezed her hand and let go, even though he didn't want to. "Of course."

"Let me go get it cleared so you don't have to worry about it." He stood and smiled at her, the most beautiful woman he had ever met.

"Thank you," she said.

"My pleasure," he said. "I'll be right back."

He was halfway across the room when he noticed the stars outside had blurred and suddenly the planet was back below the ship.

His stomach twisted as he quickly searched for someone who seemed to be in charge, without luck.

Then, as he was about to turn back to Callie, every survivor in the room vanished at once, leaving only the staff.

Across the room Doc shrugged.

Fisher just stood there, staring at the empty chair where Callie had been.

The woman of his dreams was gone.

And now she would never remember him.

Yet he would always remember her.

Part Two

Chapter Fourteen

THE LIGHT STREAMING IN the window woke Callie.

She had had the worst dream, about dead bodies and having to move them and put them in a truck.

She rolled over and yawned and stretched, then opened her eyes.

And instantly she was in full panic mode.

She was in the lodge.

It hadn't been a dream.

She was alone and everyone was dead.

She sat up in the bed and looked at the sweatshirt and sweatpants she had on.

They were a dead woman's clothes.

She lay back, pulled the covers up to her chin, and tried to force herself to just breathe.

"No panic," she said out loud to the large suite.

Her voice echoed and sounded strange to her ears.

"No panic."

Deep breath.

"No panic."

Deep breath.

That helped some.

She opened her eyes and forced herself to look around, focusing on every detail of the room to make herself calm down.

The room had high ceilings, with polished logs as beams. The walls were painted an off white and were decorated in old photos of the early days of the lodge.

There was a living room just off the bedroom to her left with large overstuffed furniture including a couch with soft cloth that looked big enough to sleep two end-to-end.

The floors were old polished wood and had area rugs on both sides of the bed and in the living room under the furniture.

A bathroom with tile floors and old-style sinks was to her right.

The sunlight streaming in the windows meant it was the middle of the day because this time of the year the sun was only over the valley directly for three hours. The rest of the times the tall peaks on three sides of the lodge blocked the sun.

The two main rooms of the suite were lit with wooden chandeliers hanging from wood beams and there were a number of table lamps in various places.

She had left the overhead lights on last night, she remembered that.

If she was going to stay here, she was going to need to replace those table lamps with oil lamps pretty soon.

Unless she could keep the generator working and there was enough fuel for it.

She climbed out of bed and in her socks went into the bathroom. Then she pulled on some slippers the hotel furnished that were in one closet and went in search of her cell phone.

It was on a wooden table in the main living room area.

No calls, so she tried to call Jim.

His phone rang, and then after a moment he picked up.

"They are dead," he said, his voice soft. "Everyone in the city is dead. My baby is dead."

"I am so sorry," Callie said.

There was a soft sobbing sound on the other end of the call and then the phone went dead.

She looked at the phone, trying to figure out if there was anyone else she could call while the power and cell phones still worked.

There wasn't one damn person outside of Oregon she could think of.

And if Bill had found everyone in Eugene dead as well, then this death had spread far, far wider than she could imagine.

She was alone.

At least for any foreseeable future.

She took her cell phone and went back to the large featherbed. She put the phone on the nightstand and plugged it in, just in case.

Then she crawled back in bed, pulled the covers up over her head, and pretended nothing had happened, letting herself just breathe in the soft smell of lilac fabric softener from the sheets.

She had been strong last night while moving the bodies.

She didn't need to be strong today.

After an hour of feeling sorry for herself and feeling very, very alone, her bladder again forced her into the bathroom. She sure didn't remember drinking that much before going to bed.

But she did need to eat. She hadn't eaten anything before going to bed, but she wasn't hungry. That didn't matter. In this situation, not eating wouldn't help anything.

And she was going to need to do some inventory. She started to run down some chores as she put on her tennis shoes.

She needed to get enough wood in to keep the fireplace going for many long months.

She needed to find oil lamps and as much fuel for them as she could find.

She needed to do an inventory of the food supplies and when all of it was going to spoil.

And she needed to see if she could find a few more clothes and some winter clothing as well.

In other words, she needed to know how long she could hole up here in this lodge before she needed to go down into the valley and then on back to Eugene and the University.

She hoped that she was going to be able to stay long enough for the smells to mostly pass.

She headed out into the hallway toward the big front desk. There would be paper there to do lists. She could use the big wooden front desk as a sort of survival command center.

After all, she was in charge of this place now.

Then, with a notebook in her hand and a pen behind her ear, she headed downstairs to the kitchen and dining areas.

She was going to survive this, whatever had happened. And to do that, she had to take care of herself.

That meant eating regularly.

Even though she just wasn't the slightest bit hungry for some reason.

Chapter Fifteen

FISHER COULDN'T BELIEVE what had just happened.

Callie was gone. Sent back into the death below, and he really had no idea where she was. She had described some lodge in the mountains near a cave.

But that was all he knew. He didn't even know what part of the planet that lodge and cave were on.

He hoped that the people running the transport beams knew where, but how would he even identify her to them?

He needed to find her, but that was going to take some work and he had a hunch a lot of luck. He was looking for one person among two million survivors on a very large planet.

And he didn't want to think about the problems he would face if he did find her. She wouldn't remember him or anything about this room.

He stared at the chair where she had been. The task of finding her seemed impossible, but those wonderful eyes and the feel of her just wouldn't leave his mind.

He had to try.

He would never forgive himself if he didn't at least try.

He went to a person who seemed to be in charge of the room and asked him what the designation for this room was.

The older bald guy who had on a white smock and who smelled like death just stared at him. The guy seemed far too tired too care about any stupid questions and he looked at Fisher like he had lost his mind. But then he said, "L-266."

"What department or which person could I talk to about what part of the planet the people in this room came from?"

"Head of transport," the guy said and turned away.

Fisher thanked him as the guy walked toward a door.

Fisher then headed back to where Doc was still talking to a couple of the volunteers.

Fisher had no idea how to move around in this big ship, or if he and Doc were even allowed to. He even had no idea how to get to *The Lady* if he wanted to. They had been transported into this room and hadn't left it yet.

Talk about feeling helpless.

And trapped.

For all he knew, this Benson guy was just going to put them back on their ship, erase their memories as well, and toss them back into orbit.

"That was one of the main people in their engineering department," Doc said, smiling and clearly excited. "Nice guy. He said he would work with me on getting our drives up a notch."

At that point Benson walked into the room, clearly looking tired, but also smiling.

"Rescue a success?" Fisher asked him.

Benson really smiled at that question. "Completely. We managed to rescue over two million people and put them back without losing one person."

Fisher just shook his head. "That's amazing."

"It is, isn't it?" Benson asked. Then he laughed.

"So, let's get you two settled so we all can get some rest."

Benson indicated that they should follow him and he led them out into a corridor outside the room.

There was a wide corridor that seemed to go off into the distance with a number of branching corridors. Fisher had no doubt he could get very, very lost in a ship this size.

Numbers of crew, many in white smocks, were walking slowly along the corridor. And then as Fisher watched, one touched a wall and vanished.

Benson stopped beside a blank panel on the wall. Fisher could see them spaced evenly on both sides of the wide corridor.

"I have given you both special crew status," he said, "so you can stay on board as long as you would like. Talk to anyone you would like, and move freely about. I will be available for questions when you have them."

"Thanks," Doc said, smiling.

"Yes, thank you," Fisher said, not really believing what he was hearing. At least not fully.

Benson pointed at the blank wall screen. "Touch it anywhere."

Fisher reached out and touched the screen. It came to life, showing his name and "Special Crew" status beside his name.

"Some key words the computer is trained for specifically," Benson said. "The main ones are Location, Destination,

and Transport. Location tells you where you are at on the ship."

He nodded for Fisher to say that to the screen, so Fisher turned and said, "Location."

A map of the deck appeared on the screen with a designation as to where exactly they were standing. There were letters with three numbers after every location. The room they had just left was L-266 as the man had told him. The panel they stood at was L-267. The next one down the hallway was L-268 and so on.

"We are on L-Deck," Benson said. "There are fifteen major decks. Your ship is on O-Deck. Actually, it is at O-110. So say to the computer the word destination followed by that number. Then say two to accompany you."

Fisher turned slightly again to the board. "Destination O-110. Two to accompany."

The hallway vanished and they were standing beside a bulkhead. "The Lady" sat looking alone and very small on the big landing deck.

"Now that's nifty," Doc said, smiling.

"Would you two like to have rooms on the ship or stay on your own ship?" Benson asked.

"I think we'll be fine on our ship," Fisher said. "We're sort of used to it."

Benson nodded. "I figured as much. Feel free to roam around and talk to as many people as you would like starting in about eight hours. It will take me that long to get some sleep and tell everyone that you two are free to come and go. And the computer board will help you find any department you want to visit."

"Thank you for your kindness," Fisher said.

"Never hurts to have young, fresh ideas around," Benson said. "So we'll be glad to help you if you two can help us in return with anything you see that can be improved on."

"How long are we staying in orbit over this planet?" Fisher asked, suddenly worried that he was going to end up a very long distance from Callie.

"I'm afraid we're going to be here for some time," Benson said. "We are the ship assigned to stay in orbit and monitor the situation. All the other ships will be heading back to their home worlds over the next few days."

"Fine by me," Doc said, nodding.

"Perfect," Fisher said. "And again, thanks."

"Thanks for your help today," he said, and with that he tapped the board, said, "Destination A-19. One to transport."

And he was gone.

Fisher just stared at the spot where he had been standing, then looked at Doc.

"Can you believe any of this?" Doc asked, shaking his head and laughing.

"I'm not sure what to believe anymore," Fisher said as they turned and headed the short distance to their ship.

But all he could really think about was Callie. He hoped she was doing all right.

Chapter Sixteen

CALLIE SPENT an hour downstairs, forcing herself to munch on an apple and a half sandwich and a fruit drink. While she ate she did a partial inventory, but decided that while it was still light and sunny outside, she needed to go look around the lodge and see what she could see.

Last night, while carrying out the bodies and putting personal effects with

them, she had pulled out and kept every key ring from every person. She had a sack of them sitting on the counter in the kitchen, so she took the sack, went back upstairs and got her coat that she hadn't worn while moving bodies, and went outside, making sure to leave the front door of the lodge open so she could get back in without breaking out a window.

The day was beautiful, the sun was bright and still an hour from ducking behind a ridgeline. She didn't need the coat, so she took it off and left it on the porch.

She walked around the lodge as much as she could, considering that it was built hanging out over a ravine, checking it and making a note to get the canned fruit she had unloaded from the truck inside when she had time in the next few days.

Then she started up the road past the front of the lodge toward the parking lot.

There was a long building just up the hill from the lodge that the rangers and some staff lived in. She went up the front steps and pulled open the main door of that building. The smell of death drove her quickly back down the steps and into the fresh mountain air.

Clearly a number of people were dead in there.

She blew her nose and stood and took deep breaths of the fresh mountain air to clear what she could.

That was what the lodge would have smelled like in a very short time if she hadn't worked quickly yesterday to clear it.

She went up into the main parking lot.

There were almost twenty cars there, plus the truck she had parked last night.

She walked a wide circle out and past the truck with all the bodies, then went to the first car, a modern Dodge van. It took her a while to find the right key ring, but she got it open.

Except for a couple of suitcases in the back, there wasn't much. It looked like it was an elderly couple who owned the van, more than likely the two she remembered seeing with the tour group in the opening to the caves. There were a couple of coats she might be able to use, some tools like a shovel and an ax, and some bags of travel snacks between the front seats.

She started to pull them out, then realized that with twenty cars to get supplies from, she might as well use the van to transport it all down to the lodge.

She opened the back gate of the van wide, put the tools on one side, the suitcases on the other, the coats in the back seat, and then moved on to the next car.

The sun was behind the mountain and the air was getting a chill in it before she had gone through every car.

She now had lots of bags of snacks and crackers and different forms of food that would last for a very long time.

She also had half-dozen small shovels and other tools, including a dozen small medical kits.

She had found over twenty winter coats of various sizes and shapes.

And she had the back of the van piled with seven suitcases with women's clothing in them.

She had also found six iPods with a lot of different forms of music already loaded on them and two car chargers that she could use to charge the iPods up when she needed.

When she found the first one she had suddenly realized that the silence around her was weighing on her.

She needed music. She often worked in her office with music going.

She needed to set music up in the lodge, make the place feel more alive.

She liked all sorts of music, so it didn't much matter.

Then it dawned on her that she might want to see if she could get any radio news.

She went back to the van, stared it up and sat, working her way through the dial. There seemed to be two stations still working playing automated play lists. Not one bit of news or emergency broadcast information.

Even though she came up blank, she was annoyed at herself that she hadn't thought of that last night. She clearly was still in shock and not thinking at times. She needed to be very careful.

She was about to close up the van and drive it down to the lodge when she noticed another building with more cars in front of it up the hill to one side of the public parking lot.

More Forest Service buildings, she had a hunch. And maybe employee parking.

She took a Snickers candy bar from one of the snack bags and headed up the hill toward the cars.

About halfway up there, it just seemed to be getting too dark, so she decided she would save those for another sunny day and turned around. She wanted to get the lodge ready for the power to go out.

And she didn't want to do that after dark just in case the power went out tonight.

Ten minutes later she had the van parked outside the kitchen exit and was unloading the supplies of food from the front seat.

Then she headed upstairs to turn on lights and get some music going in the main lobby.

And maybe she would start a fire in the fireplace.

She was going to survive this. She didn't know for what. But survival now was all that mattered.

To do that she had to stay focused.

And be careful.

Chapter Seventeen

FISHER'S DREAMS were of Callie. Her smile, her being lost on a planet covered in death.

He woke up with his sheets wrapped around his legs.

He glanced at the clock and realized that he had been asleep for almost nine hours. When they had gotten back in the ship last night, he had taken a shower and then just fell into bed.

Now suddenly, he felt wide awake and not really believing that yesterday had happened.

One minute he and Doc were visiting a new planet, the next minute they were helping rescue people and he was falling in love with a woman he lost a few hours later.

He wondered if anyone on the ship had recorded what had happened in the big meeting room with all the survivors. If so, he might be able to get a picture of Callie to hold onto, and maybe with a picture of the two of them together help convince her that he had met here when he found her again.

If he found her.

He was honestly more worried about her not believing him or talking to him than finding her, but even that might turn out to be almost impossible, depending on the records the people on this big ship kept of the transports of the survivors.

He took a shower and then dressed in casual jeans and a short-sleeved blue dress shirt, he headed for the kitchen.

Doc was there, sitting at the big table sipping an orange juice and working on something on a pad.

"Up long?" Fisher asked and Doc shook his head.

"So damned tired, I passed out."

"That makes two of us. Let me fix us some breakfast and we can do some exploring of our host's big ship."

"Sounds perfect," Doc said, his voice clearly excited. "I feel like I got a ton to learn. Like I'm starting school all over again. What about you?"

"I've got a woman to find first," Fisher said.

"The survivor you were sitting with?" Doc asked, for the first time looking up from his pad. He looked almost surprised.

"Yeah, she was amazing," Fisher said, smiling at his best friend, then turning to start some breakfast.

Over the next thirty minutes he fixed a light breakfast of eggs, toast, and some cooked ham for both of them while telling Doc about Callie. It felt great talking about her and by the time he was done, he knew for certain he had to find her and fast. Doc offered to help as much as he could.

Then they headed out of *The Lady*, across the small deck, and to the board on the wall.

"Transportation Department location?" Doc asked.

Fisher smiled. It was nice to have his friend helping him. At least to start. He had no doubt that Doc would get distracted quickly and head off into some sort of space-warp mechanics, but it was great he was willing to help out to start.

The computer showed them the deck and number.

"Security department location," Fisher asked.

The board showed him C-226.

"Wondering if they were recording the room?" Doc asked.

"Exactly," Fisher said. "That way transportation will know exactly where in the room she was."

"Perfect," Doc said. "Let me have a shot at this."

Then Doc turned to the board. "Two to transport to C-226."

A moment later Fisher found himself and Doc looking at a large room of people sitting at what seemed to be large u-shaped consoles. There had to be fifty people in the room, all seemingly focused and busy.

"Wow," Doc said. "That actually worked.

Fisher felt the same way, just staring at the board and then back at the room.

"You must be our new guests on board that Benson informed us about a few hours ago."

The voice came from behind them, so Fisher and Doc both turned to face a man in a blue jacket with some sort of insignia on it. He was smiling and extending his hand.

He couldn't have been more than five foot tall and looked like he had a gut on him that left any room far before he did. He also had white hair that seemed to ring a bald spot like someone had dropped hair removal drops right in the middle of his head.

"I'm Calvin, head of security for 'The R-12'."

Fisher introduced himself and Doc and shook the man's hand, then asked, "The R-12?"

Calvin laughed, his stomach shaking. "That's the name of this ship. We built it so fast to get here, no one ever got around to actually naming it and the construction number just stuck. So why the honor of the stop here first this morning?"

"I was wondering," Fisher said, suddenly nervous for some reason, "if you recorded the events in all the survivor rooms yesterday?"

"Sure did," Calvin said.

"Would it be possible to get an image of myself in L-266 talking with a woman survivor there?"

"Sure," Calvin said, smiling as he turned and headed toward a desk.

"Thinking of making a rescue of your own?"

"If I can find her again," Fisher said. "And if she'd come with me."

He nodded. "Not going to be easy. But it is possible. I've heard there are about ten people up in transportation working on a similar idea as we speak. Smart to come here first."

"So it wasn't possible for some people to just not be beamed back?" Doc asked, looking at me with a puzzled frown.

"Nope," Calvin said. "Transporting that many people in such a short time had to be done by a computer program. Anyone beamed to the ship had to be sent back down to the exact same position they left from. Their memories were fogged and they were put to sleep. No other way to handle that many people in time to save everyone."

"Makes complete sense," Doc said.

"That it does," Fisher said, feeling relieved that he hadn't failed Callie by not finding someone in time to stop her return.

Calvin was bent over a panel, staring at a screen that Fisher couldn't see.

"What part of the room?"

"Near the window, about in the center."

"There you are," Calvin said.

A moment later Calvin reached under the terminal and pulled up an image of Fisher sitting talking with Callie. It felt like a normal piece of paper, only the image was a top-level photograph.

"I can see why you want to track her down," Calvin said, smiling as he handed Fisher the paper.

"Wow," Doc said.

All Fisher could do was just stare at the image in his hands. It was as if the photo was taken looking over his shoulder directly into Callie's face.

She was looking at him with those fantastic eyes, and she was smiling at him.

"Thank you," Doc said to Calvin.

Fisher managed to pull his gaze away from Callie long enough to say thanks as well.

"Just tell transportation that she was in Sector 3160 of L-266," Calvin said, smiling at Fisher. "And be patient with them. They are jammed."

Fisher again thanked Calvin and then followed Doc over to the panel on the wall.

All he could do was stare at the image in his hands.

"We'll find her," Doc said. "Then it's going to be up to you to convince her to come up here?"

"If I do find her, do we have room on *The Lady*?" Fisher asked. "And will it be all right with you?"

Doc just laughed. "It's about time, don't you think, that we use some of those extra suites we built?"

Then he turned to the board and transported them to the people Fisher hoped would help him find Callie once again.

Chapter Eighteen

THE ROOM FISHER AND DOC found themselves in was crowded. It was much smaller than the huge security area and had a dozen u-shaped stations with one person behind the station and a second sitting close by looking anxious.

There were four others standing to one side, leaning against the wall.

A woman behind the closest desk looked up and smiled at them. She had bright green eyes and the shortest hair

Fisher had seen a woman wear. Being totally bald wasn't far away for her, yet it looked great the way she wore it.

"Looking for someone on the planet?" she asked.

Fisher nodded.

"We'll be with you as quick as we can," she said.

Fisher and Doc stepped over against a wall. Fisher was stunned at how many people were in the same spot he found himself in. And he wondered about all the other ships that were getting ready to leave orbit. What would he be doing if he was on one of those ships right now?

They stood there for a moment before Fisher finally turned to Doc. "No need for you to wait here with me. Head to engineering and I'll meet you back in *The Lady* for lunch in three hours."

"You sure?" Doc asked.

Fisher laughed. "I'm going to be fine. I only talked to the woman for a couple of hours. I might not even like her after I find her again."

Doc laughed. "Yeah, fat chance of that. First woman you've even noticed since you lost all the weight. Trust me, you'll like her."

Fisher glanced at the picture of Callie in his hands and knew his friend was right.

"Lunch," Doc said. He moved over to the big board on the wall and a moment later vanished, off to his real love, engineering.

Four others showed up after Fisher so that the small area around the panel was almost crowded. But people were leaving the desks, some looking sad, others just worried.

Finally a woman wearing a summer-like green dress with short brown hair and sandals came up to the group still waiting and asked, "Who is next?"

It took Fisher a moment and a guy pointing at him before he realized he was next.

He followed her back to her station and she pulled up a chair in front of the monitor and some flat panels. "I'm Raina," she said, giving him a smile that had some of the brightest and whitest teeth Fisher had ever seen. "I assume you are looking to find someone on the planet that you met yesterday?"

Fisher nodded. "L-266, Section 3160."

He handed her the photo as she turned and looked at him with surprise.

"We'll that's going to save some time scanning the room," she said, glancing at the picture and handing it back to him. "Thanks for going to security first. Now let's see if I can track back through the data on the transports to find her."

Her fingers danced over the flat panels and on the screen in front of her an area of the planet below appeared.

With each movement of her fingers the image that Fisher could see on the screen focused in closer.

The image was like looking down at a color photo of the surface.

There were red dots everywhere. Fisher assumed the dots all represented a human. There were a lot of them, scattered, and as the screen moved in closer, there were fewer and fewer red dots.

Finally, Raina stopped and sat back, shaking her head. "That's the best I can do. She's one of those thirty-four people."

She touched her board and then a moment later handed him the image that was on her screen. He could also see data on it as to the location on the planet of the image.

"Sorry I couldn't get it narrowed down any more than that?"

He smiled. "She told me enough about her location that this is more than enough. Thank you."

"Well, that's good," she said.

He stood.

She turned and smiled at him. "Glad to be of help and welcome aboard."

He must have looked shocked and puzzled.

She laughed. "Chairman Benson sent images of you and your friend with his announcement."

"Oh," Fisher said, laughing. "Again, thanks."

He started to turn away, then had a thought and turned back. "How would I find some topographic maps of this area?"

He sort of waved the image she had given him.

Her fingers again danced over the screen and she handed him another image with topographic lines and the dots still showing.

"Thanks," he said, again. "Any chance you might have some information about natural features in this area? She survived in a cave and is staying in a large lodge beside the big natural cave."

This time it took Raina a little longer, her face frowning at times in a focused study, but when she turned to Fisher, she was smiling from ear-to-ear with her teeth almost lighting up the room. "You just made my entire day."

She pointed at the image she was handing Fisher. "Big cave, big lodge, one person way up in the mountains of that area, all alone."

Fisher stood there, staring at the image in his hand of a roof of a large lodge, some big parking lots and other buildings nearby, and an area showing a natural cave.

There was a red dot in the lodge.

"I think we found her," Raina said, smiling.

"I think we did," Fisher said, smiling so hard he thought he was going to hurt himself.

He felt levels of relief he didn't realize he could feel. There was just something about Callie that drove him and now that he knew where she was the feeling of relief almost knocked his knees out from under him.

But then he suddenly realized that there might be rules about having a person from a planet come on board The R-12. Did he need special permission?

He looked at Raina. "Now what do I do?"

"You go talk with her. No rules on bringing anyone back from the surface as long as they want to come. They must be willing and want to come with you."

"Well, she won't remember me, but good to know all I have to do is convince her I'm from outer space."

Raina laughed, again showing all those wonderful white teeth. "Yeah, a challenge, but I'm betting you are up for it."

"And when I'm ready to go to the surface, who do I talk to and how do I get back?"

Again Raina gave him that bright smile. "Me. I'll help you with anything you need. It will be my pleasure."

Then she stood and hugged him and he hugged her back.

"Thank you," he said. "I can't thank you enough."

"Just introduce me to her when she comes on board," Raina said.

"Deal," Fisher said, hugging Raina once more, then turning to go.

"See you soon?" she asked.

"Soon," he said. "Very soon."

Chapter Nineteen

CALLIE WOKE with oldies rock music playing softly from the main room of her suite. Outside her window the light was coloring the top of the ridgeline that she could see. The day looked like it might be another beautiful one.

She lay there on the wonderfully comfortable featherbed, the quilt pulled up to her chin, just thinking.

Last night she had built a fire in the big stone fireplace in the main lodge front room. Then she had pulled over a couple chairs with stands and a couch and circled the fireplace at a distance where the fire would keep her warm, but not too close to take a chance of anything catching fire. She had put a quilt on each chair and two on the couch and oil lamps on both sides of the big stone mantel, two on the ends of the front desk, and lanterns on all the nearby tables.

Plus she had three flashlights that she had found so far. She needed to go search the glove boxes of the cars for more. She had put one flashlight on the coffee table in front of the couch, another on the front desk, and another in her room near her bed.

The fire turned out wonderfully, warming the big room and giving it a glowing orange look and light smoke smell that she just loved. And between the music and the crackling of the fire, she didn't feel the pressure of the silence and being alone as much.

She had taken an estimate of how much firewood she was going to need to have a fire like that every evening all winter long. She didn't have enough, so the task of finding more went to the top of her list of things to start doing. She hoped the other buildings had wood, and that there was some outside someplace, because the idea of her cutting her own wood didn't appeal in the slightest.

She had also done an inventory of all of her food right after a dinner of turkey sandwich and cherry pie. Eating the way she did, she would easily have enough to make it a full year. In fact, she guessed she had enough to make it almost two years if she had to, considering how many cans of different items were in the storage. Her diet would become very bland, but at least she had enough to make it through the winter and into the spring before thinking about what to do next.

And she had a hunch that the other buildings would have food supplies in them as well. She couldn't go into the dorm for the Forest Service people because of the smell until at least next spring. Today she would look at the other cars and the other buildings higher up the valley.

On the big board behind the main desk in the big room she had written in large letters her list of priorities.

Today she also needed to search for more flashlights and batteries and oil for lamps. She had no idea how long the power would stay on, but she bet it wouldn't be long if no one was maintaining the power grid in this area.

And she had no idea how to even turn on the generators in the basement or how much fuel they had. Finding answers to those questions were on her main list, right near the top as well.

She also needed to do a wash-load or two of clothes. She had found a bunch of women's clothes that would fit her in the cars and in the rooms, but some were dirty, as well as her own clothes from the cave. Today was wash day as well as exploring day.

She glanced at the clock.

A little after seven in the morning. Time to get moving. She had a lot to do.

By 7:30 she was finished showering and dressed in jeans, tennis shoes, a wool man's shirt, and a light jacket.

She had also put a pair of gloves in her jacket pocket.

The fire in the fireplace was down to only embers that cracked and the music she had left on in the main lobby had shut itself off.

She turned the music on again and set it to shuffle the selections through pop and country songs.

Anything to keep the silence away.

Then she went down to the old lunch room, put her coat and gloves on the counter, turned on the music she had set up down there as well, and went back into the kitchen to cook herself some breakfast.

She was going to use the food that would spoil first, so this morning it was two eggs over easy cooked in butter, a thin slice of ham, and white toast.

She had a hunch that in six months she would almost kill for this kind of breakfast. But right now she was going to enjoy it.

She sat at the lunch counter, listening to a country western album from Blake Shelton and staring out through the trees as she savored her breakfast. Damn she was going to miss eggs.

And ham. And toast.

She shook that thought away and went back to planning the day.

Chapter Twenty

FISHER WENT BACK to *The Lady* with the maps of where Callie was and the picture of her sitting smiling at him.

He spread the maps and picture out on the kitchen table and then went to working on some lunch. Doc wouldn't be back for at least an hour, but that would give Fisher time to think. And he loved to cook and think at the same time.

He couldn't believe he was even considering going after Callie. More than likely under normal, calm circumstances, they wouldn't even get along. But he doubted that.

Those few hours of talking had been really special for him. And she had seemed very interested in him as well and very happy at the idea that she might be able to stay on board with him.

So even if they didn't end up getting along, he owed her the right to decide to come aboard and out of the death below. She could go back at any time if she wanted. He would not hold her.

But the big problem was that she was isolated and wouldn't remember him at all. The only rule about anyone coming from the surface to the ship is that they must want it.

So he had to somehow come up with a way to introduce himself, let her get to know him a little, and then tell her about a spaceship in orbit that she could go to if she wanted.

Just thinking that made him shake his head and laugh. She would think him a nut case and more than likely just shoot him.

And he wouldn't blame her.

So somehow he was going to need to get to know her and that might take time.

And before he could even try that, he needed a ton more information. The biggest question he had was that if he walked up to her on the planet surface, would she understand a word he said? He was sure that the language systems that made them all seem to be speaking the same language was a shipboard feature. He needed to know if he could even talk with her, considering that they were from planets over sixty light years apart.

He took a pad and started jotting down notes of things he would need to know while he worked on a bacon, lettuce, and tomato salad with a fresh balsamic dressing.

Almost exactly on time Doc walked in followed by a tall, thin woman with thick eyebrows and dark black hair. She was almost as tall as Doc and when she smiled, her mouth seemed to just expand her face out sideways.

She had on jeans, a light blouse with a white vest over it, and a badge that said Engineering on the vest.

"Fisher, this is Kalinda from Engineering," Doc said.

He shook her hand and invited her to lunch. Luckily he had made more than enough. "Hope you are up for a bacon, lettuce and tomato salad."

"I would love that," she said, smiling. "Doc said you usually made enough."

"Always," Fisher said.

She had a great voice and a great smile and she seemed to continually be staring at Doc.

And Doc seemed to be returning the interest just fine.

"Kalinda has been helping me understand some of the basics of their trans-tunnel drive," Doc said.

She just shook her head and laughed. "That took about three minutes, then he started asking questions that a couple of us had never thought to ask. We got permission from Benson to have him work with us."

"It's going to be a blast," Doc said, the smile so large, Fisher thought he might hurt himself.

Doc had always been in his own personal heaven working on higher levels of physics and subspace and warp space technologies. And now it looked like he found a woman that might be able to keep up with him.

"Did you find her?" Doc asked, picking up the map on the table.

"Thanks to a wonderful person by the name of Raina in transportation, I found her."

Both Doc and Kalinda applauded.

"Doc told me what you are thinking of trying to do," Kalinda said, staring at the picture on the table. "She's beautiful."

"But she's not going to remember you," Doc said, sitting at the big table and motioning for Kalinda to do the same.

She went over and sat beside Doc, leaving the chair across from them open.

Fisher doubted Doc noticed, but it was clear that Kalinda wanted her and Doc to be a couple. And as far as Fisher was concerned, that was fantastic.

"Nope, she won't remember me," Fisher said as he served them salads in bowls with the dressing tossed in. "And she has to want to come back to the ship on her own free will. That's the only rule."

"Ouch," Doc said

Kalinda just shook her head. "So you can't just bring her up and then convince her to stay after she sees all this."

"Nope," Fisher said, his stomach twisting so much he wasn't sure he could eat. "I got to let her know I'm a space alien and that she should zip away with me to the stars."

Kalinda laughed softly, but Fisher could see in her eyes that she understood his problem.

"What can we do to help?" Doc asked.

Fisher just shook his head. "Not a thing I can think of. Just keep learning and I'll let you know when I head for the planet and when I get back. Think you can feed yourself while I'm gone?"

Kalinda just patted Doc's hand on the table and he looked at her with a fond smile and a slight puppy-dog stare.

"I'll show him how to use The R-12's mess and boards for snacks," Kalinda said to Fisher. Then she looked into Doc's eyes with a smile. "But trust me, he won't get anything like this wonderful salad."

"Thank you," Fisher said, nodding to Kalinda.

She smiled back and Fisher liked her even more.

And from there they talked about engines and mathematics and everything but the task that faced Fisher.

How was he going to convince a very smart woman who was alone in the mountains after seeing a lot of death that he wasn't from her world, that humans existed beyond her planet, and that she should leave the planet with him.

Yeah, that was going to be easy.

And if he did anything slightly wrong, he would lose any chance of being with Callie forever.

Scared didn't begin to describe how he felt.

Chapter Twenty-one

AFTER BREAKFAST, Callie headed out to search for firewood and other items on her list.

Near the downstairs kitchen entrance that she had taken the bodies out of was a double door that led into an area of the basement. It took her a while sorting through all the keys before she found the right one and got the door open.

Inside was a room the size of a double car garage and on both sides stacked as high as she could reach was freshly cut firewood, all up off the ground on wooden pallets.

"Score," she said, laughing and clapping her hands together. The lodge had already brought in their wood for the winter, so she was ready to go.

In the back of the garage area was another locked door that didn't take as long to get open because she now had the right key ring, more than likely from the person behind the desk upstairs, or one of the cleaning workers she had moved out.

She opened the door and was stunned. There had to be at least four rifles in there with ammunition under them and two shotguns. There were also knives and other things needed to dress out an animal.

Not once in her life had she fired a gun and didn't much care for them. But standing there, staring at those rifles, she suddenly realized that maybe, just maybe, she should have a way of defending herself.

If not from wild animals, from other humans.

The thought made her shudder, but she still picked up the smallest rifle. The boxes of shells under it said "22 caliber" it, so she took a number of boxes of shells and the gun, locked the closet back up, then locked the wood doors, and went back upstairs.

She stored the rifle under the front desk and put the shells beside it.

At some point in the near future she would practice with it a little bit, see if she could even load it.

But not today.

She went back outside, fired up the van that she had used the day before to transport supplies, and headed up the road toward the big parking lot again. She kept the windows rolled up, but still a couple times along the way she had to cover her nose from the smell coming from the bodies in the forest service building, the two still in the lot, and those down in the entrance to the cave.

She went all the way to the top of the lot to where the other building sat. It looked like it had been a large cabin at one point and had been converted to offices in the front.

She decided to go through the cars first. She found more snacks, mostly bagged chips and candy bars. She also found two flashlights and a couple more coats.

She looked up at the building, almost afraid to go up and try the door, then decided she might as well.

She climbed the ten steps sniffing with each step. So far the air was clear.

She looked through the windows along the porch into the building and could see no one dead in there. Just a few desks and a small kitchen area off to the back.

Finally, taking a deep breath and holding it, she tried to open the front door.

It was locked.

Could she get so lucky as to have no one dead in this building?

She spent a good ten minutes going through keys before she found the right one.

Again taking a deep breath, she opened the door.

No smell. Just a smell of closed up and musty.

So the cars out front were for the workers down in the other building.

She explored the four offices on the main floor, finding two more rifles, a couple flashlights, and some containers of paraffin for the oil lamps that were scattered around the room.

All of the lamps also seemed full, so they would help with light if she couldn't find more fuel down in the lodge.

In the kitchen there were more supplies, but nothing fresh. All canned and packaged food, which she was happy to see.

Upstairs there were two dorm rooms, one had women's clothes in a suitcase. But the woman had been very tall and very large and Callie just left them since she was convinced none of it would fit her at all.

More blankets, more bedding, nothing else.

She took what she needed out to the van, closed and locked the building back up, and then went down to where the cars were parked.

Moving quickly to avoid as much of the smell as she could, she checked the glove boxes for flashlights, finding two more.

By ten in the morning she was back at the lodge and had a load of laundry going in one of the big machines.

As she was taking a long drink of water from a bottle of water, it suddenly dawned on her that she was forgetting a couple of very major areas of survival that she needed to deal with first.

Water and sanitation.

With enough water she could make toilets work. And take baths. But did she have enough water?

121

And could she get it when the power failed?

The idea of not having enough water suddenly had her feeling very panicked.

She grabbed two candy bars and another bottle of water. Munching on a Snicker's Bar, she went in search of how the lodge supplied its water.

She couldn't believe she hadn't thought of that before now.

What else was she forgetting?

Chapter Twenty-two

FISHER SPENT the next few hours downloading and studying the area around where Callie was held up, including pictures of the lodge.

Then he went back to talk with Raina in transportation. She was very glad to see him and got him back to her station at once.

"You about ready to go?" she asked.

"Getting there," he said.

Today Raina had a maroon scarf around her neck that both accented her short brown hair and her dark dress. And like the first day, she was wearing sandals.

"What I need is information about how the transport to the planet surface is going to work."

She pointed toward the back of the room. "Back there we have a transport room that will transport you to any spot on the planet's surface simply by asking. No waiting."

He nodded.

She held up a small button about the size of the end of his little finger. "We plant this under your skin, normally on the inside of an upper arm where it won't get accidently triggered. You press it in

a certain set manner and it will automatically transport you back to the ship and the transport room."

"And if I can get her to agree to come up with me?" Fisher asked.

"You simply say that you have two to transport and hit the button and we bring her along. Just as it is done on the panels around the ship."

"Great," Fisher said.

At that moment he noticed that Raina's eyes got slightly bigger and he turned around in time to see Benson come up behind him.

Fisher and Raina both stood.

"Chairman Benson," Raina said, nodding slightly.

Fisher glanced at her. He had no idea why she called him Chairman. Clearly he had been so focused on getting Callie on board, he hadn't bothered to learn much about this big ship. And suddenly this little voice was warning him that maybe he needed to spend some time and do just that.

"Just wanted to check and see how it's going with your search for the woman you were talking with," Benson said, smiling at Fisher. "Now that I have a little time to breathe again."

"Raina is helping me a great deal," Fisher said. "She found Dr. Callie Sheridan and now I'm just trying to figure out a way to approach Callie on the surface without her chasing me away like I was a nut case."

Benson nodded. "The planets at this level are very suspicious and fearful of possible alien attacks. In a different universe, I suppose it would be justified. Anything I can do to help?"

"Actually," Fisher said, "Raina is doing a great job on this problem. But I was wondering if I could have a little of your time to get a few questions answered in general."

Benson laughed. "I figured you might have a few thousand questions. And your friend Doc has taken to engineering as if he has worked there his entire life. So I have time now. Let's go to my office."

"Wonderful," Fisher said. He turned to Raina. "I'll be back. Thanks again."

"You are more than welcome," Raina said, smiling.

Benson then said, "Two to my office."

A moment later Fisher stood in a huge office with an entire wall that looked like it was open out to space. Below the blue and green and whites of the planet spun by slowly.

"Never get tired of that view," Benson said, indicating a large chair for Fisher to sit in across a wide wood-looking desk.

"Can I ask why she called you Chairman Benson?" Fisher asked as he sat down, turned slightly so he wasn't distracted from the view.

Benson nodded. "In the Alliance we formed in our sector, we don't have a military structure. We run every ship as a corporation, a business venture. So what would be the Captain is the Chairman."

"Since you plan on being here for a year, how many people live on board?"

"Just under two thousand," Benson said and Fisher was stunned. "A lot of families and we are doing a lot of research and just getting used to this big new ship over the year."

"Wow," Fisher said.

Benson shrugged. "Space has no limits and power is unlimited as well. We are only limited by our imaginations. Which brings me to your partner, Doc. He's amazing."

Fisher laughed. "In more ways than one."

"Just from questions he's asking in engineering, he might help all of us advance in speeds of our ships. Glad you both are interested in staying on board for a while."

"Thanks for having us," Fisher said.

He went on to ask a dozen more questions about the ship, including the one about how everyone spoke the same language.

"Transport," Benson said. "The language is just given to the person being transported."

"That's why we could understand you and think we were speaking our own language?"

Benson nodded. "Exactly. Since all humans on all planets seem to have a basic pattern that their civilizations develop, the language aspect became pretty simple."

Something about all civilizations developing along similar paths bothered Fisher, but he couldn't put his finger on what. So he asked the next logical question he had.

"Has anyone ever gone looking for the Seeders?"

Benson laughed. "Just about every day from every planet out there that has figured out space travel and found out what happened in this galaxy."

"And no trace?"

"Not one item left behind by the Seeders. Nothing. They seeded the galaxy with humans and plants and animal life that took over on each Earth-like planet in the Goldilocks zone of each sun and then seemingly vanished."

Benson tapped what to Fisher looked like a form of computer panel on his desk, then scribbled something on a note pad that everyone on the ship seemed to have and leave around like paper.

Benson then handed the pad to Fisher.

"Doctor Jenny Sins, the top scientist in the department focused on the Seeders search. Go talk with her. Tell her I sent you."

"You have an entire department on the ship for this?"

"Every ship does," Benson said. "The question you asked is that important to all of us. We all know how the universe started. That's just science. None of us have a clue how we got here.

Or for that matter, why?"

Chapter Twenty-three

FISHER WAS STUNNED when he entered the Seeder Research area of Benson's big ship. There had to be fifty people working in the large room at different stations. He had no idea what they might be doing.

An elderly man with white hair and a formally white lab coat that seemed smeared with some sort of strawberry jam sat at the first desk closest to the entrance. He glanced up and then smiled with a perfect set of teeth. The smile made his face turn into a mass of loose flesh and wrinkles. "You're one of the explorers from this sector, aren't you?"

"I am. Doctor Vardis Fisher," Fisher said, extending his hand. "But everyone just calls me Fisher."

The older man took his hand and shook it, but before he could say anything a woman's voice behind Fisher said, "Well, Doctor Fisher, The Chairman warned me you would be coming."

Fisher turned around to face one of the most beautiful women he could have ever imagined wearing a white lab coat. And over the years he had imagined some

pretty amazing women in white lab coats. Never met one, but imagined many.

She looked more like a model that should be posing half-nude in magazines.

"I'm Doctor Jenny Sins," she said, extending her hand and smiling. The smile reached her blue eyes and made her seem radiant. She had long brown hair pulled back into a ponytail, and seemed to be about Fisher's height.

And she was Fisher's age as far as he could tell.

He took her hand and as he said he was pleased to meet her he noticed her wedding ring.

She held his hand for a few seconds too long while she stared into his eyes, then nodded and let go and turned away. "Let me show you what we do here."

Fisher had no idea what that was about.

He followed her and her flowing brown hair and white lab coat as she introduced him to three others in the lab. All seemed very happy to meet him for some reason.

Finally they ended up in a large open office built into one wall of the large room. It was clearly her office and from it she could pretty much see the entire room.

She went around and sat behind a large desk that seemed to have grown out of the floor. She indicated Fisher should take the chair across the desk from her, which he gladly did.

"Well, Doctor Fisher, ask me anything and I'll see what I can tell you."

"It's just Fisher."

She smiled again. "Jenny."

He took a second, then decided which question he wanted to ask first.

"So is it clear where the Seeders started and where they stopped in the Galaxy?"

She nodded and with a few quick taps on a control panel on her desk, an image of the Milky Way Galaxy appeared on the wall to the right.

"They started in this area," she said, and on the map an arrow appeared pointing at some stars on the outer edge of one of the spiral arms of the galaxy.

"They went around the galaxy clockwise, working inward and then outward, and ended in this area."

Again on the image of the galaxy another arrow appeared near the edge of the galaxy.

It was amazing and almost more than his mind could handle. She was talking about an entire galaxy like it was a neighborhood. Billions of stars and more distance than he could almost imagine.

He forced himself to not think of the size they were dealing with and pull his mind back and pretend the galaxy was actually only like a round city.

"Looks like they came into the galaxy," Fisher said, continuing to stare at the image, "did their work, and then left."

She nodded. "Sure seems that way."

"How far into the core of the galaxy did they push?"

"Only as far in as human populations could stand the radiation levels," she said. "But very few of those civilizations in close have survived for very long. Just too much going on in closer to the galaxy core that causes planet-wide destruction."

"Like what we saw below," he said.

"At a vastly more frequent and violent scale," she said, nodding. "The closer to the core of this galaxy, the nastier it gets for human life. They stayed pretty much in the zone conducive for human growth over long periods of time."

"So where do you think they went?"

"Andromeda Galaxy and all the smaller galaxy clusters around it," she said without hesitation.

The map of the galaxy shrunk down to the size of a small dinner plate on the wall allowing the closest neighboring galaxies to be shown. "Looks like they came in from the Large Magellanec Cloud and then headed to Andromeda and all of its satellite galaxies."

He had to admit that it looked that way. Like following a map on a bunch of country roads.

"Anyone go after them?"

"Not that I know of," she said. "Our ships don't have the speed to cross that much distance in a time that would allow us to catch them, even if we were sure where they were headed."

"So how did they do all this?" Fisher asked, trying his best to keep his mind clear and the scale of what he was thinking about under control. "Are we all genetically the same? Everyone on every planet?"

"We all started from the same basic gene pool," she said, again nodding. "And no degradation over time. Every planet's human and animal population started with the same genes, the same diversity, the same numbers. One hundred and forty-four thousand."

There was that number again. He just couldn't seem to make any logical sense out of any of this. There was something very clear he was missing. He knew that feeling. He just had to find what was between the obvious.

"Did they grow our ancestors or something?"

She shrugged. "Lots of theories on that. But what we do know is that it took them six major visits to each planet to accomplish what they did."

"Six?"

She nodded. "On the first visit they shoved some asteroid or something large into every planet that caused a vast extinction event of most of the animal and plant life that was natural to the planet."

"You're kidding?"

She shook her head no. "On the next four visits they covered each planet with new plants at first and then stages of animal life that quickly took over, including early primates."

"How long between that last animal seeding and the introduction of humans?"

"About three thousand years," she said, not even breaking into a smile.

Fisher shook his head. "That is so against all science I know that it's scary."

She nodded. "We are convinced they also seeded historical evidence on every planet of both human, plant, and animal history."

Fisher started to open his mouth to object, then realized where he was sitting and that he was talking to a beautiful human scientist on a huge spaceship light years from his home and even farther from her home.

Historical evidence could be planted. Sitting here was very real and hard to discount.

But wow, planting historical evidence was sure going to make Callie's work as a paleontologist seem almost impossible. Unless maybe she could help find some clues in the planted evidence. She might be able to help him on all this if he convinced her to come on board.

Fisher closed his mouth and just sat there.

"Hard to get a grasp on it all, isn't it?"

Fisher laughed. "I imagine you grew up with this knowledge. I've just been coming to grips with it over the last two years that we have been out here in space exploring."

"That would be difficult," she said, a look of worry suddenly in her blue eyes.

"I'm sure I'll come to terms with it," Fisher said, even though he wasn't so sure. "So how long do you think the Seeders were in this galaxy?"

"Only about fifty thousand years," she said.

That number made no sense to Fisher. "How many planets did they do this to?"

She shrugged. "No firm count. Maybe upward of a hundred million in this galaxy. Maybe ten times that number. No one really knows."

"In fifty thousand years? Holy smokes, how many Seeders were there?"

She shrugged once again. "No one knows that either, but they just finished about five thousand years ago as far as we can tell."

That stunned him even more.

"How long have the races in your sector been in space?"

"About two thousand years," she said. "We just missed them."

"And they didn't leave a trace?" he asked, stunned at what she had told him.

"Just us," she said. "Just us."

Chapter Twenty-four

CALLIE FOUND the water supply for the lodge in about thirty minutes. As she feared, it was an electric pump that seemed to draw water up from a well.

The entire well was tucked in a large room in the basement and off the side that seemed to almost hang over the ravine. She studied the pump for a moment, noticing that it looked fairly new.

Also, on one side of the pump was a small generator.

She opened the fuel cap on the generator and as far as she could tell, the tank was full. That was good because so far she hadn't found any extra fuel to run any of the generators in the lodge.

It would have been logical that they would have set up this generator to run only when water was required and the power was off. Otherwise, she was going to have to be down here turning it off and on regularly.

From the big well pump, she followed a white-wrapped pipe through a wall and into a large room next door. There was another smaller pump there and the pipe went straight up.

She tried to mentally mark her position in the building and then went upstairs.

The pipe was exposed in a back service area coming from the floor and going through the ceiling to the next floor above.

So she went upstairs.

The pipe again came from below and went directly up through the ceiling.

The pipe didn't seem to be like any vent, but if it wasn't, that meant there was another floor up there under the eves of the lodge.

It took her almost a half hour of searching and opening doors before she found the service staircase.

She followed it up, a flashlight in one hand just in case the power chose this moment to finally go out.

She could stand up under the peak of the roof and there was a wide walkway there. She followed it back to the center of the hotel and there she saw something she couldn't believe.

A large tank. Maybe ten steps across and almost as tall as she was.

The white pipe she had followed up from the basement came up the side of the tank and curved and went into the tank.

There were a couple of metal stairs on one side and she climbed them and opened a metal hatch she found at the top.

Water.

A full tank of water.

All gravity fed. All she had to do was run the generator for the pump to refill the tank at times. And the tank was large enough that it would last her for a very long time.

Her decision to stay in the lodge had clearly been a correct one.

So she closed up the tank and headed back downstairs. Then for the next hour she checked every faucet in every room in the building, making sure nothing was on or even dripping.

Now she needed to find more fuel for the generators. The small one running the water pump had gas in it, so she knew with all the cars in the parking lot, she could refill that one.

But the two larger generators she suspected didn't run on gas. More than likely diesel.

She went back into the basement and checked both fuel tanks on both generators. She was right, both ran diesel and both were thankfully full. Clearly the lodge had been getting ready for the coming winter.

She went back outside. It was just noon and the sun was now hitting the top of the lodge and the valley floor. It was a beautiful day once again.

She started slowly around the lodge, looking for any sign of an underground fuel tank.

Nothing.

She went from the service entrance all the way around past the front door and to the uphill side and out onto a balcony built there off the main lobby.

Cave Creek ran below the lodge, but there wasn't even a trail down the ravine that she could see. All the guests normally went up the hill to the caves. Not down into the ravine.

She went back to the kitchen, made herself a quick turkey sandwich and then, eating it and carrying an apple in her pocket, she headed back out and up the hill, looking alongside the road for any sign of a fuel tank.

There was nothing around the Forest Service dorm building with the bodies in it, so she climbed up through the parking lot and walked around the building above the top of the parking lot.

Nothing there as well.

So the only fuel she had for the two big electrical generators were in them.

She would have to make that last. And charge her electrical devices in the cars.

It wasn't going to be the best, but she could make it work through the winter.

And then next spring she would deal with that future when it got here.

Chapter Twenty-five

FISHER WENT BACK to *The Lady* and just sat in the kitchen area, munching on the remains of the salad from lunch and trying to figure out what was the best way to approach Callie.

After talking with Benson and then Jenny in the Seeder Research, he was even more convinced he was just flat missing something that was obvious and right in front of him. He hated that feeling. And he had a hunch that from what he understood of Callie's mind and spe-

cialty, the two of them might be able to solve what he was missing.

He just didn't know how he was going to convince her to come back here with him.

Finally he hit on an idea.

He spent the next hour studying the area around the lodge, the towns below it, the road in, and the distances involved. And he memorized all the names as best he could.

Then he made sure that his jeans and shirts would match the look of the area and that he had a few days of clothes with him.

He packed that in a backpack, contacted Doc that he was leaving, and with the picture of Callie smiling at him in his pack, he headed for the transportation department. His stomach was twisting in fear, but unless he tried this now, he never would.

And he didn't want to lose the chance of getting to know Callie more. And if nothing else, rescuing her from a very tough number of years on the planet's surface.

Raina greeted him with a smile as he appeared in the transportation department.

"Ready to give it a try?"

"I am. But a couple of questions to make sure my plan will work. If I come back, how quickly can I return?"

"It would take us about thirty seconds to send you back to the exact spot," she said.

Then she smiled. "Vanishing in front of her might well help her decide."

"Or scare her to death."

"Yeah, it most certainly will do that," Raina asked.

"One more favor? Do you have access to the security images of that day when she was on board?"

"Sure," Raina said, sitting back down at her station. "What room again?"

"L-266, area 3160."

Her fingers flew over her board and the same image Fisher had of Callie in his pack came up on her screen.

"Is there a camera showing us both talking with the planet in the background?"

"Again good thinking," Raina said. On the screen an image appeared a little farther away from the two of them. They were talking and both of them were very clear. Beyond them, out the window, a clear image of the planet.

"Perfect," Fisher said.

She printed it out and he folded it and put it in his pack with the other one.

Then she took him back to the transportation room. It was a giant area with a hundred small platforms lined along both walls separated by narrow partitions.

"Where do you want the return chip?" she asked. "And how many times do you want to hit it as a return call."

"Two clear pushes," he said. Then he raised his arm and showed her where he wanted it to be. Under his arm on his left side, so that his right hand could reach over like he was grabbing his arm and his thumb could push the return key.

She nodded and then before he could worry about something being inserted under his skin, it was already there.

He stared at the slight lump under his skin and felt it, amazed.

Raina smiled. "We can transport full humans and anything we want just about anywhere. Easy to put something just under your skin."

He shook his head. Of course it would be.

"Ready?" she asked.

He nodded.

She had him step up on a nearby platform and as he did a control panel slid up out of the floor in front of the platform and Raina stepped to it.

"Where exactly?" she asked.

"It's midday in the area she's at, correct?" He had checked that a few times, but he wanted to be very sure he didn't arrive in the middle of the night.

"It is," Raina said.

"How about a short distance down the road below the lodge?"

"Perfect," Raina said. "I show her in the lodge right now. Good luck. And remember, two pushes on the return and you come right back here to this platform."

"And no problem going back and forth?" he asked.

"None," she said, smiling.

"Then let's do this before I chicken out."

Raina nodded and her fingers danced on the board and the next moment Fisher found himself standing in fresh mountain air on a narrow paved road.

"Oh, man, now what have I done?" he said out loud as he looked around at the tall pine trees and mountains that towered over the narrow valley.

No one answered.

Chapter Twenty-six

IT WAS JUST AFTER ONE in the afternoon and Callie had just finished making a salad from the last of the lettuce in the fridge when she heard the call. She had added in part of a tomato and hard-boiled an egg and crumbled it over the salad. She had a choice of dressing that had been made up and in the fridge for a few days, but she didn't trust them and used the oil and vinegar instead.

She had just tossed the entire thing realizing she had made far too much for one person when she heard someone shouting. At first she didn't recognize the sound, but then a second "Hello!" echoed through the air outside the lodge.

All she could think about was rescue was here.

Could that be possible?

She left the salad sitting on the counter and scrambled up the stairs and to the main door of the lodge that led out onto the big road.

"Anyone home?"

Another shout echoed through the canyon as she opened the big wooden front door and went out onto the porch.

A lone man stood there in the middle of the road about thirty paces from her, a pack on his back and a smile on his face. He wore jeans, a dark shirt, and what looked like tennis shoes.

He wasn't any sort of rescue, that was for sure. But he was another survivor.

She felt her knees get weak as she smiled back at him.

He was one of the best-looking men she had ever seen. His short brown hair and wide shoulders just made him look sexy standing there in the sun holding the pack on his shoulder. And the smile on his face didn't hurt the look either.

He could have been a model in *GQ Magazine*. Wow!

"Hi," he said, waving, but not coming any closer, which she respected. "My name's Fisher."

His voice was low and sexy as well.

And there was something about that name and his looks that dinged the back of her brain. She felt like she knew this guy from somewhere. She couldn't place where, but she was sure she had seen him or met him before.

Completely sure of it.

"Callie," she said.

"I was hoping others would be alive up here," Fisher said. "I figured the cave might have saved a few."

"It did," Callie said, not telling him that she was the only one here. "Where are you from?"

"Eugene, actually," Fisher said. "I was at the coast when all this happened, so decided to come up here to hole up for the winter. That is if you and the other survivors don't mind more company. If you do, I can go back to the coast."

"Not at all," she said, her heart leaping at the idea she might have company all winter long. "More the merrier."

He stood there, not coming toward her, just staring at her.

And she just kept staring back as the silence of the hills and the warm afternoon closed in around them.

Finally she realized it would be up to her to welcome him. He was being very courteous and not trying to just come up.

Wow, the guy was smart.

And her little voice told her that there wasn't a threatening thing about him.

Sexy yes, but not threatening.

And over the years she had come to trust that little voice when it came to creepy men.

He was far from creepy.

"You hungry?" she asked, breaking the silence of the mountains. "I just made a salad and I got enough for two."

He smiled, looking relieved, and nodded. "I am, actually. Thanks."

"Come on in."

She stood to one side and held the door.

She couldn't believe she was trusting this stranger this much. But he seemed so familiar and nothing about him felt threatening at all. More than likely she had seen him in Eugene around the university.

As he got closer she could see his wonderful green eyes and the smile never seemed to leave his face.

Then suddenly he looked embarrassed and looked down and went past her into the lodge.

As he went inside he said, "Wow, this place is really something."

He stood there, just inside the door, sort of looking around at the high ceilings and massive stone fireplace and log construction.

"It is, isn't it?"

She pulled the front door closed and then indicated that he should follow her down the wooden stairs.

When he saw the old fashioned café with the nifty old counters and the view of the ravine, he again shook his head. "Amazing, just amazing. And the electrical is still on."

"I'm betting not for long," Callie said, leading the way into the kitchen. "You're going to have to tell me what it's like out there beyond this hill."

"Not pretty," he said.

He didn't elaborate, so she grabbed an extra bowl from the cabinet and again tossed the salad, then filled both bowls, still having some left over.

"Last of the lettuce," she said, handing him a bowl and leading him back out into the lunch counter area. "Mixed with a tomato and egg."

"Perfect," he said. "Thanks."

All she could think was that it wasn't the salad that was perfect. He was, and maybe she was dreaming all this out of fear of spending the entire winter alone up here on the side of a mountain surrounded by nothing but trees and death.

He put his pack on the top of the counter and they sat at a table in front of one window.

They ate and talked some, both clearly being careful. She just staring at his strong hands and then up into his green eyes.

Finally she said, "Do I know you from somewhere?"

"It does feel like we have met before," he said, nodding.

And then he smiled and she just laughed.

"I'll remember where," she said.

"I hope so," he said, staring down into his salad.

Chapter Twenty-seven

FISHER COULDN'T BELIEVE IT when Callie came running out of the front of the lodge when he shouted. At first he didn't think she was going to answer him.

But then when she came out of the lodge without a gun, he both breathed a sign of relief and was stunned at her beauty once again. Her short brown hair and dark eyes just seemed to draw him in and he had a rough time keeping his voice level.

She was dressed in jeans, tennis shoes, and a heavy blue work shirt that almost looked like it had been a man's shirt with the sleeves rolled up. Last time he had seen her she had been in sweat pants and a sweatshirt and socks. She looked good like this and in the sweats. He had a hunch she would look wonderful wearing anything.

And now, standing in the middle of a road on a different planet, he remembered completely why he was risking so much to try to rescue her.

He was drawn to her more than he had ever been drawn to another person in his life.

He gave her his cover story about being over on the coast, but thinking this might be a good place to find survivors. He felt odd having to lie to her, but at this point he had no choice.

Finally she had invited him in for some lunch and had served him a salad.

Over lunch he managed to get her talking about how she survived in the cave. She had told him the story before, so he was careful to not say anything to get ahead of her.

"You want to see the entire place?" she said after lunch and he had offered to wash the dishes, which she let him do while he asked her questions about her job.

He just liked listening to her talk and it seemed she was very happy for company.

"I'd love to," he said. "How's the water situation?"

"Big tank up under the eaves," she said, smiling like she was happy she had the answer. "Pump from a well on this level with a small generator on it keeps the tank full."

She pointed back behind the kitchen to where the pump room must be.

"So that's good," he said. "How about food supplies?"

"More than enough for the winter," she said.

She led him back upstairs. "I haven't found any reserves of oil or paraffin for the lamps yet, but all of them are full."

She pointed to the lamps she had placed around the lodge and on the front desk.

"Lots of wood?" he asked.

"Again more than enough to make it through the winter."

He nodded.

She stood, staring at him for a long moment. "Where did you teach? You look so familiar?"

"Eugene," he said, sticking with his cover story. "Math department." She nodded, then indicated he should take a seat on one of the couches. "I got some questions I need to ask you."

"Sure," he said, dropping his pack on the couch and sitting beside it. There were two big couches there, all with blankets over the back, and four large, overstuffed chairs. All were grouped around the big stone fireplace and a large wooden coffee table clearly made out of cut pine.

As he sat down, Fisher could feel something had shifted and darned if he knew what or why or what had gone wrong.

She moved around the counter, then quickly pulled out a rifle from behind the counter and aimed it at him.

His stomach twisted into a knot. Somehow he had screwed up and screwed up big time.

"Okay," she said, staying behind the front desk and keeping the weapon leveled at him. "Now for some truth from you before my friends get back."

"Didn't buy my cover story, huh?" he asked, shaking his head and smiling. His best bet was to just remain calm. He doubted she would shoot him, but anything was possible. She was a very strong woman and he had no doubt she would do what she had to do to survive. Including killing him.

"Not in the slightest," she said. "Or at least not for very long. And I know everyone in the Oregon math department. So how about some truth and where do I know you from?"

"Truth?" he asked, deciding to take a chance. "Like you have no friends coming back?"

"Truth," she said, nodding, the rifle in her hands waving.

"You are not going to believe me."

"Try me," she said.

"We met just a day or so ago," he said, doing his best to keep his voice calm. "You were wearing sweat pants and a green sweatshirt and socks. It was the first night when you came out of the caves and had finished clearing the bodies away from inside the lodge."

"I…" she started to say something, but he stopped her. He could tell his statement shocked her, and it hadn't been the best way to start into the truth. But he had to keep going now.

"I know you don't remember that. None of the survivors do. But you were wearing those clothes that night, correct, as you slept?"

She just stared at him.

"I said you wouldn't believe me."

"All right," she said after a moment. "Start at the beginning. What happened to cause all the deaths?"

He sighed. He hated to think about all the death that covered this planet right now. "A star about twenty light years from here exploded, sending out an intense electromagnetic pulse that hit this planet directly and short-circuited human and some animal brains, killing everyone who was out in the open instantly. Only those underground, in ships, bank vaults and places like that survived. There were just under two million survivors of the first pulse."

"First pulse?" she asked, looking very puzzled, but seeming to follow.

"There was a second pulse," he said, glad she was staying with him through

133

this, "so other human planets mounted a rescue operation and got all two million survivors of the first pulse out of the way on ships until after the second pulse went past."

She started to interrupt him, but he kept talking. "Then they erased everyone's memory of the event and put every person back where they were a few hours before. Asleep. You and I spent a number of hours together talking during that rescue operation."

She opened her mouth, then closed it.

"I knew you wouldn't believe me, so I brought pictures, if I may?"

He pointed to the pack, hoping she would let him get out the pictures and not just decide to start shooting.

She nodded and he took out the two pictures and then carefully stood with his hands in the air and put them on the end of the counter away from her, then went back to the couch.

She stared at them, shaking her head.

He had no idea how she would feel about those pictures, but he knew without a doubt they were his best shot at convincing her.

Finally, after what seemed an eternity, she looked up at him with those wonderful brown eyes.

"Who exactly are you?"

At least she wasn't chasing him down the road yet with the weapon.

"My name is Vardis Fisher, but everyone calls me Fisher. I am a mathematician and inventor."

"And where are you from?" she asked. "And is this your natural form?"

He laughed, because he had wondered the same thing when he first met Benson.

"I am from a planet about sixty light years from here. And yes, this is my natural form. My friend and I were exploring

when we stumbled onto this rescue operation. We offered to help, but we didn't do much. Except that I talked to you. And I caught you when you turned around too fast and fainted from not eating. And I got you some food."

She again looked blank, but he could tell his truth was getting through a little.

So he went on. "The people up there who are in charge of the big ship I am visiting tell me there are no alien life forms above low-level animal life anywhere in the galaxy. Humans with the same exact genetic make-up as you and I have settled the entire galaxy."

She looked at him for a moment, shaking her head, then back at the pictures, the rifle on the counter in front of her seemingly forgotten, even though it was still mostly aimed at him.

"What reason would you tell me this story?" she finally asked.

"Because you asked for the truth," he said. "Remember?"

"So, if you are telling me the truth, why are you here?"

"Because," he said, "when we were talking, we got along very well. And you said you wanted to stay on board the ship instead of coming back here. I went to get permission from those in charge of the big rescue ship to have you stay, but you were transported back and your memory erased before I could."

"So why don't you just transport me back up to the ship?" she asked, again the gun in her hands.

"Can't," he said. "Anyone coming on board must want to come on board. So I'm here to try to convince you to at least come and take a look. No strings attached."

"And you would erase my memory again when you sent me back here?"

"Nope," he said, shaking his head. "You would be free to stay on the ship or come and go as you wanted."

"And what's in this for you?" she asked.

"Honest answer?" he asked. He was deathly afraid she would get to this question and he wasn't sure how he would answer it.

"After all this, I can't imagine you saying anything that might shock me more."

He took a deep breath and decided on just flat continuing to tell her the truth.

"I was very attracted to you, but we only had a few hours to talk. I would like to have longer to get to know you. And with your brain, I think you would do your planet a better service from space than trapped here in this lodge."

With that she opened her mouth, then just closed it again.

"Second, I have a problem I'm sort of just starting to study about humans settling the entire galaxy. I could use someone with your knowledge and skills to help me figure it out. So that's two reasons. One personal, one professional. But honestly, the personal reason is my number one reason."

He held her gaze and she held his.

Finally she slid the gun a few feet away from her down the counter and he let himself take a slight breath of relief. He had never had a gun pointed at him in his entire life and he didn't much like it at all.

"Can you jump back to this mythological ship at any point, or do you need to wait for a shuttle or something?"

"I can go and come as I want," he said, again holding her gaze.

"Then go back to your ship and give me time to think about all this. Come back tomorrow."

He wanted to jump up and down for joy, but he maintained his composure.

"Can I bring you breakfast and meet you in the kitchen in the morning?" he asked, hoping that she would say yes. It would be more than he could have hoped.

"Why not? Eight a.m."

Again he almost jumped to his feet and shouted "Yes!" But he refrained.

"White or wheat toast?"

She laughed, shaking her head. "White."

"Orange juice?"

"Sure, why not?"

"See you downstairs in the kitchen at eight your time."

With that Fisher touched his return point in his arm twice and the lodge and Callie vanished and the next moment he found himself standing on a platform in the transport center.

Raina ran over to meet him.

"How'd it go?"

"She saw right through my cover story in a flash," he said.

She laughed. "Smart woman."

Then Fisher smiled at Raina, his grin almost hurting his face. "But I'm taking her breakfast tomorrow morning."

Chapter Twenty-eight

CALLIE STARED AT THE SPOT on the couch where the handsome and very weird stranger named Fisher had been. He had simply vanished, leaving the pictures and his pack behind.

"Holy crap, Callie," she said out loud, her voice echoing through the lodge. "You're going crazy."

She didn't let herself look again at the two pictures of herself sitting on some sort of spaceship and went around to the couch to look through his pack. There was nothing in there that would confirm that he was either a nut case or a space alien. Just clothes. Two changes of clothes, actually.

And nothing that would tell her that he had the slightest worry about survival. He was clearly someone who had only expected to stay for a day or so, not survive an entire winter.

"Think!" she said. "Think! This can't be real."

She left the pack on the couch and headed out the front door.

The afternoon had turned warm and the sun hadn't yet dropped behind the ridgeline. The warm smell of pine was something she loved as a child and it comforted her now.

She turned and headed up the road toward the parking lot, her footsteps echoing in the silence of the mountains. About halfway to the parking lot the smell of death stopped her cold. She didn't want to see the two bodies in the parking lot and what the heat and animals would be doing to them.

That was real.

The death here that had happened suddenly was very, very real. Not a one of those bodies she had moved the first day out of the lodge had a mark on them.

Something like an electromagnetic pulse had killed them, of that she had no doubt. So his story fit on that one detail.

And somehow he had pictures of her in that dead girl's sweatpants and sweatshirt sitting in a lounge with an image of the planet behind her.

How could he do that?

And why? And how could he be so damn good looking?

She was going crazy.

She turned around, walking fast down the road, away from the lodge and the death.

Finally, a quarter mile down the road she saw a small sports car in the ditch to the inside of the road. A couple was in it, dead, slumped over, their seat belts holding them upward. They looked young. Not as young as the couple she had taken from the bed.

But young.

They had clearly died instantly and their car had just run off the road.

She remembered the call from Jim, how he was sobbing that his wife and kid were dead in Eugene.

She sat down in the middle of the road and just stared at the car and the two bodies inside.

This was very real.

All of it.

The death, the smell, the fact that she was alone.

She hated being out of control and yet now she felt completely out of control.

Her world had ended.

The world she trusted, had depended on, had worked inside.

It was all dead around her.

And now some total stranger claiming to be from space had offered her a way out.

But how could she believe him?

How could she trust him?

She couldn't.

She knew that. She hadn't been good at trusting anyone back when the world was normal. She sure couldn't do it now.

But he had said he was there, sitting in the lodge, talking to her, trying to convince her to go with him.

He said he was attracted to her.

He said he also needed her help professionally on a project.

136

And he had simply transported away, so clearly he had the technology to transport her as well if he wanted.

But he said she had the choice.

What choice?

She stared at the two bodies in the car. Except for survival, at this point she wasn't sure she had any choice.

But she was going to need more information before she would agree to be spirited away by anyone.

Especially some alien.

Even if he was the most handsome man she could remember seeing.

And unlike the two bodies in the car in front of her, he seemed to be very much alive.

Chapter Twenty-nine

FISHER KNEW THAT the next eighteen hours were going to be eighteen of the longest hours he had ever spent. He hated waiting. So he went to find Doc in engineering.

Both Doc and Kalinda came rushing over to ask how it went and why he was back so quickly. So he told them, then he listened to what they were working on.

From what Fisher could tell, Doc had an idea of putting one trans-tunnel inside another to speed up all flight, and he had everyone buzzing with the idea.

"If this works, *The Lady* will be the fastest ship in this sector," Doc had said at one point.

"Can you get it to stop coming out of a trans-tunnel flight?" Fisher asked, remembering their scary entrance into this system.

"That's easy," Doc said, shaking my head. "Amazed I didn't see how to do that myself."

Kalinda smiled her full-face smile at Doc. "You would have."

Fisher had no doubt that those two were a couple for some time to come. Doc might not know it yet, but Kalinda knew what she was doing and would make it happen. And that made Fisher happy for his friend.

So after killing a half hour with them, he decided to visit Jenny in the Seeder department and let Doc and Kalinda get back to their work.

Jenny managed to get him a number of papers on theories as to why no evidence of the Seeders had ever been found.

And Fisher took two of the top authorities on the theories of how the plants and animals were seeded, as well as how historical evidence was also planted to let cultures think they had been there a very long time. He figured Callie would really be interested in that, once she got over the entire idea of Seeders. And spaceflight. And humans on every planet.

She had a way to go to get through an entire forest of shocking facts. Fisher just hoped he could help her some. And not drive her away by simply telling her some of the stuff.

By the time he got back to *The Lady,* he had used two hours of the eighteen hours.

Somehow he had to keep himself distracted to keep going through the rest of the day and eventually get some sleep before going back to the surface.

So with one of the papers on Seeder evidence playing in his ear, he went to the gym on *The Lady* and worked out for almost two solid hours.

Then after a shower, he cooked Doc and Kalinda and himself a dinner of fresh fish and a special potato dish he had gotten two planets back. They had a wonderful dinner conversation about trans-tunnel flight and how it might be possible to take the speed of a ship up a thousand times by opening tunnels inside of tunnels.

Fisher tried to focus on the conversation and not think about how he wished Callie was sitting there with them. If he was lucky, that would happen at some point.

He wasn't sure when. But he was willing to go slow to make it happen.

Chapter Thirty

CALLIE SPENT the rest of the afternoon sitting in the café, at the counter, just staring at the pictures Fisher had left with her.

She had found a magnifying glass behind the main desk in a drawer and studied them up close. They didn't seem to have been altered in any way.

And the pictures seemed to be on some sort of paper she had never felt before. Under magnification, it didn't really have a grain.

Then, as the ravine outside the window got dark, she went up and turned on lights in the main area, put Fisher's pack with the pictures behind the main counter, so she wouldn't have to look at them, then started the fire in the big fireplace.

She changed into the same sweats she had on in the picture and then made herself a light dinner. After that she just curled up on the couch, a blanket wrapped around her.

She had no idea how long she sat there thinking about her friends at the university, and about her parents who had died three years ago.

But it seemed that every other thought was about Fisher. And how he looked.

And his smile.

And how much she wanted to get to know him, just as he said he wanted to get to know her.

Slowly, she felt like the memory of the night was coming back, but she honestly wasn't sure if they were real memories or just her making something up from the pictures.

It might have been hours, but she ended up dozing.

Some whistling from the basement café area woke her up. The sun was up, but barely and the fire in the fireplace was nothing but embers.

She looked at her watch. It was 7:30 in the morning.

She scrambled for her room down the hall, took a quick shower, and put on clean jeans and one of her own blouses. The building was chilled, but she didn't care. From the looks of it, the day was going to turn warm.

She made it to the basement just at eight.

It smelled wonderful, as if someone had been cooking for hours.

The big wood table they had sat at yesterday now had napkins and silverware on it. There were two large glasses of orange juice at the table, something that the lodge did not have. He had brought the juice from somewhere.

A moment later Fisher came out of the back room carrying two plates of food.

"Good morning," he said, his smile almost melting her. Oh, my god, how could one man be so damned good-looking?

"Morning," she said, so stunned that all she could do beyond that was nod back at him.

"Grab a seat."

He sat two identical plates on the table, then he headed back to the kitchen. "Just have to get the toast."

She watched him go, then turned back to the table.

Ham, eggs, hash browns, orange juice.

She just shook her head as she took the same seat as the day before and he came back out of the kitchen smiling. "Pretty nice kitchen in there," he said as he slid the toast onto the table. "Not as good as my kitchen on *The Lady*, but pretty close."

"*The Lady*?" she asked.

"The ship my friend and I built on our home world about two years ago."

"Not one of the rescue ships?" she asked, almost afraid to touch her silverware, even though her stomach was rumbling and the food smelled wonderful.

"Oh, heavens, no," he said, laughing. "We thought our ship was big when Doc and I built it, but right now *The Lady* looks like a tiny flea in one of the big ship's landing decks. The big ship is called *The R-12* because they built it too fast to name it yet. It has about two thousand men, women, and children living on it."

Callie couldn't imagine a ship that size.

Fisher went on. "It held almost twenty thousand more, including you, in the rescue."

"Where is it from?"

"From what I have been told, a very distant section of this galaxy."

"Wow," she said, not really understanding or even imagining what he was trying to tell her in what seemed to be normal conversation.

"Yeah," Fisher said, nodding. "I honestly have no idea how really big that ship is."

"So how did you get on it?" she asked, clearly not believing she was having this conversation.

He indicated that she should eat, then he dug into his eggs before answering her.

"They saved us just as they saved you and all the survivors on this planet."

She shook her head and nibbled at a piece of wonderful toast, made from fresh bread, something she had convinced herself she would not see in any near future.

He was eating, clearly hungry. And he seemed to be in a wonderful mood.

"You said there were almost two million survivors on this planet. How could one ship save them all?"

Again he laughed softly. "There were almost one hundred of the huge ships in orbit, built just for the rescue by over fifty different human planets' cultures. *The R-12* just had over twenty thousand of the people from here."

"And not your planet?" she asked, tasting the wonderful eggs. He had a slight pepper taste on them which made them perfect.

"My planet doesn't even know Doc and I are gone. My planet is about at the same place as your planet was before this tragedy, maybe ten or twenty years behind. All the planets we visited in this area are at the same level in development, or behind where your planet was before this tragedy."

She started to ask him something and he held up his hand with his fork in it for her to stop. Then he smiled that wonderful smile. "Trust me, don't ask. Doc and I flew around out there for two years and visited almost two hundred human worlds. And I don't believe the answer to what you were about to ask. But it's part of the project I could really use your help on if you decide to take a look."

"So what is your friend doing while you are down here slumming?"

He waved an arm around the place. "Far from slumming and great company."

She smiled and kept eating, enjoying every bite. And enjoying company more than she wanted to admit, even with the strange conversations.

"Doc is working with the engineers of the big ship, more specifically a young head engineer named Kalinda. He's learning how to make our ship even faster and I have a hunch he's going to be helping them out as well."

"He's that good?"

"Better," Fisher said.

"And why aren't you there working with him?" she asked.

"Trans-tunnel drives and warp-space calculations are past me for the most part. I tend to like working to find things that are clear, but not seen in both mathematics and the real world."

"I like to do that as well, only without the mathematics," she said, smiling.

"I know," he said. "You told me that during the first night, which is another reason I think you could help me on my little quest."

"But first I have to agree to transport with you to the ship."

"Not really," he said. "You can stay right here if you want. I can bring down supplies and some very powerful computers and everything we would need to see if we can find some answers. If you wouldn't mind some company at times, that is. This place is really special and very comfortable."

"It won't be when the power goes off shortly," she said, trying to comprehend what he had said about not really needing her to go back with him if she didn't want.

He laughed. "My specialty is seeing things between other things. Between light and dark matter there is unlimited energy. The big ship uses it, I invented it for my planet, but no one took me seriously. So we built what we thought was a big spaceship and left. No one noticed."

He reached into his pocket and pulled out a small device that looked to be no bigger than an apple, with two square sides on it and terminals.

He set it on the table between them. "When the power goes off, we hook this up to the power grid for the lodge and we'll have unlimited power for as long as needed."

She stared at the small device for a moment, then said, "Why are you making this offer?"

"I'll give you full honesty," he said.

"Please."

He nodded. "Same two reasons I said yesterday. I am really attracted to you and would like a chance to get to know you better."

"Flattering," she said, and it was. Her heart was beating faster than she could remember. She was scared to death of this stranger, yet wanted to get to know him as well.

She had never been the type to go for dangerous types. And no warning signal about him was going off for her. Even though he was telling very strange and unbelievable stories, he didn't seem dangerous in the slightest.

"Second," he said, "I could really use your help on something I feel is wrong with what I have seen on that big ship and during the two years that Fisher and I flew around before coming here."

"Wrong how?" she asked, suddenly even more worried.

"Wrong with the history they are telling me and that they all believe. Since I am an outsider and you are an outsider, I think we can see things that they are not seeing, even though they are hundreds and hundreds of years more advanced than we are."

"And you wouldn't mind staying down here and working?"

"Not in the slightest," he said, smiling. "In fact, the more I'm here, the more I like this place and after seeing it yesterday, was going to suggest that even if you came back to the ship with me, we work here."

"Seriously?" she asked.

"Seriously," he said, smiling at her with that wonderful smile of his. "It will keep us from being influenced by the 'truths' they have built up in their belief systems."

"Then let's work here," she said, smiling at him. "But on a couple of conditions."

"Name them," he said, smiling as well.

"You and your people help me move the bodies that are within a half mile of this building to someplace safe and respectful to them."

He nodded, now serious. "I don't really have any people to speak of, but I think the people on the ship can do that. I would have to check."

"Good," she said. "Secondly, you show me the big ship and your ship."

At that his smile looked like it was going to break out of his face.

"When?" he asked.

"How about now, before I chicken out?"

He laughed. "I remember saying that exact same thing before I transported down here yesterday."

He reached for her arm.

His touch was gentle and sent shivers up her spine.

"Two to transport."

And the old diner around her vanished.

Part Three

Chapter Thirty-One

CALLIE FOUND HERSELF standing next to Fisher on a wide platform in a large room. The place was the size of two large gymnasiums and had a large number of the platforms around the outside of the space. The fact that she was standing there like that scared her more than she wanted to admit.

The big room had a clean, antiseptic smell and was colored in tans and whites, with a soft surface of some sort on the floor. It was in a very, very stark contrast to the old wooden lodge they had just been sitting in.

A short-haired woman wearing sandals and jeans came running over to the platform from a door into another room. The smile on her face seemed to be almost infectious.

"You must be Doctor Callie Sheridan," she said, extending her hand to Callie. "I'm Raina, the transport advisor who's been helping Fisher. Welcome to *The R-12*."

"Nice to meet you as well," Callie said, shaking the woman's firm hand and then stepping down from the platform with Fisher.

Callie couldn't believe she could even talk, but her politeness gene must have kicked in overcoming the sheer terror she was feeling.

"Let me call The Chairman," Raina said, turning to a podium that had come up out of the floor facing the platform. "So he can get you special crew status and into the system."

Her fingers moved over the slick board, then Raina looked at Callie again. "Fisher can show you as much of the ship as you like, but if you ever need anything, or need to go to the planet again, just come to me."

Before Callie could say anything, Fisher asked, "Is there any way that we can get special permission to just transport to the lodge below and back, kind of like my return button under my arm, without coming in here?"

"Planning on staying there?" Raina asked, that infectious smile of hers making Callie relax just a little.

Fisher smiled. "It's beautiful in the lodge, an amazing place. A good place for us to both work."

Raina nodded. "I think we can work that out, but I'll have to get permission."

"Permission granted," a man said as he appeared out of thin air beside Raina.

Callie knew it was going to take some time for her to get used to people doing that. If Fisher hadn't gently held her elbow, she would have stumbled back right there.

The man who had just appeared looked directly at Raina. "And permission for them to take to the surface the instruments they need for their work as well."

"Understood," Raina said, smiling. "I'll work with them for whatever they need."

The new man who was clearly in charge was about Fisher's height, but a lot older, with silver hair and a wonderful smile. He extended his hand to Callie. "Welcome back to *The R-12*, Doctor Sheridan. Just call me Benson or Chairman. We were all hoping you would come and tour our little ship."

"I hear it's not so little," Callie said, smiling at Benson as she shook his hand. Her stomach was so tight, she felt she needed to just sit down. But everyone was being so nice, she did her best to stay with them, as if this were just a normal event.

"Thank you," Fisher said to Benson.

Benson laughed. "All of us on this ship are going to owe you and your partner a great amount by the time he and Kalinda are finished."

Fisher laughed. "Yeah, set Doc loose and you just never know what's going to happen.

"It's clear why you two are the first ones to explore this area of the galaxy," Benson said. "With your energy device and his grasp of trans-tunnel mechanics, no planet was ever going to hold you."

"Thank you," Fisher said, nodding and from what Callie could see, he seemed slightly embarrassed. She liked that. He didn't take compliments well.

She forced herself to take a deep breath and try to focus on what was going on.

"I have you into the system as a special crew status, Dr. Sheridan," Benson said, looking at her. "And the rest of the crew is getting a notice to answer any questions or help you in any fashion you like."

"Thank you, Mr. Chairman. And it's just Callie."

"Welcome aboard, Callie," he said. "I hope we can get a chance to talk at some point in the future."

With that he just vanished and Fisher again had to hold her elbow slightly to keep her from stepping back. She was never, ever going to get used to people just vanishing like that.

Raina was smiling as she went back to the board on the podium. "Go take the tour and I'll have your special transport buttons ready in about an hour."

"Thank you," Callie said, not knowing what to feel or say.

"I'm just glad that we could find you," Raina said, "and that you were courageous enough to come look around."

"As am I," Fisher said, smiling at Callie.

"Now, go take a tour," Raina said, turning back to her board. "I got work to do."

Fisher led them out the door and through an office with about twenty people working. Some of the closer ones looked up and said, "Welcome aboard."

And they were all smiling and actually seemed happy to have her on board. They all looked like just normal office workers, but unless Fisher was pulling a very large scam on her, this office was in orbit over her planet.

And every one of these people were aliens.

Fisher led her through to what looked like a reception area and to a wall panel. There he explained the simple commands on the panel, showing her how to find her location on the big ship.

"Now this is the fun part," Fisher said, smiling. "How about we go meet Doc and Kalinda in Engineering?"

Callie nodded, doing her best to just pay attention. She could feel she was beyond overwhelmed at this point.

"Ask for the location for engineering," Fisher said.

She turned to the board and asked and the map showed her the area.

"Now watch," he said, smiling. "I honestly don't think I can ever get tired of this."

"Two to transport to engineering."

Callie felt nothing, but an instant later they were standing in what looked like a

waiting area against one wall of a huge engineering lab area.

Parts of it seemed to go off into the distance with people in white coats, mostly bent over consoles. The ceiling was high and even with dozens of people talking, the sound seemed to be dampened by something.

It looked so normal, so human to Callie, she was having a very difficult time realizing she was on a big ship from another planet.

"Doc's the tall skinny one in the middle of that group," Fisher said.

Callie took Fisher's arm. "He looks busy and I'm a little overwhelmed to be honest. How about you show me your ship after you show me the room where I was that night."

He turned to face her, suddenly worried. "I'm sorry, I know how I felt the first time I came into this ship and Doc and I had already been in space for years."

Without letting her say a word he tapped the board. "Two to transport to L-266."

Callie found herself standing next to Fisher in a large hall that looked like it could hold hundreds. Chairs and tables and cots were stacked against one inner wall.

The other wall was a floor-to-ceiling window looking out over Earth.

The scene of the planet below was stunningly beautiful with all the blues and whites and browns. Her area of the West Coast was in solid sunlight and she could almost pick out Portland and other West Coast cities.

Fisher had gone to the wall and gotten them both chairs, then he motioned that she should follow him over toward the window. At one spot he put the two chairs down facing one another.

"There were between over two hundred or so survivors in this room," he said as she sat down. "They had food against

the wall on tables and medical staff back in those rooms. People were sitting and laying down everywhere. And it smelled like death."

She nodded, looking around at the room. She knew that smell too well already.

"You transported in right here in the sweats and sweatshirt," Fisher said. "When you spun around to look at the window, you fainted. The medical person said it was from not eating and shock."

"Not eating," she said, not wanting to believe that she could faint from shock. But she was feeling pretty light-headed right now, she had to admit. And she had just had a great breakfast.

Down there.

On the planet's surface.

"I happened to be nearby," Fisher said, "and I caught you and got you checked and some food."

"And we talked?" she asked, trying to remember. Everything around her had that familiar feeling, but she just couldn't put a memory to the feeling.

"We did, for about two hours," Fisher said. "Then you said you wished you could just stay here and when I went to check, the ship came back into orbit and you were transported, erasing your memory of the hours on board."

"I'm glad you came to get me," she said, reaching over and squeezing his hand. It felt wonderful and she could see in his face that he liked her touch as well.

She had no doubt that this was a very gentle man with very little experience with women. And that made him even more attractive than he already was, if that was possible.

"I'm glad you agreed to come see this place," he said.

"And now that I'm here, you still want to work in the lodge?" she asked.

"Very much," he said. "I'll explain why when we are back in the lodge."

"Fair enough," she said.

She stood and walked over closer to the big window, staring down at her planet below. The ship's orbit was taking it over parts of Europe now and she could see large areas of blackness where lights used to shine.

Earth was slowly shutting down. And there was no telling how many centuries it would take to come back to what it was, if it ever would.

She had been fantastically lucky to meet Fisher.

She turned and looked at the most handsome man she had ever seen, staring into those deep green eyes. She really, really wanted to get to know this man.

And she really, really wanted this all to be real, and that she wouldn't have to spend the winter alone in that lodge, worrying about survival every day.

"Thank you," she said.

He only nodded, clearly not sure what to say.

"Now, let's go see that ship of yours."

He smiled, a twinkle in his eyes. "With pleasure. After seeing this ship, it will be like seeing a townhouse inside a large city."

"But it's your townhouse, right?" she asked, laughing.

"Exactly," he said, grinning at her as they put the chairs back against the wall and headed for the transport panel.

She felt a lot better. Still overwhelmed, of that she had no doubt.

But after seeing the big room and imagining that night, she now was starting to believe Fisher.

And she was falling for him more and more every minute they were together.

Chapter Thirty-two

FISHER COULDN'T BELIEVE he was showing Callie his ship. He felt like a proud parent. He tried to make the tour short, but at the same time he hoped it would last for a very long time.

Finally, after about a half hour of the control room, engine room, storage areas, and his suite, they made it back to the kitchen and dining area.

"Oh, my God," Callie said, standing in the kitchen and looking around. "This is amazing. You designed this?"

"Every detail," he said, about as proud of that statement as he had ever felt about anything he had done. "As I said, I love to cook."

"I guess so," she said, studying the details of the kitchen.

Suddenly he realized something that hadn't occurred to him before. "You are the very first person I've ever had the chance to show this ship to."

She stopped and turned to look at him, her deep brown eyes holding his gaze.

"I'm not kidding," Fisher said. "Back home we built this ship in secret in a warehouse, me and Doc doing all the work. And on all the planets we've visited, we never had guests until now. You are not the first to be in this kitchen because I cooked dinner last night for Doc and Kalinda. But you are the first to get the full tour."

"I am honored," she said, smiling at him and bowing slightly.

"Actually, the pleasure is all mine."

They stood there staring at each other for an awkward moment in the silence before Fisher finally found the nerve to speak.

"Let me fix us some lunch."

"I'd love that," Callie said. "Rest room?"

Fisher pointed down the wide corridor leading off the kitchen and along the spine of the ship. "Bathroom is the second door on the right. Look around the other rooms in there as well and tell me what you think when you get back."

She nodded and he turned to get some bread from the pantry and turkey and fixings from one of the fridges for a simple lunch. If she felt like he had felt his first time on *The R-12*, she wouldn't be able to eat much. But she needed something.

And so did he.

He sat the table and poured them both water and iced tea and had them on the table when she returned.

"That's an amazing suite," Callie said, coming into the kitchen. "Really comfortable."

"It is, isn't it?" Fisher asked, pointing to the table to indicate she should sit down.

She did as he said, "It's your suite if you want it if you need to stay up here."

"Mine?" she asked, frowning.

"I know it can't compete with that incredible old lodge, but when we are working, if you want to stay up here, that suite is yours. Doc and I have never had guests on board, even though we added seven suites similar to that one. We would love to have different company at times."

"Seven of those suites, plus your own suites? Wow, you did build this ship big."

"We thought so until we saw *The R-12*. As Benson said, space and energy are in abundant supply in space."

"And you know how to get the energy," she said, staring at him as he worked on the sandwiches.

"On my planet I invented a source of unlimited energy, yes. But no one paid any attention. They will eventually."

"What's the name of your home planet?" she asked.

Fisher took a deep breath and laughed as he finished the sandwiches and cut them into halves. "Now we're getting into the part you won't believe. And where I'm going to need some help."

"At some point you got to start telling me," she said, laughing as he set the sandwich in front of her. "I am here seeing all this. Not really believing it all, but seeing it."

He sat down, worried about what he was about to say, then just decided to go ahead and start. "It's called Earth."

She looked at him, the sandwich halfway to her mouth.

"Every planet we visited, every society, called their planet Earth, or something in their own language that meant Earth. Benson and everyone on this ship from another sector of the galaxy is also from a planet called Earth."

Her green eyes bore into him and then she just shook her head. "You aren't kidding, are you?"

"I'm not kidding, but I didn't say I was believing any of it either," he said. "But I've seen it. And if you are up for it after lunch, I can show you images of some of the many planets Doc and I visited before we came here."

"I think I might need to see some of that," she said, nodding.

And then she took a bite of her sandwich with delight, something Fisher knew he would never get tired of watching.

Chapter Thirty-three

CALLIE LET FISHER SHOW her about an hour of recorded visits to other human planets. With each recording he showed her on a star map where the world was.

He said that she was sitting in Doc's chair and he was in his in the control room. He used the big screen between the chairs on the main panel to show her.

"We investigated mostly yellow dwarf suns like ours and yours staying in our neighborhood of the galaxy," he said. "In fact, compared to how large the galaxy is, we haven't left the home street yet in the neighborhood."

She thought she had some idea of the size of the galaxy before, but now she was starting to understand just how big it was.

After showing her about ten worlds, all about the same level of human advancement as her world and his, she had him stop. Her brain wasn't allowing anymore in.

"Background first," she said, sitting back in the comfortable command chair and closing her eyes. "How many human cultures did you visit on how many planets?"

"Just over two hundred," Fisher said.

"All were at the same level of advancement?"

"Generally, yes," Fisher said.

"How is that possible?" she asked, opening her eyes and looking at him.

"That's exactly the big question I was hoping you would help me with," Fisher said. "Something doesn't feel right about all this, but the people of the world that built *The R-12* and ran this rescue have been studying this for centuries."

"And you don't like what they have come up with as an answer?" she asked.

"Oh, the basics, I agree with," he said. "And when you are ready to hear it, there's someone on board who can help with those. She helped me. But it's as overwhelming as this."

She nodded. She was feeling completely overwhelmed.

And she wanted to know for certain that she could go back to the planet's surface when she wanted. She was trusting Fisher more and more, but now she needed that final feeling that she wasn't trapped before she could relax a little.

"How about we go meet your friend Doc, then go get our transport devices and head back to the lodge. You can give me the basics there."

"Sounds perfect," Fisher said, smiling.

On the way out, he showed her how to get into *The Lady* if she needed to, which she thought was an amazing amount of trust.

A few moments later they were standing in the engineering section of the big ship again.

This time Doc and a woman were alone, so Fisher led her toward him. As they got close, this very skinny man glanced up and broke into a huge smile that seemed to completely fill his face and almost made his nose vanish.

The woman beside him, also tall and very skinny did the same. And they both came to great her like she was a lost friend.

"Welcome back, Doctor Sheridan," Doc said, smiling and shaking her hand. "Very glad you decided to join this craziness."

"Callie," she said to Doc and Kalinda. "Just call me Callie."

"We heard you were on board," Doc said. "Getting the tour?"

"*The Lady* is really something," Callie said, feeling completely at ease with both of these new people. Fisher clearly had great friends and she liked them both at once.

Doc smiled like he was a kid and she had just given him a big piece of candy.

"It's going to be a lot faster pretty soon," Doc said.

"How much faster?" Fisher asked.

"Well, it would take us now about thirty hours to go the sixty light years to get home."

Fisher nodded and Callie could see that Doc and Kalinda were both bursting with pride at what Doc was about to say next.

"We can cut that to thirty minutes," Doc said, smiling.

Fisher actually seemed rocked back at that news.

"And with what we are working on," Kalinda said, "we might cut that to only seconds."

"Wow," Fisher said. "That is really something."

"We got half the room working on it now," Doc said. "I haven't had this much fun since back when we built and first tested *The Lady*."

Callie didn't know what to think. She was having a hard time just imagining so many things, let along going sixty light years in a matter of seconds.

"Well, keep going," Fisher said. "You two are really amazing."

"Thanks," Doc said. "And great meeting you, Callie. I hope we get a chance to talk at some point."

"Me too," Kalinda said.

Feeling totally stunned, Callie agreed and turned with Fisher back toward the panel on the wall. Fisher walked with her in silence, obviously stunned at what his partner was doing.

A moment later they were back in the transportation department with Raina who planted a button under Callie's skin without so much as even touching her. Callie was really impressed with that.

Then Raina did something to Fisher's control as well.

"I set both buttons for the kitchen on your ship and the front room of the lodge where you left from yesterday, Fisher."

Callie and Fisher both nodded.

Callie was having trouble even understanding that was only yesterday. She had to slow down some and catch her breath and think. Things were moving far, far too fast.

Raina went on. "Two distinct pushes take you to the lodge. One distinct push takes you to your ship's kitchen area. That way you don't have to go through here all the time."

"But we like seeing you," Fisher said, smiling.

Raina laughed. "Thanks. If you want equipment in either location for whatever you are going to work on, you will need to come to me."

"I can't thank you enough," Fisher said.

"Yes, thank you," Callie said. "It's been wonderful meeting you."

Raina gave her a hug and then whispered in her ear. "Take care of him. He's a real catch."

Callie smiled at the woman. "I hope to."

"Good," Raina said. "Now off you go. Test those buttons."

"Lodge?" Fisher asked, looking at Callie.

"Lodge," Callie said.

Then she felt for the button as Fisher vanished.

With one last smile at Raina, she pushed it twice.

And ended up standing beside Fisher in the main room of the lodge, right in front of the big front desk. The fire from last night was just embers in the fireplace and the sun was still lighting up the room.

It felt like she had been gone forever, yet it had only been a few hours.

"Well, that worked," Fisher said.

Callie moved over and dropped on the couch.

"How about I head back to the ship and give you a couple hours alone and then bring us some dinner. You up for dinner? Or do you need more time."

She looked up at the worried expression on his handsome face and smiled. "Dinner sounds wonderful."

He nodded and smiled as well. "Back in three hours."

He touched his arm and vanished.

She pulled a blanket off the back of the couch and covered herself and just lay there staring at the logs of the ceiling over her.

Numb.

None of this could be happening.

She was attracted to an alien from another planet who lived in a spaceship inside an even bigger spaceship full of really nice aliens from more planets.

And most of the people on her world were dead.

All of her old life was dead.

Yet Fisher was offering her a new life, far more exciting than her old one.

And he was so damn handsome.

She closed her eyes.

She just needed to rest and think.

Just for a short time.

Chapter Thirty-four

CALLIE AWOKE AS FISHER was quietly trying to put firewood in the fireplace and get the fire started. She lay there, smiling at him as he worked to stack the wood and start it, clearly not having a clue what he was doing.

It was dark outside the windows and he was trying to start the fire while holding a flashlight in one hand.

He was amazingly good-looking and clearly in shape. He had told her he used the gym on his ship all the time, and she could tell that he did just from how he moved with the grace of someone in shape and control of his body.

And he was also clearly a very considerate and sweet man. That had been obvious from the first moment she had met him. Raina was right, he was a catch.

"Not the outdoors type?" she asked, not moving from her position on her side on the couch.

He glanced back. "I'm sorry," he said. "I didn't mean to wake you. Just wanted to get a fire started and let you sleep. After everything today, you need it."

She sat up and stretched, realizing as she pushed the blanket back just how chilly the lodge had become. No wonder he was working on the fire for her.

"I did need that," she said, stretching and yawning again. "But you promised me dinner, remember?"

He laughed. "I did. It's downstairs."

"If I get the fire started, can we eat it up here?"

"Easily," he said.

"Light switch near the staircase for the overhead lights," she said as she stood.

"I'm going to splash some water on my face and then I'll get the fire going."

"I'll be back up in ten minutes with dinner," he said, smiling at her in the light of his flashlight.

On the way down he flipped on the overhead lights.

"Power's still on?" she asked as she headed for the hallway.

"Nope," he said as he vanished down the stairs.

She just shook her head. The entire lodge was being powered by a cube the size of a saltshaker that he had invented on another planet. How was this perfect man even real?

She had the fire going strong and lights around the lodge turned on when Fisher brought the dinner up the stairs on two plates balanced on a large tray with two glasses of some juice and a bottle of water.

It smelled heavenly, like a wonderful pot roast that had simmered all day in the oven.

She went over and sat down in one of the big overstuffed chairs, pulling it closer to the big wooden coffee table where he set dinner.

He sat in another chair facing her and said, "Hope you like a very tender steak."

She could tell the steak had been sliced thin with a sampling of white sauce along one edge. Fresh asparagus spears were coated in a light cheese sauce and some tiny red potatoes coated in butter filled the rest of the plate.

"Oh, my, this is wonderful," she said. "And it smells heavenly."

"Dig in," he said, grabbing his fork and knife and easily cutting the steak on his plate.

While they ate, they talked about her past and his past, both mentioning their parents. She learned how long he and Doc had been friends and how they had been laughed at for their projects.

She understood that feeling and had seen it a number of times where she taught. Professors could sometimes be so petty that it had stunned her.

She liked the fact that he was willing to tell her about his home and his money and how he and Doc had built *The Lady*.

"What did you expect to find when you left?" she asked.

"Honestly, not much," he said, finishing up the last bite of potato on his plate. "We hoped to find some alien life, maybe plants, on different planets, that sort of thing. We were just out exploring with every intention of going home when we got bored."

"That didn't happen," she said, laughing.

"Actually, it almost did," Fisher said, sitting back in the big chair. "After a couple hundred Earth-like planets with all human civilizations about the same level, it was getting boring."

Now that surprised her. And the idea that all those planets were at the same level bothered her more than she wanted to admit.

"I'm still not seeing how that is possible," she said, shaking her head as she finished the last bit of her steak and pushed the plate away. "And that was a wonderful dinner. Thank you."

He smiled. "You are more than welcome. Not often I get a chance to really cook for someone besides Doc, who tends to eat everything."

"And he stays that skinny?" Callie asked, again feeling stunned.

"Drives me crazy because he doesn't exercise," Fisher said, shaking his head. "I'm in the gym three hours a day on most days because I love it and I like to eat like this. Doc never exercises and yet eats all of my cooking and doesn't gain a pound."

Callie laughed. She was falling for this man even more with every passing minute.

Fisher stood and started gathering up the dishes. "Let me take care of these dishes, get them washing, and we can talk if you like, or call it a night. Up to you."

She didn't want him to leave yet, since her brain seemed to be slowly returning. "Let's talk for a time."

"Would you like some tea or wine?"

"You have wine?" she asked, surprised.

"Red or white, some great choices from about twenty different planets," he said, his smile filling his face.

"A glass of red would be wonderful," she said. "Not too heavy."

"Got a perfect one," he said.

He put her dishes on the tray, leaving behind her half-finished tea and the bottle of water. "Be right back."

Balancing the tray with one arm, he pinched his arm and vanished.

She just sat there staring at the space where he had been standing a moment before. "Callie, what have you gotten yourself into?"

Only the crackling of the fire answered her back.

She stood and headed for her suite to change into a pair of slippers, turning on the music to a low level to cut the silence.

She sort of had a date for a drink with a man from space.

And she was looking forward to it.

Chapter Thirty-five

FISHER FOUND DOC and Kalinda sitting in the kitchen of *The Lady* when he jumped back to get the wine. They were both eating sandwiches and had data pads on the table between them. Clearly it was a working dinner for them, which didn't surprise Fisher at all. Doc seldom didn't work.

"Dinner with Callie, huh?" Doc asked.

Fisher nodded, putting the dishes to one side of the sink.

"How's she doing with all this?" Kalinda asked.

"Actually adjusting pretty well. I haven't really tried to explain the Seeders to her yet, though. Not sure if I completely understand them myself."

"Yeah, good luck with that," Kalinda said, shaking her head. "I grew up with this knowledge, I can only faintly imagine what it must feel like to just be learning all this."

"It's weird," Doc said, smiling at Kalinda.

"Very," Fisher said. "I'm going to head back down. If you need me, Raina in transportation knows exactly where I am."

"Have fun," Doc said.

Kalinda just smiled as Fisher turned and headed back into the pantry to get the wine and a couple of glasses. A moment later he was standing back in the big main room of the lodge.

The fire was going strong, there was faint music in the background, and Callie was seated in one chair facing the fire.

"Thanks for the great dinner," she said as he opened the wine and poured it, then took another one of the overstuffed chairs facing the fire and half turned to face her as well.

"My complete pleasure," he said.

They spent the next thirty minutes just talking more about their families and how her parents had been killed in a plane accident. Then she finally turned the big chair to face him more.

"Okay, you've been avoiding telling me about what you want me to help you with. Time to get to that."

He nodded and sat his glass of wine down on the coffee table.

"Now please realize that I've only been seeing this for myself for a few years now, and only had a nice person named Jenny on the ship try to explain it to me just yesterday."

"So we both have fresh eyes on this." Callie said.

"Exactly," Fisher said. Then he took a deep breath and started into this explanation that might lose him Callie. But at this point, he had no choice at all.

He explained how he felt while he and Doc were seeing all the civilizations at the same level. Then he told her Jenny's explanation of how a race they called "The Seeders" seeded all the human planets in the galaxy and then left.

"Aren't there something like one hundred billion stars in this galaxy?" Callie asked, shaking her head.

"Closer to two hundred billion," Fisher said. "A large part of those are outside of what our astronomers called 'the habitable zone' for human life, meaning they are too close in toward the center of the galaxy. And the vast majority of stars in this galaxy are red dwarfs, not yellow dwarfs as our sun. And a few of the yellow dwarfs Doc and I found didn't have planets in what our astronomers called

'The Goldilocks Zone' meaning inside an area where it wasn't too hot or too cold for life."

Callie just nodded. "That still would leave a lot of stars and human planets."

Fisher nodded. "More than I want to think about. Hundreds and hundreds of millions at least."

Then he went on to tell her what Jenny had told him about how the Seeders had wiped all older life from the planet with a big asteroid impact, then basically planted all animal and human life over a period of a few thousand years in numbers of visits to each planet.

Callie just shook her head. "Too much."

Fisher just nodded. "Do I understand that feeling. How about tomorrow you and I go talk with Jenny and then I can tell you what is really bothering me."

"Besides the fact that this changes every belief I've ever had and it is impossible to boot."

"Yeah, besides that," Fisher said, smiling.

Chapter Thirty-six

CALLIE SAT, sipping the wonderful glass of red wine and letting herself relax. They had changed the conversation away from all the strange stuff and had it back on more normal stuff.

Fisher had asked her about her two days in the cave and exactly what she had been looking for and then seemed actually interested as she explained. His green eyes kept looking at her.

She was so attracted to him, it almost felt unnatural. She had never really felt like this for any other person before and she wasn't sure if it was because of the situation or simply because he seemed to be the perfect person for her.

After talking about her cave dig, they talked about exercising and he told her about his former weight problem. The fact that he had dropped it all and kept it all off impressed her even more.

She desperately wanted to ask if he had had girlfriends in the past, but didn't.

And he didn't ask her about any of her short relationships either, which she was thankful for.

Finally, after almost two hours of talking and after the entire bottle of wine was gone, he said, "I suppose I had better get back and let you get some sleep."

"Stay," she said.

She was surprised that word had come out of her mouth, and he looked surprised as well.

"There is a suite across from my suite down the hall here," she said. "You offered me a suite in your ship, it's the least I can offer in return."

He smiled.

She went on before he could politely decline. "Besides, to be honest, it would feel good to have someone else in the building."

"Now that I understand," he said, smiling. "I would love to stay. And breakfast on *The Lady* in the morning?"

"Wonderful," she said, feeling excited at the idea that he would be close by.

She led him down the hall and into the suite across from hers. The bed there was freshly made up, ready for guests that would now never come.

It had a small sitting room to one side and a large bathroom with tile floors like hers. Plus a huge bed in the bedroom with four wooden posts carved out of pine trees.

He went over to the bed and pushed on it, then smiled at her and sat on it. "A real featherbed?"

"Seems they are in every room in the place," she said, smiling.

She really, really wanted to go over and sit on the bed beside him and kiss him, but she didn't.

"So you'll be all right here?" she asked.

"It's wonderful," he said, smiling at her. "Thanks."

She then said goodnight and as she started to pull the door closed he said, "It's all right to leave it open."

So she did, going back to her suite.

She once again got into the sweat pants and sweatshirt she now wore to bed, then crawled in and shut off the light. She could hear him moving around a little, then silence.

She lay there, staring up into the darkness. Out the window, she could see some stars up through the pine trees. They seemed bright and welcoming now, for some reason.

What in the world was she doing? The man of her dreams was across the hallway. He had flat told her he was attracted to her. And he was so damned shy and respectful of her feelings, any move for them to be together would be up to her.

"Callie," she said softly to the darkness, "this is stupid."

She pushed back the heavy quilt and sheet, found her slippers, and headed out into the hallway.

His door was open but the light was off. The only light was one they had left on in the big room, plus the last light flickering from the fireplace.

She had only known this man, this alien, for a few days. Yet this felt right.

That might be the half bottle of wine talking, but she didn't care.

She eased open his door and whispered, "Fisher?"

"Yes," he said from the bed.

Before she lost her nerve, she walked to the bed and slid in beside him.

"Just hold me if you wouldn't mind."

"I will never mind," he said softly.

She turned her back to him and he wrapped his arms around her and she snuggled back against him. Except for a pair of underwear, he was naked.

"This is wonderful," she said as his strong arms held her. "Thank you."

He kissed her softly on the neck. "Thank you. Now rest."

She tried.

She really tried.

But those firm arms, that fantastic body pressed against her just were impossible to resist.

Finally, she rolled over and kissed him.

And he kissed back.

She got lost in his kiss. Like no other she had ever felt. Gentle, yet insistent.

She could feel his arousal as he kissed her and she stroked his naked shoulders.

Under the big quilt and sheet it was getting warm. Too damn warm, actually, to be wearing as many clothes as she was wearing.

Finally she pulled away from one more fantastic and long kiss, panting.

Then she pushed the covers back, stood, and turned on the lamp next to the bed. She took off the sweatshirt and sweatpants as Fisher watched, his eyes wide and his smile big.

"You are fantastically beautiful," he said, his voice slightly raspy.

"Get rid of those pants," she said.

And he did.

Then she crawled back in bed with him, kissing him and letting him feel her body against his and guiding his hands to places they needed to go.

She hadn't been with very many men before, but it had never, ever come close to how wonderful making love to Fisher was.

She belonged with him. She knew it and she felt it.

Almost two hours later they finally dozed off in each other's arms, only the sheet pulled up over them.

And even with everything that had happened, she felt safer than she had ever felt in her life.

Chapter Thirty-seven

CALLIE AWOKE as Fisher was working to ease himself away from her. The morning light was just starting to brighten up the trees outside the window and she felt wonderful, better than she could ever remember feeling waking up. She normally wasn't a morning person.

As Fisher moved, she turned and pulled him in close and kissed him, long and hard.

And he kissed her in return, just as hard and just as passionately.

The man could kiss. The two of them just fit perfectly together. How was that even possible?

"Where did you think you were going, mister?" she asked after letting him come up for air from the kiss.

"Get us some food," he said, smiling at her.

"Not yet," she said, kissing him.

She could feel his body had the same idea as hers.

She climbed on top of him and they made love again, quick and intense and even more incredible than the night before.

Finally, as they both lay there trying to catch their breaths, she raised up on her elbow and looked into his wonderful green eyes. "I hope I wasn't too forward."

He laughed. "One of us needed to be and I was too damn scared to even suggest anything."

"And why am I so scary?" she asked, smiling.

"Because you are the most beautiful woman I have ever met," he said, looking directly into her eyes with those intense green eyes of his. "And the smartest and bravest."

"You know the exact right thing to say to a woman."

"Just the truth," he said. "Just the truth."

She kissed him long and hard once again, then rolled out of bed and picked up her sweat pants and sweatshirt, standing there naked in front of him. "I'm going to take a long, hot shower and get dressed. I'll meet you on *The Lady* for that promised breakfast?"

"Perfect," he said.

With one last look at the naked man stretched out on the bed staring at her, she turned and headed out the door and across the hallway.

Thirty minutes later, she pushed her transport button under her skin and appeared in *The Lady's* kitchen.

Fisher was already there dressed in fresh clothes and with wet hair, working on starting to cook something.

"You are right," she said. "I don't think this transport thing will ever get old."

He laughed, put down what he was working on and came over and kissed

her long and hard. Then he finally pulled away and said, "Sit and I'll cook."

"I feel like I should do something to help," she said, moving over to the table and sitting.

"Eggs, ham, hash browns, toast, and juice," he said, smiling at her and making her want to just jump back up and kiss him again. "Not much to help with. But I could use your feedback on a few things."

"That was really nice last night," she said, staring at his broad shoulders and tight butt in the jeans.

"Nice doesn't begin to describe it for me," he said, smiling. "Thank you for taking the chance."

She laughed. "I doubt I would have gotten much sleep there in my own bed alone with you so close."

"I was feeling the same way when you came in," he said, smiling over his shoulder at her as he worked on starting the hash browns in a small pan.

"So what can I give you feedback on?" she asked.

At that moment, before he had a chance to answer, Doc and Kalinda came in. Both of them looked like they had just gotten out of the shower and Kalinda was wearing the same clothes she had on yesterday.

"Good morning," Fisher said to the new arrivals, indicating that they should sit at the table with Callie.

She smiled at both of them and then winked at Kalinda, who just smiled fondly back at her. Callie knew that feeling. She was feeling it right now herself.

"Sure I can't help now?" Callie asked.

"Nope, just twice as much of a very simple breakfast is all. Thanks."

"So are you starting to believe all this craziness?" Doc asked Callie as he and Kalinda sat at the table holding hands.

"Still in shock about a lot of it," she said. "But another day or so and it will all just feel strange instead of completely impossible."

"How did it go yesterday with the new drive equations?" Fisher asked.

Callie could see both Doc and Kalinda brighten up, as if their minds were returning to their bodies.

"We should have the speed of *The Lady* up so that we could be back in our home system in thirty seconds," Doc said.

Callie watched as Kalinda nodded.

Fisher just shook his head in clear amazement.

"And *The R-12*," Kalinda said, "should be able to cover the six hundred light year journey home in a few days once everything is upgraded and tested."

"How long did it take you to get here?" Callie asked.

"Fourteen months," Kalinda said. "And we barely made it in time."

Callie watched as suddenly Fisher turned around, staring at Kalinda.

Callie stood and went over to him and took the spatula out of his hands and worked the eggs. She could tell he had suddenly gone into his own mind, thinking, and if she didn't take over, the breakfast was going to burn.

He started to object, but instead she pushed him toward the table. "Sit, I got this."

He nodded. Then as he sat down, he said, "Maybe using all four of you as a sounding board would be a good idea."

"Fire away," Doc said. "I'm not going anywhere until that wonderful-smelling breakfast is served."

"Glad to help," Kalinda said.

Callie nodded to Fisher that he should go on as she put the toast down and turned over the hash browns.

He started to say something, then just shook his head. "Never mind, the answer I'm looking for is obvious."

He stood and came to help Callie finish with breakfast. Then when all four of them were sitting at the table and eating, Callie had to keep the conversation going.

"So what's so obvious?"

Fisher looked at her and shrugged. "Everyone wonders how the Seeders could have done what they did and just left, moving on to another galaxy."

"Is that the theory?" Callie asked and Fisher and Kalinda both nodded.

"They left cultures to fend for themselves?" she asked, clearly not understanding what he was saying.

"That's what everyone believes on this ship, right?" Fisher asked Kalinda.

"That's what we were taught in school," she said, working on her ham.

"Not possible," Callie said and Fisher smiled at her. "None of these human cultures could have come up in such exact ways and so close in development and technology without a vast amount of guidance. Especially through the really tough turning points."

"Exactly," Fisher said, smiling. "What's obvious is that the Seeders, at least some of them, never left."

Kalinda just shook her head, now the one having trouble believing the facts in front of her. Callie felt good that it just wasn't her for a change.

"Then where are they?" Kalinda asked.

"Right here," Fisher said, waving at the entire table. "We're Seeders. Or we will be when we get a little more advanced."

Kalinda shook her head. "That theory has been considered and discarded a number of times over the years."

"No hard evidence, right?" Fisher asked.

She nodded.

Callie knew, without a doubt that the hard evidence was the simple fact that so many cultures had grown at the same pace, in exactly the same way.

Fisher looked at Kalinda who had stopped eating. "Think about it. Your culture has pretty much invented everything needed to be a seeder. And you built ships that held over two million humans on short notice."

Again Kalinda nodded, a little more slowly.

Doc was keeping out of the conversation, which Callie thought to be very smart.

"From what I have read of the articles that Jenny gave me," Fisher said, "looking for Seeders seems to have always been an outwardly directed hunt. But Callie and I have specialties that allow us to be able to see things where there isn't supposed to be anything."

Callie was honored that Fisher included her. What she was seeing didn't seem to be hidden.

"So what evidence have we all missed for a thousand years of studying this?" Kalinda asked.

Callie was glad that Fisher just ignored the barbed question and went on calmly while eating. "Assume the Seeders are humans just like us. Any evidence would be human evidence."

"We've thought of that," she said. "I can give you some of the papers discounting those theories. We got them all in basic school."

"Written by Seeders, of course," Fisher said, smiling at her frown.

Then not giving her a chance to go on, he said, "Just look at the cultures. Now I know math, and I wouldn't want to even try to calculate the chance that every culture on every Earth-like planet would become over centuries of war and fighting a democracy and a capitalism-based culture. Or that every planet would devel-

op along the same exact lines and at the same basic speed."

Fisher turned to Callie. "Doctor, in your expertise, could cultures of any animal species, separated by light years of distance, develop at exactly the same pace and way and genetic mutation?"

"Not a chance," Callie said, smiling at Fisher. "Not without a lot of help. Vast amounts of help, actually."

"So every culture we visited was directed and helped?" Doc asked. "That's your theory?"

Fisher laughed. "It's the only thing that explains anything I've seen in the last two years. And what I see on this big ship as well. The Seeders are still here and still helping and you've met them."

Now it was Callie's turn to be shocked.

Both Doc and Kalinda were flat staring at Fisher.

"And just how are you so certain of that?" Kalinda asked, clearly upset. Callie could tell that Fisher was challenging one of her hardest held beliefs.

"Because I've met one as well," Fisher said.

Fisher glanced up at the ceiling and said just slightly louder, "Am I correct, Mr. Chairman?"

At that moment Benson shimmered into view. He pulled over a chair and sat down at the head of the table.

"Smells wonderful," he said.

"You hungry?" Fisher asked, clearly not surprised at all that Benson was sitting there with them.

Callie was shocked, but she managed to somehow just take a deep breath and watch Fisher.

"Nope, already had breakfast," Benson said. "So what gave me away?" He was smiling and ignoring the completely shocked look on Kalinda's face.

Callie watched as Kalinda's mouth was opening and closing and nothing was coming out. Callie knew that feeling well from the last few days.

"A couple of slips," Fisher said. "You knew about me and Doc ahead of time."

Benson laughed. "I had hoped you had missed that. Not sure what I was thinking on that."

"And the look in your eyes when you looked at the planet below. It was a personal failure to you that you couldn't save everyone."

Benson nodded. Callie could see that Benson's eyes filled with sadness. Fisher was right. Benson did take all that death down on her world personally.

"It was my failure. This area of the region is mine to watch and I just couldn't mount a rescue operation fast enough, get the right people on advanced enough planets involved quick enough, get them here fast enough. At least we saved some of those poor souls."

"The speed of the travel to where *The R-12's* home world was another thing that gave you away. How long ahead did you know what was going to happen?" Fisher asked, his voice respectful.

Callie was impressed.

"A good three hundred years," Benson said, his voice soft. "We had to push culture advance on a number of planets faster than we wanted to even save as many as we did."

Then he looked directly at Fisher and shook his head. "I knew from the moment you two started building your ship that you would be problems."

Fisher laughed and Doc looked stunned.

"I think your secret is safe with the four of us," Fisher said.

Everyone at the table nodded.

"But I'm betting the really big problem for you is Doc and Kalinda here, right?" Fisher asked, smiling at his best friend who was really looking puzzled.

Benson nodded. He turned to Doc and Kalinda. "You two are a rare combination and very advanced. This galaxy isn't supposed to develop the kind of speed you two are working on for another two thousand years. It's about then we'll be needing help in the major part of Andromeda."

And Benson turned to Callie and Fisher. "And you two worry me even more. We could really use you both, to be honest."

"So you can use a little help a little earlier?" Fisher asked.

Callie was just flat stunned. Now she completely understood what Fisher was talking about. Benson was a member of the race of humans who started humans on all the different planets, including hers.

And now Fisher was saying that the main force of the Seeders had moved on to a completely different galaxy.

Benson laughed. "Seems like we're going to get it even if we don't need it, huh? But before then, we could use help here in the Milky Way if you four are up for the task. There are a lot of wars going on right now on the developing planets. And there's only so many of us to go around who stayed behind to help here."

"To make sure all the cultures develop to a peaceful way of life," Callie asked, trying to imagine the vastness of that task.

Benson nodded.

"So if the four of us agree to help," Fisher asked, "how long until you teach us that teleportation trick and the long-age secret?"

Callie was now completely lost again.

Benson just shook his head. "You don't miss anything, do you?"

Then he addressed the entire table. "You all agree to become a Seeder and it might be a lot sooner than later."

With that he smiled at Kalinda's open mouth and stood.

He turned to Fisher and extended his hand. "I'll let you explain what just happened," he said. "But do it down in the lodge where no one can overhear you. I've got a war to try to stop about fifty light years from here. We can all talk tomorrow if you want."

With that he vanished.

And the silence in the kitchen of *The Lady* was so thick, Callie figured she could cut it with a knife.

Chapter Thirty-eight

FISHER LOOKED AROUND at the three people sitting over a mostly finished breakfast in the kitchen of *The Lady.* His three friends were shocked, to say the least.

Doc looked at him. "You want to explain to me what just happened?"

Fisher nodded. "I will, just not here."

"Four to transport," Fisher said, and pushed his button under his skin for the lodge.

All four of them ended up in front of the big desk in the main room. There was a bite to the air, since the sun hadn't really hit the valley floor yet to warm up the place.

"I'll get the fire going a little," Callie said as Fisher indicated that Kalinda and Doc take a seat on the couches.

"This place is really amazing," Kalinda said, looking around. "Really,

really comfortable-feeling. I love the feel of the big logs."

"That it is," Callie said.

Fisher went over and sat in one of the big chairs, saying nothing until Callie had the fire coming back up and she had sat near him on a couch.

"What just happened," Fisher said, "is that a Seeder asked us to become Seeders and help them with directing all the civilizations in this galaxy in their growth. And then maybe eventually go on and help them in Andromeda and beyond."

Kalinda just shook her head. "As a child I learned that the Seeders were mythical advanced people who built entire civilizations and then left."

"They are," Fisher said.

"As with any garden that is planted," Callie said, "it must be tended to grow the way the gardener wanted."

"And they want us to join them, help them tend the garden of all these civilizations they have planted," Kalinda said.

"That's it in a nutshell," Fisher said, nodding.

"And what do we get out of doing that?" Doc asked.

Fisher smiled at his friend. "Well, for starters, I'm betting that Benson is a few thousand years old at least."

"You're kidding me?" Doc said.

"We can ask him tomorrow," Fisher said, smiling at his friend and then looking at Callie who clearly just realized that as well. "And he basically said that if we join the Seeders and help out, we'll live a very long time as well."

Now Doc only shook his head.

"Second," Fisher said, "I'm guessing that he has the ability to transport over great distances without mechanical help. He seemed to hint as much."

"Now that would be cool as well," Doc said, nodding.

"So we can't say anything about this. Remember? We can talk with Benson tomorrow."

Doc shrugged and smiled at Kalinda. "You up for going and working on some engines?"

She smiled back and took his hand as they both stood. "I would love that, but first I want a tour of this wonderful lodge."

Callie gladly gave them a tour and Fisher jumped back to *The Lady* to do the dishes. Twenty minutes later, Callie brought Doc and Kalinda back up from the surface and then after they left, she sat at the table and watched him finish up.

When he was done, he turned to her.

"What would you like to do today?" she asked, smiling at him.

He could tell that even though it was still early in the morning, she was already overwhelmed. He was as well, to be honest.

"How about we go back to the lodge and just curl up on a couch and do nothing until lunch?"

"Perfect," she said. "Then what?"

"We come back up here, have lunch, and return to the couch."

"Perfect," she said, smiling. "And then what?"

"We come up here and have dinner and then return to the couch in front of the fire with a bottle of wine and a promise of a featherbed."

She smiled at him. "Have I ever told you how I like how you think?"

He moved over, helped her stand, kissing her long and hard, and then transported them to the lodge and the big couch in front of the fire.

Chapter Thirty-nine

OVER THE NEXT MONTH, as *The Lady* was having her engines upgraded and her shields worked on, Doc and Kalinda moved into the lodge with Fisher and Callie. Doc was going to end up being right. *The Lady* would be the fastest thing flying in any part of the galaxy.

All four of them had met with Benson on the second day and he had made his offer clear. He wanted all four of them to become Seeders and work together to help civilizations walk a moderately peaceful path toward the future. They had all agreed.

Callie loved the company and with Fisher doing a lot of the cooking in the lodge kitchen and them meeting all the time in the dining area, the lodge felt like it was actually alive.

A crew from *The R-12* had cleared out all the bodies around or near the lodge, moving them to a respectful place down in the valley below. So as the fall days got shorter, Callie and Fisher had started taking walks along the road and on some of the trails.

Callie loved those walks through the crisp mountain air.

She actually had come to love this lodge a great deal, even though it was the most isolated place on a very injured planet. But with her ability to jump up into space to *The R-12*, and the other three around, she didn't feel the isolation.

One evening, as *The Lady's* engine and shield upgrades were nearing completion, Fisher seemed bothered and worried about something. Callie decided she would just wait and let him tell her.

They were walking along the roadway, both wearing coats against the crisp of the fall air. She could almost see her breath in the clear air.

"I've just assumed," Fisher said, clearly working up the courage to ask the next question, "that you would want to come along on this crazy new world and be with me. But I never really asked. Are you sure you want to join me out there?"

Callie stopped and somehow managed not to laugh. She turned Fisher so she could look him directly in the eyes.

"I love you," she said.

"I love you as well," he said. "You know that."

"You have saved me," she said, "and given me a new life where I can help millions and millions of people to find a new life as well."

He nodded.

"Of course I want to go with you. But on one condition."

"Name it," he said, looking worried.

"For as long as we are still in this galaxy, we keep this lodge up and come back here once in a while."

He broke into a huge smile.

Wow, did she love that smile and that man and the brain behind those intense green eyes.

"I have another idea as well," he said, smiling at her.

"I'm listening."

"Assuming you don't get tired of me after a few years of traveling around in space all over this galaxy helping people..."

"Yeah, that's going to happen," she said, laughing.

"Then maybe, in a couple of years, we can talk with Benson and come back here and have him marry us."

Callie just stared at the man of her dreams, her mouth open. She wasn't really sure she had heard that right.

"Well?" he asked, smiling.

"Vardis Fisher, are you asking me to marry you?"

He smiled. "I am. Too forward? Too soon?"

She grabbed him around the neck and kissed him as hard as she had ever kissed anyone before.

Then she leaned back, not letting him go. "How about having Benson marry us before we set off to save the galaxy?"

His smile now was radiating.

"I'd like that," he said.

She would like that more than she had ever imagined.

And with that they stood there in the road to the old mountain lodge, kissing, until the chill of the evening air finally drove them inside and to the big featherbed.

— ᵕ —

The novel you just read will be available
in trade paper and electronic editions
from all your favorite booksellers in February, 2014.

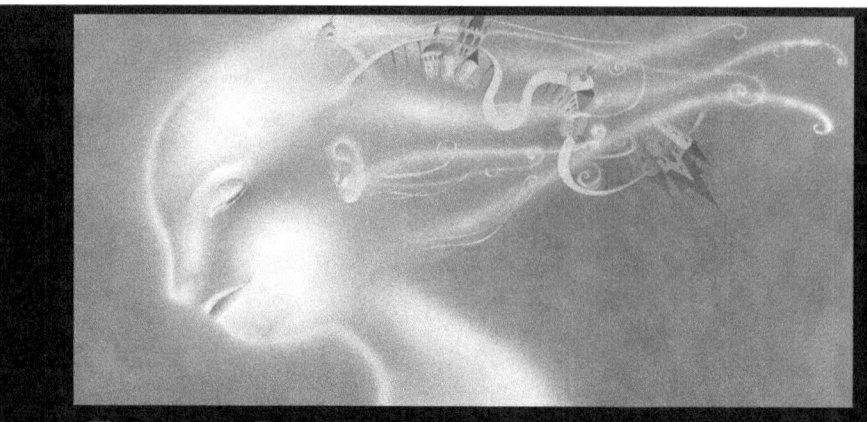

Poems by DEAN WESLEY SMITH

The First Cat in Space

The first cat in space was named Bob.
Not Morris or Schrodinger or Galallio
or Starry or Moonbeam or Alpha.
Just Bob, a black-and-white alley cat.

It was a bad idea
that must have sounded fun at one time.
Why not have a pet on the space station
to curl up with, to play with, to have purr?

They neutered Bob,
made sure he had no deseases.
Then they declawed poor Bob,
all four feet for fear he might puncture something.

Bob got space-sick within the first hour in no gravity,
screaming and floating in the middle of his cage,
all four feet extended, eyes wide in terror
his black and white fur covered in his own vomit.

Then Bob peed,
and it covered his fur as well.
The smell was so bad they had to seal Bob's cage
and pump air in to keep him alive.

Bob went back to Earth and gravity on the next shuttle,
since no one dared open his cage and touch him.
After a few baths and some good grooming, Bob went home,
where he has lived out his life crouched close to the ground.

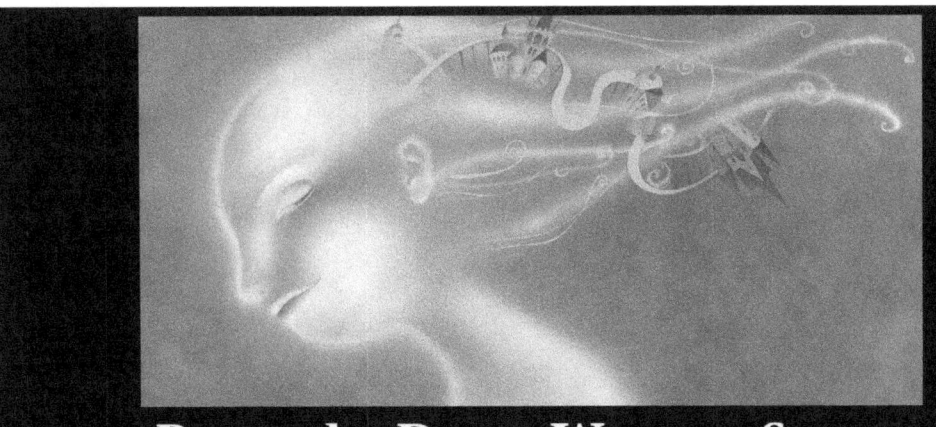

Poems by Dean Wesley Smith

The Second Cat in Space

The second cat in space was named Fluffy,
even though it had been shaved to such an extent,
the cat looked like a rat with wrinkles,
and big green eyes.

They put Fluffy out cold for the lift-off,
for fear the rumbling and all the force of the shuttle
would scare the cat into being useless
for the experiments on adapting to falling.

They didn't feed Fluffy for a day ahead of the flight,
then strapped her into a specially made harness,
to keep her upright and her feet pressed to the ground
when they reached zero gravity.

In the shuttle's first pass over Northern Africa
one astronaut went to see how Fluffy was doing.
She was dead. Growing stiff.
Too many drugs? Not enough food? No one knew for sure.

Two nights later Fluffy reentered the atmosphere,
over the southern coast of Oregon, above the redwoods,
flashed briefly in a puff of flame
that only a child on his front porch noticed.

The kid made a wish on the falling star, hoping for a cat.
His dad overhead, the next day brought his son a kitten
which the kid named Bright Fluffy,
after the cat the newspapers had said had died in space.

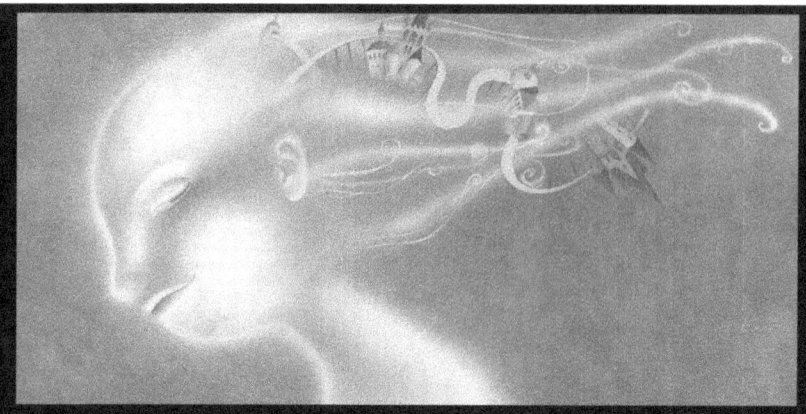

Poems by DEAN WESLEY SMITH

The Third Cat in Space

After the first two attempts to take a cat into space,
no one thought a third try would ever be,
until John Davis Davis needed something live
to ride along in a test of his auto-piloted space-plane.

The third cat in space was named Sweetie,
because that's what they called it at the pound
when John Davis Davis went there to get a passenger
no one would miss if things went wrong.

Sweetie got to be the first to ride in John Davis Davis's
three-million-dollar experiment using hydrogen thrusters,
and a saucer-shaped body with magnetic sections
spinning for lift and stabilization.

John Davis Davis strapped Sweetie's cage into the pilot's seat,
remote-flew his new ship into low orbit,
went around the Earth the same amount as John Glenn,
and landed his ship safely.

Sweetie survived just fine, was released by John Davis Davis
into the neighborhood where an animal control man
found him and returned Sweetie to the pound,
where he stayed for the next two weeks.

Three weeks later John Davis Davis told the world
about his new ship and Sweetie,
who had been put down the week before
because no one wanted to adopt him.

www.ingramcontent.com/pod-product-compliance
Lightning Source LLC
Chambersburg PA
CBHW080543180626
46818CB00008B/3107